BLUE RIVERS OF HEAVEN

THE TALES OF ZEBADIAH CREED, BOOK 3

BLUE RIVERS OF HEAVEN

MARK C. JACKSON

FIVE STAR
A part of Gale, a Cengage Company

LIBRARY OF CONGRESS CATALOGING-IN-PUBLICATION DATA

Names: Jackson, Mark C, author.
Title: Blue rivers of Heaven / Mark C. Jackson.
Description: First edition. | Waterville, Maine : Five Star, a part of Gale, a Cengage Company. September 2022. | Series: The Tales of Zebadiah Creed ; book 3 |
Identifiers: LCCN 2022007300 | ISBN 9781432896997 (hardcover)
Classification: LCC PS3610.A3543255 B58 2022 | DDC 813/.6—dc23
LC record available at https://lccn.loc.gov/2022007300

First Edition. First Printing: September 2022
Find us on Facebook—https://www.facebook.com/FiveStarCengage
Visit our website—http://www.gale.cengage.com/fivestar
Contact Five Star Publishing at FiveStar@cengage.com

Printed in Mexico
Print Number : 1   Print Year : 2023

Dedicated to Fayette Glass, a poet and my grandmother

ACKNOWLEDGMENTS

Thanks so much to my mother and collaborator, Judith Ann Jackson. Three books in and still has as much passion and love for Zeb as I do.

Thanks to my wife, Judy Walsh-Jackson, for completely embracing the life of a writer. Ten years at the desk and going strong.

Thanks to Denise Liebl, Joshua Jackson, and Sarah Jackson for supporting their dad.

Thanks to Linda Fowler, Kim Skinner, and Dawn Varner for supporting their brother.

Thanks to my great friend Pamela Haan for her endless encouragement and insight into how a book should be written . . . for the reader.

Thanks to my dear friend Peggy Lang, who offered time and time again a deep understanding of who Zeb is.

Thanks to the members of the San Diego Professional Writers Group, who for ten years have listened to the exploits of ole Zeb, chapter after chapter, offering critiques with only the best of intentions for the writing.

Thanks to my agent, Cherry Weiner, for her patience, constantly reminding me that the story comes first and not the deadline.

Acknowledgments

Thanks to Tiffany Schofield and Five Star Publishing for again taking the chance on a writer of only three books, who from the beginning just liked the name Zebadiah Creed.

And, thanks to Hazel Rumney for her stellar editing.

INTRODUCTION

There comes a time of morning when, if one listens close, the river sounds like conversation. Between two folks or a thousand depends on the water's calling, and who shows up to do the deeds necessary to tell the tales. Through our adventures come simple, meaningful lessons for us all to heed, to live another day or die by our thoughtless, selfish acts, only to find that it may be a simple conversation that saves us from ourselves.

Thus, up and down the river we shall go until we find a landing suitable, though brief, for one to call home, to share a joyous word or two each morning and evening with those we have come to love . . . and to listen closely to the tales of all rivers, blue rivers of heaven.

I wrote these words nearly forty years ago. As they seemed appropriate to the telling of the story, I added them to the introduction of this book. I would not write a new paragraph for another thirty years, and only after countless evenings spent with Samuel Clemens in a native tavern on the island of Hawaii, in the dead center of the Pacific Ocean. (How I came to be there, I will leave for another day.) Through his prompting, I wrote paragraphs upon paragraphs and now, years later, claim to have written three books. My small story, my own true tales sold to the world.

Now, I am tired. Yet, I am restless at the same time. How can this be, you may ask? I have lived in this hotel through winter and summer with constant waves crashing the cliffs below my balcony; the day and night barking of deckhands manning the dog schooners hauling timber off the shore and sold down the coast to San Francisco and beyond. Am I finished writing? Do I have more words to share? Can I conjure up more paragraphs to write into books sold across the nation? I do not know.

The book you are about to read is the third in a series; please read the first two, for all three tell a tale as complete as one can write about a young man of twenty-five.

Tomorrow, I catch a schooner south to San Francisco and by clipper ship, on to Hawaii, where I shall retire, and consider whether I have more words in me.

Samuel says the stories of our lives do not have to disappear when we die. If we write them down, they can live on forever . . . or at least until the books fall out of print! For the most part, I have always heeded his sage advice.

Zebadiah Creed
The Continental Hotel
Mendocino, California
July 1884

CHAPTER 1

Orleans Parish Prison, Early May 1836

Day and night had disappeared. I did not know when the sun rose, or the moon shone. All was dark but for the flicker of an oil lamp in the passageway and a torch as the guard brought food, slop I would not feed to a dog. I ate every bit. There came a constant moan from somewhere deep within the prison, behind walls as thick as the expanse of my hand. An insane agony I could not fathom. I wondered, this person must only sleep when I sleep, and I slept in fits and dreams. Sometimes, I woke thinking it might be me with the moan, and insanity.

For the murder of Benjamin Brody, I sat in this place. I admitted taking his scalp while fighting an honorable duel months before, over stolen furs and my brother's death. Though I could have easily slit his throat, I left him alive.

The clothes I wore still stank of Texas. Battlefield blood soaked into the cloth and dried; a stain map of my recent plight could hardly be seen for the rot, the holes and tears uncovering scars. Yet, no matter how threadbare these clothes became, I smelled of Texas.

How I yearned for buckskin, clean air, and cool water.

A rustle in the next cell and I knew his questioning, then his stories would begin anew.

"Hey, Scalper, you awake?"

I did not answer. I never answered.

"I can hear ya breathing different. You ain't much of a snorer.

11

Good for you. I heard some men die in their sleep from snorin', just stop breathin'." He laughed, sounds from the back of his throat caught between his teeth. "Hell, I killed a bastard once, for snorin' too loud. We was on a hunt. Slept like a tiny baby after." He laughed again. "Not him, I tell ya, *me, me*. I slept like the tot, not him. He could no longer sleep; the bastard had a knife in his throat!" He howled, as if his words were the funniest ever said.

Of the many men I had met who were true killers, this one bragged the most. He reminded me of Grainger. Less convincing perhaps, and less conniving, for it was because of Grainger and a five-hundred-dollar bounty that I sat in this black, shithole. *I will kill him.* The thought spun constant through my mind; my gut filled with rocks. *I will find my way out of here and kill Grainger.*

"Hey, Scalper . . ."

He had leaned closer toward my cell, within the distance of a few feet. But for the wall between us, I could reach out and shut him up for good.

"I know why you're here." His voice changed, becoming deeper, serious, hard.

"Oh, not what they told ya as to why you're here, but the truth."

"Why should I believe you?" I asked, the first words I spoke to the man in the cell next to me.

"You have nothing left to lose, my friend. For they will hang you, with no ceremony, no spectacle to show the fine men and women of New Orleans that your travesties will be accounted for, as well be theirs. You will die and no one will know." His words carried a different tone, a cadence to his speech he had not shown until I asked my question, as if a new man had taken his place.

"You call me Scalper, why?"

He laughed with a much gentler, refined sound than before. "Ah, Mr. Creed, your reputation most certainly proceeds you."

He knew my name.

There came a silence between us, for how many minutes I did not know. Time meant nothing to me. My own breath and heartbeat were all I heard. I stood and reached for the wall. Though this prison had been built only a few years before, the rough-cut stone felt ancient, with a thin layer of slime coating the rock. As I followed the wall from corner to corner, then finally to the iron bars of the door, the scurries of the rats told me that I was not alone in my cell. In the darkness, I faced the passageway.

"Who are you?" I asked. "And how do you know who I am?"

He laughed again, then sighed. "Why, I thought you knew. Everyone knows who the Scalper is." He must have stood at the same place in his cell as I stood in mine, side by side, not three feet from each other. "Your tales have become famous, my friend. Here in New Orleans and beyond."

"Who are you?" I asked again.

"In some circles, this question might get you killed."

"I ain't afraid, with or without this rock between us."

Another sigh, and he said, "Ah, Mr. Creed, you are afraid else you would not have engaged with me. Besides, this rock will not stand between us for very much longer, my friend."

I cringed at him calling me this. The last friends I had either betrayed me or were killed.

"I ain't your friend."

"Hmm, no, not yet. Though, we will have history together."

I felt obliged not to acknowledge him any further, my mind shaken as to how this man imprisoned next to me knew so much. I stepped to the back of the cell and squatted against the wall. *I will not speak to him again.*

How soon after our conversation the light appeared, I could

not tell. A guard stood at my cell door holding a torch. Behind him, a shadow moved, then a man in top hat appeared, short, rotund, breathing heavily. Sweat glistened on his forehead and chubby cheeks. He removed the hat and brushed a hand across his bald head. There came over me a vague recollection that we had met before.

"Mr. Creed, I am here to serve as your attorney, appointed by the court. Though the judge is obligated to provide you with defense in trial . . ." He cleared his throat. "It is customary to pay as you can for my services. Have you any coin, sir?"

I laughed. The last of my coins had been lost in a poker game six months before near San Antonio.

"I take that as a no." He placed his hat back on his head and tapped it down. "I will do what I can then, sir."

"When is the trial?" I asked.

Impatience sounded in his voice, high, whining. "Tomorrow. Mr. Creed, your trial is tomorrow morning. So, now I must ask you, did you murder Benjamin Brody?"

"No, I did not."

"This is how I thought you might reply . . . that is all." He began to turn away, then took out a handkerchief and wiped the sweat off his brow. "If you were to plead guilty, sir, I can promise the hanging a man would be proud of."

He paused, as if waiting for an immediate answer, then turned to the guard. "I will be bringing him fresh clothes. Ensure that he is properly washed. We don't want him stinking up the courtroom . . . courthouse." With another wipe of the brow, the lawyer and the guard left, leaving me again in darkness.

From the next cell came a sigh, then, "Ah, I wish you luck, Mr. Creed."

"Ain't no luck," I said.

"Then, Scalper, I wish you the best."

I leaned back against the wall, and waited, listening for the moan. But for the scurry of the rats and the snores of my fellow prisoner, all was quiet.

CHAPTER 2

With my next meal, came a biscuit. Its aroma filled the cell, reminding me of the biscuits Deaf Smith had made the night I sat with him at his campfire in Gonzales, before the massacre of Goliad, before the victory at San Jacinto. I never knew if he was a friend or just someone to confide in during a war. That night, I learned how valuable the land was that Grainger owned, the land he won from James Bowie in a poker game. The land Judith Lee claimed to be her own. I sat in that stinking cell because I was a terrible poker player and allowed Bowie to take my place at the table. If I had somehow stayed in the game, maybe I would have won the land.

Deaf Smith and I both agreed, Jim Bowie cheated to lose. Perhaps he knew his fate. Perhaps he knew the fate of us all.

I took tiny bites, to savor the biscuit's crunch. Not until later did I ask myself how it came to be on my plate. *Who would be so kind to me here?* I whispered. *Or is this part of my dying rites.* I held the last crumbs to my mouth, then on my tongue, chewed and swallowed, licking my fingers clean. I tasted the blood of a scalped Mexican, for I had not washed my hands since before the battle of San Jacinto. No matter, I was not to miss a single bit of the biscuit.

The clang of the door woke me. The pale-faced guard held a torch in his left hand and a club in his right, in case I tried to escape. I would not have gotten far. The skinny guard, his sunken cheeks filled in with sideburns connected to a drooping mustache, held chains. The leggings and wrist cuffs he struggled to put on me hung heavy as I shuffled out the door. Passing my neighbor's cell, I peered into darkness. By the flicker of the torch, I saw him for a second, only a dingy, gray smock showing, his long, matted hair pulled back, his face turned down toward the wall. An animal hiding from the light.

Would I ever see him again as he claimed I would?

The passageway smelled of tar, the floor sticky, making it impossible to slide my feet. Each time I peeled a foot up and stepped down, the chains rattled, as if I was stomping my way to the gallows. Myself and my fellow prisoner must have been special for we passed no other cells, no windows or doors. The few minutes we walked, I noticed a growing light. We turned a corner to face a barred gate to the street. The sunlight hurt my eyes. I tried to shield them but could not raise up my hands to my face. Both guards extinguished their torches in a sand barrel. Another guard standing outside unlocked the gate, and we stepped into the street. A prisoner's wagon waited.

"You come back, you don't go to the cell, we bring you here," said Paleface, and shoved me toward an arched opening. A platform with a noose hung above lay just inside the building's façade, on display and ready. I had seen a guillotine in use, and just one hanging. *Is it better to lose one's head or to have one's neck merely broken?* I thought, trying in my mind to make light of my current situation. My hands began to shake, then I stood very still, not allowing my fear to be seen.

"I will not die this way."

All three guards laughed. "Is what they all claim," one said.

I was shoved into the back of the wagon. Skinny joined me, and the iron door swung shut.

"We forgot to wash his ass," he hollered out.

"To hell with him, and the lawyer. He'll be dead soon enough," Paleface said, and nudged the driver. With the crack of a whip, we were off.

The first cabbage hit square on the side of the wagon, busted into pieces by one of the iron bars, its torn leaves hitting Skinny in the head. Hurled by an old woman as we rounded a corner onto Jackson Square, she screamed out a few words in French and made what appeared to be an obscene gesture. A small gang had gathered in front of the courthouse and began pelting the wagon with rotten vegetables, thrown mostly at the guards. I could not tell if this was a single event just for me, or if this was a common thing, to throw moldy food at the local municipalities.

The horse pulling the wagon, along with several marshals from the court, helped to disperse the crowd enough for us to stop at the entrance. All the while, the angry folks chanted *Back to yer own Parish*, then repeated in French what the old woman had said. It was not until the guards pulled their clubs and threatened to knock heads did the gang truly break up. One more tomato was thrown, by a young boy, hitting Paleface in the side of the head. He swung down but the child was gone. Wiping his cheek and slinging the bits of peel to the ground, he cried, "Goddamn Creoles!"

I wondered why I was untouched by the barrage.

My lawyer stood at the doorway spinning his top hat round and round, his face a bright red. "Come on now, come on, we mustn't be tardy! Judge Bermudez will become quite angry."

I was helped down from the wagon and shuffled up a few steps, both Paleface and Skinny on either side of me, the lawyer all the while motioning at us to hurry. Paleface stopped just short of the doorway and rattled my chains, tearing my shirt a bit more. "We ain't lettin' him escape," he said, smiling.

The lawyer shook his head, then sniffed. "I told you to wash him."

"We thought that airing him out with the breeze might be

18

'nough," Skinny said.

I asked, "Why were those folks so angry?"

"Why, Mr. Creed," said the lawyer. "You seem to be quite the hero for killing Mr. Brody like you did."

"But I didn't kill him." I had grown numb to the feelings of betrayal and the resentment I held in my heart. A simple denial was best, rather than showing my true emotions.

My lawyer continued. "We shall see, Mr. Creed, we shall see. As I said, my intentions are to defend you with the best of my ability, then the court will decide." He reached out his hand, offering a shake. I could not raise mine to meet his. "By the way, sir, I have not introduced myself properly. My name is Simon Baumgartner, former lawyer for Mr. Benjamin Brody . . ." He paused to look me up and down, scowling. "And the brother of Amos Baumgartner, the man you killed in Sophie le Roux's parlor last October." His scowl turned to a smile, his perfect teeth gleaming in the late, morning sun. "Can't say as he didn't deserve it, right, Mr. Creed?" He leaned in close. "But blood will be blood, sir, and his I can account for."

I could not think of anything more to say in my own defense.

Damn! If it ain't one thing, it's another, I mumbled to myself, then lowered my head, and shuffled on into the courthouse.

CHAPTER 3

If I did have luck, it was all bad. And if I had ever been in a worst circumstance, I could not, at the time, remember when. Though later, I was reminded of being tied to a chair and tipped off a bluff into the Mississippi River. Then, I had a knife, Frenchy's knife, pulled from the belt of John Murrell, to cut loose the rope. Scuffling into the courtroom in chains beside my defense lawyer, who happened to be the brother of the man I killed who murdered my brother, I truly felt defenseless.

Baumgartner paused at the door of the courtroom to discuss something in private with, I presumed, his assistant. I peered into a room filled mostly with a mix of blacks and Creoles, not so different from the angry folks outside. Along with them, a contingency of white, well-dressed men sat behind a desk on the right, facing the judge's bench, in deep discussion with the prosecuting lawyers. To their right, hanging from hooks on the wall, were top hats of all shapes and sizes with the tallest showing in the front. It glistened in the sunlight streaming through the high windows. *Who might that one be owned by?* I asked myself, and then recognized Broussard. *That bastard,* I thought. He greeted me with a nod and a smile and went back to talking with the other men. I did not acknowledge him.

As we entered the room, everyone became silent. The chains jangled with each step I took. Baumgartner led me to a desk on the left. Nine empty chairs sat against the wall. As I began to sit, he motioned me not to. I stood next to him feeling all eyes staring at me. The chatter slowly took up the silence of the courtroom and I heard mentioned two words over and over, *scalper* and *hero.*

Baumgartner whispered, "Your reputation precedes you, Mr. Creed." He looked me up and down again and sniffed. "You are a mess, sir. I suspect that you are condemned from the start."

I glanced at our opposing attorneys. One, perhaps senior to the rest, stared at me as they continued their conversation. "I suspect I have been doomed from before the start," I whispered, then leaned in and said, "You know your brother killed my brother, murdered him, shot a ball straight through his head while he leaned against me dyin', both of us tied to a tree. Then him an' Rudy stole our furs. They ain't been returned."

Baumgartner hung his head for a few long seconds, wiping sweat from his brow with a handkerchief. "I know Amos was a scoundrel, and a murderer, always had been. Still, he was my brother." Another long pause. "And a good father, leaving a wife and three children destitute."

A marshal stepped through a door behind the judge's bench, leaving it open. "All rise for the honorable Judge Bermudez," he stated, his voice cutting through all the chatter. With a single stomp, everyone rose to their feet.

"I will do my best not to hold his death personal, Mr. Creed, but . . . did you have to scalp him?" my lawyer asked.

I shrugged. "At the time, sir, I could not help myself."

"Thus, the name Scalper . . ." he said, nodding.

The judge entered the courtroom with an air of superiority, wearing black robes. He stood behind his bench, surveying the crowd, turned to me for a long second, staring, his face expressionless, then gave a quick glance at the prosecuting attorney and his white congregation, frowned, and sat down. He poured a glass of water from a crystal pitcher, the only two items that sat on the bench beside a wood block. With a whack of the gavel, the man who was to decide my fate brought his court to order and said, "All may be seated but for the defendant and his lawyer."

I stood still, as did Baumgartner.

"Zebadiah Creed, you are brought here today to my court charged with the deliberate murder of Benjamin Brody; how do you plead, sir?"

Again, I glanced at my lawyer. He stared straight ahead.

"Mr. Creed, this is a preliminary hearing with the trial set for this afternoon, if we can finish rounding up enough jurors. What you are accused of doing has been, to say the least, quite a popular act here in this municipality, as you can see, sir." He waved his hand toward the crowd of spectators. "So, I will ask only one time more and if you don't answer, I will hold you in contempt. Now, did you, or did you not kill Benjamin Brody?"

"Last I saw him, he was missin' his scalp. But he was very much alive, sir."

There came a couple of cheers, then boos as the crowd realized that I did not confess to the murder.

With a stern glare toward those folks, he asked, "And where did his scalp end up, Mr. Creed?"

"Hung on my belt, sir."

"Hung on your belt along with several others, for I hear you have quite the reputation of leaving men you are not fond of without their hair. In fact, it's come to my attention that yourself and your lawyer have a rather interesting relationship. An event that has bonded the two of you together, perhaps for life?"

"I killed his brother, sir . . . and scalped him."

A collective gasp, then snickers rose up from the audience. Without any reaction, the judge turned to the prosecuting attorney. "Mr. Gilbertson, why wasn't this man charged with the murder of Amos Baumgartner?" He sounded as if he might have known him personally.

Gilbertson stood, his chair screeching as he pushed it back across the wood floor. "Your Honor, at the time of poor Amos Baumgartner's unfortunate demise, there seemed to not be enough evidence for conviction, as there were no witnesses to the murder, sir." He continued standing, staring at me.

"That's a lie! There was a whole whorehouse full a witnesses, town officials an' the like. I only wish I could remember the names of the ones I met. You'd have to ask Sophie le Roux about them. 'Sides, I killed him fair an' square. Fact is, when we started to fight, I was unarmed and he carried a knife he stole from me way up on the Missouri River, after he shot my brother in the head, sir . . ." Through clenched teeth, I said, "And stole my furs."

The courtroom was quiet. I glanced at Simon Baumgartner. He stared straight ahead, a frown creasing his face. He seemed truly pained by the conversation.

"Hmm . . ." said the judge, rubbing his chin. "What an interesting situation we have here. This man stands before us charged with a murder he claims he did not commit, leaving Mr. Brody alive after a good scalping. Yet, confesses to killing a man in a room full of townfolk who won't bear witness, revenge for the killing of his brother." He shook his head, then looked at the prosecuting attorney and asked, "Sir, do you have witnesses to the crime this man is charged with, and are they ready and willing to come forward and testify?"

"Yes, sir," said Gilbertson.

"And you, Mr. Baumgartner, do you, sir, have witnesses willing to testify to the contrary of the charges brought against your client?"

"Yes, sir," answered Baumgartner.

"And can you set aside all your prejudices you might feel against Mr. Creed for killing your brother?"

A long pause with not a sound in the courtroom.

"Yes, sir, I can."

"I will hold you to it. And, I might add, what strong character you exhibit, sir." Again, he looked at Gilbertson, frowned, and said, "This trial will commence at three o'clock this afternoon. Sirs, I expect to have the jury deliberating in time for supper, do you understand?"

Both Gilbertson and Baumgartner nodded.

"And Mr. Creed, speak to your attorney about getting some decent clothing. It will not help you to be looking such a mess," said the judge, and he slammed the gavel down.

The marshal exclaimed, "All rise." As if awakened from a dream, everyone in the room stood. With his black robes in a flurry, Judge Bermudez exited through the door he had entered from just a few minutes before.

My lawyer stared straight ahead. "A young woman named Juliette will be our only witness today. I believe you know her."

Yes, I did know Juliette. My life hung in the balance by a girl who was deaf and could hardly speak. Though feeling damn near hopeless, I thought, *it sure will be good see her.*

Baumgartner nudged me. "I have clothes for you," he said, and with another nod from Broussard, we left the courtroom.

CHAPTER 4

I did not know she was watching until I was fully dressed. Sophie le Roux, the madame of the most infamous bordello in New Orleans and half-sister of Olgens Pierre; the confidant and fellow conspirator of Billy Frieze; the lover of Jean Laffite and mother of his child; also, the lover and attempted murderess of Benjamin Brody. And twice my seductress. I was not surprised that she showed herself. I thought she might somehow be a part of this deadly charade. She smiled, curtsied, and walked away, back through the outside door, and disappeared onto Jackson Square.

I crouched in a cage, set up in an alcove down the hallway from the courtroom. A couple of tattered, horse blankets kept me partially shielded from the prying eyes of the crowd that followed Baumgartner and me out of the courtroom. Skinny removed the chains that bound my wrists and ankles. A bucket of warm water with a brush lay just inside the door to wash with, along with a comb to untangle my matted hair and beard. Pouring water the best I could over my chest and arms, I finally scrubbed the bloodstains off of my body. After dressing, I turned over the empty bucket, combed out my hair, and sat down to wait.

Baumgartner's assistant brought a plate of rice and beans, the first food I ate since sitting in my prison cell the evening before. Not being given a spoon, I scooped with my fingers, eating every bit. I finished my meal and glanced up. Young Juliette stood before me. Though she wore the same plain, cotton dress I remembered, printed with lavender flowers, her hair tied back with a yellow ribbon, there seemed a hint of rouge on her cheeks to go with an air of experience. In the months since we had seen each other, she had grown into a woman. I did not know if it was my peculiar predicament, the fact that I might be dead by sunset, or her beauty shining on a new set of eyes, that I, in that instant, grew deeply fond of her.

"I . . . I am glad you are alive," she said, haltingly, speaking in the off-kilter way a deaf person would talk.

Taken aback by her speech, I stood, gripped the bars of the cage, and said, "Me too." I noticed she held a small handbag, the same bag I remember her carrying when, months before, she cut my hair.

Her shy smile could not hide the fear showing in her eyes. "I will tell what happened, the . . . the truth."

To go back to the morning I fought Benjamin Brody in a dual with long knives, tethered together like two raging dogs . . . I did scalp him, left him alive, his blood seeping into the ground below the towering oaks. His wife had laid on top of him, stabbed through the shoulder by Sophie as she attempted to finish what I was unwilling to do. Together, Juliette and I stopped the woman's bleeding, saving her life. *Maybe I shoulda killed him*, I thought. In a fair fight, I would not be called out for his murder. *The bastard would still be dead, and I would not be locked in this cage.*

Juliette turned swiftly and looked back down the hallway, as if she felt someone watching us. An older man stood staring our way. She turned back to me and reached out, gently wrapping a hand around mine. "I must le . . . le . . . leave now," she said, then, "I was to cut your hair, but they would not allow it."

Before I could say thank you, she was gone, walking close to the stranger I had never seen before. My heart sank. I lowered my head and rubbed my fingers, her touch the first from a woman since Francisca two months before. I felt so alone.

It seemed that I sat for hours. The folks so interested in me earlier had disappeared. *'Least I ain't sittin' in the dark with rats an' a cold-stone killer braggin' away in a cell next to me.*

With the waning light shining through the windows, I knew it was past three. Down the hallway, a door opened and out stepped Baumgartner and Gilbertson.

"Gentlemen, there will be no hanging today, maybe tomorrow, but not today," came the voice of the judge from inside the room.

Baumgartner called for the guards and Skinny brought the chains. I stepped out of the cage and he snapped the cuffs back into place. At the closed door to the courtroom, a marshal asked us to wait. I tried to catch my lawyer's eye, but he would not return my glance. With the judge's words ringing in my ears, a shiver ran up my spine. *This ain't good.*

"What's next?" I asked.

He did not answer and continued to avoid my looks. The tap of his shoe echoed down the hallway. He stopped, wiped his brow, then the tapping continued. Now that I was clean, I could smell his body odor, garlic. The sweat stains under his arms seemed to grow larger as he stood there, shading the black coat he wore to a chalky gray. Outside, the church bell tolled from across Jackson Square. I counted four rings. A knock came at the door and was opened from the inside. But for the judge, prosecutor, and marshal, the courtroom lay empty. I was led to the center, between the two lawyers' desks, to stand alone in front of the judge.

"Mr. Creed, we have encountered circumstances that, quite frankly, I am not fond of. However, we must continue with what we are presented with." He turned to Gilbertson, then to Baumgartner. "The facts, gentlemen, the facts just don't add up here, and the witnesses in this case are weak at best and corrupted at worst." He squared his gaze at me. "Today, your lawyer has shown exemplary restraint, for I knew his brother, and though Amos was indeed a bad man, and by all accounts, you killed him in a fair fight, he was still his brother. Yet, in private, Mr. Baumgartner did defend you as a true and just defense lawyer should." He paused to take a sip of water. "There are certain aspects to this situation that are undeniable. Though not sworn under oath, just this morning, you have, in front of a courtroom full of witnesses, admitted to participating in an illegal dual at the Oaks in October of last year, scalping Benjamin Brody and leaving him to bleed yet alive. Do you still hold this in your heart to be true, sir?"

I nodded.

"Mr. Creed, a nod of the head is not good enough for my court. Please answer yes or no."

"Yes, your honor, I did fight Brody in a dual, leavin' him alive."

"Sir, there are three witnesses that have corroborated under oath that you did do what you said you did. And with your confession . . ."

I was not understanding what this man was saying, except that, on this day, I hoped I was not to be hanged.

"Do you, Mr. Gilbertson, drop the charge of murder against Mr. Creed?"

He hesitated, then, "Yes, sir."

"And does your client, Mr. Baumgartner, except the charges now brought against him for the illegal dual he participated in, and the rather egregious act of taking Mr. Brody's scalp?"

"I haven't conferred with him, sir. I'm hoping that with your explanation, he will come to his own conclusion about his fate."

"Mr. Creed, these two men, one who wants you hanged no matter what the truth is, the other, who has set aside his own prejudice to defend you, have come to an agreement, sir."

I stood a little straighter.

"The charge of murder has been dropped. You are currently charged with participating in an illegal dual punishable by time in prison. I find you guilty, sir, and hereby sentence you to six months at the state penitentiary in Baton Rouge." Again, he glanced at Gilbertson and frowned. "Mr. Creed, I'd like a word in private; you may approach the bench."

I looked to Baumgartner. He appeared to be in a much better disposition than just a few minutes before, as if the compliments laid upon him and the outcome of the trial meant everything. A slight grin creased his face, and he gave me a nod. I shuffled to the front of the bench, my chains jangling. The judge leaned across and with a finger, motioned me closer. Gilbertson took a step toward the bench, as if to try and hear our conversation.

"I have to say, your lawyer saved your life, for you would have surly hanged if this trial had proceeded. He is a man with noble cause. He and I happen to agree on most of those causes." He shook his head and sighed. "This city . . . was once a great *municipio* at the bend of a mighty river, where folks of all colors and heritage could live together and get along. My family has been here since Spain owned the territory, two generations of judges besides myself. Now, split into three municipalities, offering more power to the plantation owners . . . I'm afraid, sir, that this situation is ripe for revolt."

I stood as close to the edge of the bench without touching and listened. I was not at all sure why he told me these things. It was as if, for that one moment, he needed to share with a confidant his disappointments and misgivings of his city, and I was the one.

He continued. "Mr. Creed, Benjamin Brody was in the middle of fostering this revolt along with other," he glanced past me to Gilbertson, "well-heeled men. Now whether you did or did not kill him is immaterial. The fact that he is dead is the more prominent issue. If I were to sentence you to hang, a martyr you would become to all the colored and Creole folks and the possible spark needed to flame bloodshed in the streets. The Washington militia would put down the uprising and those well-heeled bastards would have the whole city. And I, sir, will not allow that spark to become a flame. Mr. Baumgartner helped to remind me of this."

With his elbows on the bench and no longer sitting in his chair, he motioned me to move even closer, and whispered, "Mr. Creed, I know your recent history, sir, escaping with your life from the tragedy at Goliad. You went on to win victory against the Mexicans. I invested some in that revolution, sir, but with far different motives than the slave owners." He stopped and lowered his head, as if he were giving too much away of his personal life. Then continued, "You, sir, are a hero of sorts, though your reputation as being a mere savage makes shadow of this. Time will tell . . ." Again, he glanced past me to Gilbertson, then to Baumgartner. "For these reasons, you would not have hanged."

He sat back in his chair and said aloud, as if for all to hear. "Mr. Creed, you have been given a reprieve, sir. May I suggest, that when you have disagreements with a man, you make peace with words and not take a knife to his scalp."

I could not tell if he gave a frown or a smile.

"And when you have finished your short sentence, I also strongly suggest you go anywhere other than New Orleans; there are folks in this city who would have you . . . well, let me say, I cannot guarantee your life as I have this afternoon.

"Marshal, take this prisoner away. Court is now adjourned," Judge Bermudez said, and slammed his gavel down one last time.

CHAPTER 5

The tomato seemed to be thrown squarely at me. I ducked and it splattered onto Baumgartner's chest. He hardly acknowledged the insult and wiped the fruit off his coat.

"Well, well, seems you're no longer the hero, Mr. Creed," he said, tipped his hat, and walked into the courthouse.

Skinny shoved me into the back of the prisoner's wagon. I sat alone. As we left Jackson Square, the old woman yelled the same French words and showed her obscene gesture, her finger pointed at me. Skinny drove us through the narrow streets of New Orleans, past the opera house, the only building I recognized. Its monumental arches and stained-glass windows stood as splendid as when I first saw it the night Sophie and I attended, the night I broke Brody's nose and challenged him to the infamous duel. A memory that I would have gladly forgotten. Being sent off to prison, the business with Benjamin Brody was finished. I would do my time and head west . . . to find Grainger.

We pulled up next to the gallows, the platform barely visible in the shadows of the waning twilight. Yet, by the flickering light of an oil lamp hung near the prison's entrance, I could see the hangman's rope swaying ever so slightly. I closed my eyes and, in the quiet, heard the creak of the wood beam, the last words and cries of condemned men. The absolution recited by a priest. The floor giving way, the rope growing taut, and with the twist of a body, silence. The crowd cheering.

"No hanging today," Skinny said, mocking the judge. He stood at the locked door of the wagon. The guard standing watch at the prison gate joined him, slamming his club into his hand. A couple of blocks away, the angry voices of a crowd rose with a clamor, their torches lighting up the night sky, painting the sides of buildings yellow and red, drawing closer. They would not be a pretty parade.

Skinny continued, "He'd be dead in a minute if we did it ourselves. Stick him back in his cell with a broke neck an' no one would know."

I crept to the middle of the wagon, squatted on the narrow floor between the wood seats, and prepared the short lengths of chain hanging from my wrists. *Just enough slack to wrap this bastard's scrawny neck with. Only one can enter at a time, figure I can kill him before the other gets to me.*

Down the street, a familiar voice rose above the others. From around the corner of a building, two figures ran toward us. A pistol shot echoed through the streets; one man fell to the ground, the other dashed into an alley. The yelling stopped and the mob did not come closer toward us. It was then that I understood why I was sent back to jail with one guard. It would take only one ball shot into the wagon to kill me.

Skinny gave me a glance, then said to the other guard, "Go in there an' drag his ass out."

The guard peered through the bars. "He ain't my prisoner. Last I asked a favor from you, getting me your woman's sister to give a little comfort on these lonely nights, you told me to buck off. Now, I ain't sayin' he don't deserve to be hung." He turned toward the man who lay shot in the street. "Besides . . ."

I rattled the chains and beckoned him to come and get me. He shook his head, then walked to the gate, opened it, and leaned against the wall.

"Damnit, Jim, you owe me," Skinny said, his voice shaking.

Jim shook his head again and stood silent.

Skinny unlocked the wagon door and flung it open. "You lucky tonight, you get ta sleep in your cell rather than dyin' by the rope."

I stayed where I was. "If you enter this here cage, I will kill you. If you back the hell away, I'll go peacefully. Do we have a deal?"

He scratched his head, as if he had to think on this, then quickly turned toward the prison gate. From inside, came a faint moan echoing out to the street, as if the insane prisoner was calling us to join him. Neither guard seemed to notice.

The mob up the street had disappeared.

Stepping down to the road, I said, "Ya made the right choice tonight," and I shuffled into the dark passageway. Skinny followed with a torch.

When we reached my cell, he opened the door and nodded for me to enter, making no attempt to remove my chains, as if he was scared to approach me.

"I have to eat and can't touch my mouth," I said.

He slammed the door shut and motioned me to stick my hands through the bars. The wrist cuffs and chains fell to the floor with a clatter.

"The leggings can stay," Skinny said.

"Why did you want to hang me? I'm nobody to you," I asked.

He stared at me, and said, "Because you're famous for killin' my friend."

"Brody was your friend?" I blurted out, nearly laughing, *this skinny, frightened little man?*

"He helped a lot a folks an' I was one of them. He didn't deserve what you did to him."

"The bastard shouldn't have stolen my furs," I said, and retreated to the rear of my cell.

Skinny stood for a few, long seconds, perhaps pondering my

words, then walked away carrying the light with him.

I do not understand how anyone could respect a man like that.

My fellow prisoner snored, then coughed, hacked, and sniffed hard, as if he had lost his breath.

"Hey, killer, you awake?" I asked. "Don't be dyin' in your sleep now, this ain't the place for it."

He coughed again and said, "Well, how 'bout that. They didn't hang you after all."

"Not yet."

"Tomorrow?"

"Nope, off to prison for unlawful duelin' and scalpin'."

"I'll be damned . . ." he said, "So there, Scalper, you ain't the one who killed Brody?"

"No."

"Hmm . . ." I could hear him stand, make a noise as if he were stretching, and walk to the front of his cell. "Come closer, friend."

I walked to the barred door. Again, we stood only a few feet from one another.

"I know," he said.

"You know what?"

He whispered, "I know who killed Benjamin Brody."

"And you're gonna tell me."

"Not now. Figure you'll find out soon enough."

There was silence between us. I sensed his presence stronger than ever. As if he had grown from the small, yakking man in the cell next to me into a powerful confidant.

"You seem to be feeling much better, Zebadiah."

"I didn't die this evening," I said.

"Hmm, it's still early." He laughed, I did not.

We stood in our cells facing the bars a while longer. Finally, I asked, "Ya never told me your name, and why you're here in prison."

"No, sir, I have not."

"Well . . . you gonna tell me?"

Another long pause, then a cough, and he said, "Willie Dan, to make your acquaintance. And it's not what I've done, it's what I will do."

I thought about this for a few seconds and said, "I ain't a part of it, am I?"

"Not yet!" He laughed again, harder, from the gut. "Soon enough, I expect."

His laughter echoed into the passageway. I moved to the back of my cell, our conversation finished.

The torchlight shone, not on a guard, but on someone there to visit, a man with the tallest top hat, one who I briefly met on the ship that brought me back from Texas in chains, who handed Grainger a bag of coins for my capture. The owner of the plantation where I helped steal back and free Olgens Pierre's dead brother's wife and sons. A man whom I cared not one bit to talk with.

"*Monsieur* Creed, sir, we have met briefly. Though I grieve for my dear friend and partner Benjamin Brody's death, I am glad the judge saw fit to spare your life. Revenge is indeed not so sweet, and I fear the hangings in this great city have grown far too plentiful, and, quite frankly, tiring." Broussard stood perfectly still, holding the torch in one hand, the hat in the other, awaiting my response. When I offered none, he continued. "Sir, I saved your life tonight, for a mob was on their way here to lynch you. I persuaded them to let justice run its course."

I said nothing and remained at the back of my cell. *If he wanted to step in and have a word, perhaps I might welcome him with a good bashing. Justice be damned.*

"*Monsieur* Creed, I would like to show you my hat, sir." He held it up to the light. There was a sheen surrounding its black material that I did not recognize. "I know of your life as a trapper by trade, beaver to be exact. For many years, this gentle creature has given us its premium hide to be sent back to England and made into the finest hats the world has ever seen. Well, *monsieur,* the beaver's day has come and gone, for this startling piece of headwear is made of pure silk from India. The price for beaver skins plummeted earlier this year, while you were off to war."

"Why are you telling me this?" I asked.

"Ah, he does speak, *Monsieur* Dan."

"Yes, sir . . . quite well."

"The meaning of my visit and why I'm truly here, is to tell you that if you were to ever receive back your precious furs, they would be worthless."

He was taunting me, and I was not to bite. He lowered the torch and placed the silk hat on his head and stretched an arm up to tap it down to his ears.

He turned as if he were leaving, then said, "The nigress and her boys you stole from me, well, sir, they are on my plantation, right where they belong. I went down to Haiti and snatched them back myself.

"And Brody . . . The man in the cell next to you took care of him."

Broussard bowed and walked away, leaving me again in darkness, and in shock.

I imagined Willie Dan's face, and his smile.

CHAPTER 6

Another warm biscuit came with my next meal, doused in butter and with a hunk of fatback. Someone was being quite generous. My thoughts ran about who this person might be. Olgens Pierre perhaps, come to break me out so I will help free his deceased brother's wife and two sons . . . again. Maybe Olgens was dead, killed by Broussard himself as he reclaimed, by law, his rightful property. Frenchy? Hell, Frenchy seemed to only give a damn about his whores, torture museum, and by then, I was sure, his new, pet wolverines. And lastly, it was not Sophie. She cared about no one but herself.

Whoever sent the biscuit, I was grateful to them. I did not let a single crumb fall to the floor and licked my fingers clean.

I listened to Dan's breathing until I knew he was awake.

"So, how'd you kill him?" I asked.

"Oh, now, I wasn't nearly as fanciful as a knife through the throat like you did with ole Amos. I simply went to Mr. Brody's home and shot him in the face."

I was not surprised at how simple the murder was, a ball through the head. A way to be done with the one you are killing. I was some surprised that he knew about Baumgartner, though he did seem to know everything else about me.

"The goddamn African saved your life," he said.

"How do you know this?"

"Hell, man, I was there."

I tried to remember that night, the faces of the men and their ladies as they stood on the stairs landing in the parlor of Sophie le Roux's bordello, watching me fight and kill the murderer of my brother. I did not recognize any of them.

"I know why you helped with freeing his family, beholden to him as you were." A long pause. "I don't blame you for what you did."

"I did what I thought was right."

"Hmm . . . Mr. Broussard is not as understanding as I am. He was not so angry that you stole his slaves, is that you burnt down his slave quarters. He had no place to keep 'em 'til he built new houses, so they slept in the fields. Cost him money and he doesn't suffer losing money. Hell, he prides himself in keeping his slaves well rested."

I was not much interested in Broussard's troubles because of me, especially about how well he treated the folks he kept in chains.

"Why did you kill Brody?" I asked, steering him back to my questioning.

"Ah, now that's the question everyone wants to know. Why did Benjamin Brody have to die?"

I waited, and no answer came.

Twice, Simon Baumgartner visited. Once, to tell me when I was to be taken off to the Baton Rouge penitentiary. ". . . in three days' time," he said, offering no ill or kind words, only a slight smirk when I said thank you for getting me out of a hanging.

The last time I ever saw him, he brought a visitor.

By torchlight, Mrs. Katharine Brody looked stunning, wearing a bedazzled, black dress, tight at the waist, cut low, her veil covering only half her face. She appeared to be in mourning, however . . .

"Good evening, Zebadiah."

I walked to the front of the cell to get a closer look at Benjamin Brody's widow.

"You appear to be healed from your unfortunate wound laid upon you by Sophie le Roux." I did not know whether to offer my condolences. Or to tell the truth, that I was glad her husband was dead.

"Your loss . . . must be hard for you, ma'am," I said, gripping the bars of the door with both hands.

She nodded, though the shine in her eyes did not match her sad face.

There was silence for a few long seconds.

"Why are you here, ma'am?"

"I wanted to see you and to say . . . thank you, for saving my life. You helped me to see his waning ways."

I nodded. "No one was to die that day."

"I have become great friends with Juliette, though I sometimes find her hard to understand," she said.

"Yes, I saw her yesterday; her speech has gotten better, but . . ."

I imagined them together in a parlor, in awkward conversation, Juliette wearing her plain dress, remaining quiet and still for most of the visit; Mrs. Brody becoming impatient, wanting to say or do something, anything, as long as the attention was on her. Part of me wished to be wrong, that she was changed by her sudden loss, for Juliette's sake . . . if they indeed were friends.

We stared at each other and she smiled. Any sorrow that she may have felt for her husband's death seemed to melt away.

She reached out, hesitated, then gently caressed my knuckles with a finger. "When you finish with prison, Zebadiah Creed, please come back to New Orleans, for a visit?"

I slowly opened my hand and she backed away.

Katharine Brody gave me one last glance over her shoulder as Baumgartner escorted her away.

I smiled to myself. *Now, I wouldn't mind a quick trip back to this corrupt city, if only for one night.* A deeper, nagging thought had me wondering if she knew that her husband's murderer slept in the next cell. *Hell, if it don't matter to her, it don't matter to me . . .*

Again, I lay in darkness, alone but for the presence of a cold killer; the sounds of a man continuing to moan through his insanity; and the rats. I thought of Billy Frieze. Deep inside, I wished for his friendship. I wished him to be alive, to have gone to Texas with me, to have shared in the suffering, to tell great tales when we were old. I was not dead from a hanging. I was alive, yet truly alone.

I woke thinking it must be too early for my departure. *Had it been three days?* By the constant dark, I could not tell, nor could I remember how many meals I had eaten since leaving the courthouse. From the passageway came flickering light. I moved to where the stone wall and bars met to see two guards standing outside of Willie Dan's cell. Paleface held a club and oil lamp. Skinny held a torch in one hand, with chains and a ring of keys jangling from the other.

"Time to go, Willie," Paleface said.

No answer.

Paleface raised the lamp closer to the bars and peered into the cell. "Hey, Willie!" he hollered. Then to Skinny, he said, "He's not movin'. Hell, he ain't eaten in five days, he might be dead. Go ahead an' open the door."

Skinny hesitated, glanced to Paleface, and inserted a key into the lock. With a squeak, the door slowly swung open. He stepped back into the middle of the passageway. "You go first."

Paleface lowered the lamp and charged into the cell saying, "Willie, goddamnit, get up!"

There came a punch to the gut, a sudden, forced exhale, no inhale but for a wheezy gasp, then groan, and the lamp hit the floor with a clang but did not go out. I heard a couple of empty swooshes of the club, a third stopped, the club wrestled away, then one swift wallop and bone cracking. Paleface took a gulp of air and screamed. Another strike, probably to the face, his jaw and teeth fracturing from the blow, his scream silenced. By the light of the torch, I saw the stupefied look on Skinny's face as he watched his friend being pummeled to death. Willie Dan burst through the door and struck Skinny, a full blow to the head with the club. The torch, chains, and keys fell to the floor with a clatter and Dan yanked Skinny back into the cell. One strike after another. I imagined Skinny falling to his knees, his skull caved into mush. A shattering of glass and Dan's cell burst into flames. Within seconds, the smoke and smell of scorched flesh filled the passageway and cells. But for the crackle of burning clothes and skin, there came a quiet only death could bring.

With a long squeak, the door to Dan's cell closed and latched shut. He stood before me with the torch in one hand, the ring of keys in the other, his mouth and nose wrapped with a piece of cloth, the swirl of smoke surrounding him.

"Scalper, we'll be on our way," he said, and inserted a key into the lock. My door swung open. With the torch held close to his face, though the lower half was covered, I could see his eyes, the brightest of blue. Exposed just above the cloth, on his left cheek, a cut had turned to scar. I absently reached up to touch mine. I could tell that he smiled.

We shared the mark of Rudy Dupree. The very act of us both surviving the cut bonded us forever.

"We must leave now," he said.

I crept deeper into my cell. He entered and raised the torch. The rats scurried to find their way back to the darkness; the insane moan rose in pitch, echoing through the prison passageways to die inside the stone walls we stood between. The fires of the dead men settled into charred flesh and bones. Willie

Dan pulled down the cloth. His face was that of a young boy's, no older than twelve. From his talk and murderous acts, I was not to be deceived by his innocent appearance.

"I'm not going with you," I said.

His laugh was familiar to me, the torchlight reflected in his piecing, blue eyes. Beyond lay a shadow I felt only I could see, yet could not see past.

Dan's smile lessened a little. "You must. It's a part of the plan."

"I ain't part of no one's plan." I crouched ever so slight into a fighting stance.

He slid his feet toward me and lowered the torch a bit.

"You must," he repeated, and dropped the ring of keys.

I raised my arms, my hands clenched into fists. "You gonna kill me if I don't?"

He shook his head and brought the torch closer to his face and touched the scar on his cheek. He looked as if he had aged five years in the few seconds we talked.

"I see you have survived Rudy Dupree, as I have done," he said.

I suppressed the urge to caress the cut on my face and stood stone still.

"Yes."

"Before I shot him, I noticed Brody's scar; I hear you cut him."

"Yes."

"Hmm, Rudy's legacy lives on."

He moved closer; I did not back up.

"You would rather go to prison than be free?"

I nodded.

"You know you will die in the swamps."

I shrugged.

"We have work to do, you and I."

Again, I shrugged.

"I was told to kill you if you refused to come with me."

"You can damn well try," I said. "But I ain't one of those yahoos you just beat and burned to death."

The moaning stopped for a second. Then, it was as if the fellow prisoner was there in the cell, a ghost we could not see, his bewailing come upon us. Willie Dan winced and looked away, as if he saw a wisp of the man. He turned back to me and said, "Before I leave here, I will kill him."

"It seems that's what you do best."

"For good reason," he said. "As do you, Scalper."

His blazing eyes burned into my soul, piercing my shadow, knowing all of who I was. He clenched his teeth, skin stretched tight over the bones of his face, and he leaned closer. The moaning ceased again, leaving a quiet not even the scurry of the rats could break. I did not flinch a muscle. He hesitated. The moaning started anew.

Willie Dan picked up the keys and took a step backward, toward the cell door. "We could have been friends, good friends."

With a swoosh of the torch, he was gone.

A few minutes passed, the moan became a bloodletting scream, then silence.

There was no biscuit at my next meal. There was no meal. The bodies of Paleface and Skinny were taken out, walls and floors washed down with buckets of water, and within an hour, a new prisoner occupied the cell. The only evidence of the murders was the smell of burnt flesh that lingered in the stagnant air. The rats came back.

Later, two guards locked me in the same chains that Skinny had carried and escorted me to the gate. A prison wagon waited.

Past the gallows, down the street a ways, in the early morning shadows, stood a man dressed much like a pirate, wearing a drooping mustache and a billowy, white shirt with pantaloons tucked into knee-high black boots. A cutlass hung from his waist. A girl stood to nearly his height, holding his hand. She also wore a cutlass. Frenchy gave a quick wave, his daughter did not.

CHAPTER 7

Ascension Parish, Louisiana, Early June 1836

The prison in Baton Rouge was twice the size of the Orleans Parish prison, split into two sections, one for white men and the other for Negroes. I understood the need to lock up white criminals. The fact that most all the black men were already slaves and needed to be locked up, I did not understand. I supposed at the time that this was another way to keep them held in chains.

Only once did I see any of them.

The first few days, I worked a garden near the fence that separated the prison yards, along with two other inmates, chained to a heavy spike driven into the ground. Three guards stood nearby, to ensure no other prisoners could get to me, for as soon as I had entered through the gates, there began the death threats. I did not know why someone would want to kill me and I did not care. I was to do my time and be on my way.

The sun was merciless, burning through the thin cloth of the prison stripes I wore, soaked to the skin with sweat, and with no hat. *The cool stink and darkness of my New Orleans prison cell might bring some relief.* Then I remembered Willie Dan and cringed. The cell I was thrown into at the penitentiary was as hot and stifling as a brick oven, with no ventilation. Nighttime was the worst, for I lay on a canvas cot listening to the rattle of keys as the guards walked past my cell, and the constant fear of waking to a knife at my throat by the hand of my cellmate. Not

45

a person was to be trusted, and if I had to kill someone for trying to kill me, so be it.

As I tilled the soil, I noticed a smell, the same odor that
drifted up to James and me a couple of months before, in Texas,
as we stood gazing down at the slave quarters at Groce's plantation. The very aroma I smelled while releasing Margo and her
boys from Broussard's plantation: ancient soil and eternal sweat.
Yet, this time, while tending a patch of sprouting squash, I
smelled blood. Then I noticed the swish of a whip and the slap
of leather breaking on skin. I stepped to the fence and pulled
back a wood slat. There before me slumped a man, his forehead
nearly touching the dirt, his dark-skinned back bare to the sun.
A guard stood over him wielding a bullwhip. With several vi-
cious lashes committed, the prisoner had held his tongue until,
finally, he could not. His scream curdled my ears. As I watched
the whip slice into his back again and again, he whined like a
beaten dog, grunted in rage, then began to whimper. He raised
his head once, to stare straight at me, his glare a mix of hopeless despair, then defiance. Lowering his head again, he rolled
over, and with the next strike, took hold of the whip and sat up.
The guard let go, backed away, and shouted, "Shoot him!"
From the closest tower came *Shhh-Boom*. The Negro's head
jerked sideways, and he collapsed to the dirt. A couple of prisoners moved toward the guard. Another shot and the one closest
fell to the ground. The guard glanced at me; I had not seen
such hate-filled eyes since the battle at San Jacinto. I did not
move. He picked up the whip, and slowly coiled it, still staring
at me. Hands grabbed my arms, yanked me around, and shoved
me against the fence. Two guards stood before me; one held a
club, the other a bullwhip, uncurled and ready to strike.

The man pressing me said, "Ain't your business, boy."

I shook him off. The other two moved closer with the club
and whip raised. I still clutched the hoe I was using. There

came a sharp whistle from the balcony of one of the buildings that enclosed the prison yard. A man who I assumed might be the warden shook his head, then indicated that they take me to him. I dropped the hoe.

From the other side of the fence, one last shot rang out.

Walking past the other prisoners, I felt their cold hostility toward me. Somehow, I had betrayed them. The only glimmer of understanding I received was when one of them hollered out, "You ain't no killer."

"You coward. Run away, boy, we catch ya. We scalp you!" another said, and they all laughed.

Chained and shackled, I was led to the warden's office. The guard knocked, then stepped behind me. The door opened and there stood a young man, more like a boy, of maybe sixteen or seventeen, wearing clean, perfectly fit prisoner garb. Behind him, the warden sat at his desk, head lowered, reading. He gave a nod to enter. The guard stayed in the hallway and shut the door.

"He is my assistant," the warden said, without looking up.

Though I was accustomed to wearing chains, the room was so quiet that I heard every clink as I walked to the front of his desk. The young prisoner moved to stand behind the warden. Behind them, hung a large painting of men on the hunt, with dogs, chasing a Negro into a grove of trees. After what I had just witnessed, at least the man in the picture had a running chance.

"Do you know why you are here?" the warden asked.

"For duelin' and scalpin', sir."

"Hmmm . . ."

He raised his head. A white-bearded man he was, but trimmed very close against his face, maybe forty in age, his hair cropped shorter than most men of his stature. Perhaps to weather the heat, though it did make him look the dandy, wearing a velvet jacket and vest, and a black ascot with a cream-colored shirt. The top hat hung on a hook gave off the same sheen as Broussard's. The fine clothes seemed out of place for such an insular job.

He said, "I know that, in fact, you are here for other reasons . . . you don't know about."

"I'm confused, sir. I am to serve a six-month sentence and be gone."

"Hmmm . . . you killed Benjamin Brody."

"No, sir, I did not."

"Then you were accused and found not guilty of his murder."

"There was no trial," I said.

"And you ended up here instead of staying at the parish prison."

I had wondered about this. Most prisoners where I was previously were there waiting to stand trial or to serve out their sentences for rather minor offenses, or for not paying their debts. With my sentence of six months, I would certainly have fallen into this lot. Yet, there I was, held in the largest prison in Louisiana.

"A man escaped during your stay in New Orleans; the prisoner in the cell next to you killed two guards, burned them, killed another, and walked out of the prison. Your cell was found unlocked with you still in it."

"Yes, sir."

"You did not choose to leave with him . . ."

I could not tell if this was a question or a statement. "No, sir, I did not."

"Hmmm . . ." he said again.

The young prisoner laid a hand ever so gently onto the back of the warden's chair.

"Sir, may I ask a question?" I asked.

"By all means, Mr. Creed."

48

"You said you know why I'm here. You gonna tell me?"

The warden smiled for the first time and glanced down at what he was reading, then shooed the boy's hand away. "You were in Texas, for the fight, were you not?"

"I was."

"And you fought bravely I am told."

I shrugged and said, "Depends on who you ask."

"You survived Goliad," he said, staring at me.

I hesitated. No one had mentioned that place in a long while. I swallowed and said, "Yes, sir, I did."

"Well then, you are a hero, isn't he, Georgy?"

The boy smiled, leaned into the warden's ear, close, and whispered, "Yes, sir."

"There are rumors that refute all of what I just said, that you are in fact a coward and did none of those things we speak of. Or at the very least, you were inconsequential to the fight."

I sucked in a breath and said, "Then they are lies, sir."

"You may have to prove yourself, again, Mr. Creed; I suspect it will be a struggle, however, you will be successful. We are counting on you."

I was not at all sure what he was talking about; I had nothing to prove, and why would he have any interest in my doings. "If there are folks that want to speak lies about me, then I will explain my point or ignore them."

"Do you have any honor, sir?" the warden asked.

I thought about this for a second, then said, "I'm tired of offering my honor to dishonorable men . . . sir."

He nodded, as if agreeing with me. "Mr. Creed, there are far more dishonorable men in this world, and we must somehow get along despite this fact."

It was my turn to nod in agreement.

"You are to join a gang, to build a road."

"A road, sir?"

"Yes, a road," he said, and hollered, "Guard!" The door opened. "Take this prisoner to Mr. Persimmons."

"Why me?"

"You have been summoned by John S. Preston."

Who the hell is he?

The last I saw the warden, he resumed his reading. The boy again laid a hand on the back of the chair and smiled at me as I was escorted out the door.

CHAPTER 8

The road we were to build would wind from the back sugarcane fields of the Hydras plantation, through a cypress swamp, to the Amite River. Not a long road, only a few miles, but a road that would be built around and over black water, by way of bridges, and with what little solid land could be found. Why a ragtag gang of fifteen prisoners were doing the labor, and why I was chosen, I did not know, for I had never built a road before in my life.

Along with my fellow prisoners came the guards, two per gang of five with one foreman by the name of Mr. Persimmons. He was also the master road builder, or so he claimed.

One of the guards for my gang was the man who whipped the Negro prisoner, causing him to be shot. His name was Roy Messenger, who we were to call Mr. Roy.

Leaving Baton Rouge at daybreak, by flat barge, we were chained to iron rings embedded in the deck, in case we were so inclined to take a swim in the Mississippi River. According to one guard, during the last float downriver, a rather dumb lag had thought he would try and escape by taking advantage of a broken clasp. He slipped into the water, his chains weighing him down. "The fool never saw blue sky again."

I gave the heavy chain that bound me a swift tug. With a broad sweep of his hands, the guard offered me the river, then turned away laughing.

We arrived at the dock of the Hydras plantation by late

afternoon, wedging our way between two larger barges. Again, I smelled the deep richness of sweat and soil wafting off six or seven slaves as they loaded sugarcane. They were not in chains for they must have understood that to escape was to die in the river or swamp. I felt a sudden kin to these men. The only exception was that I would be free in several months. They would never know freedom.

Mr. Persimmons stepped off the barge and shook hands with a man who must have been the master. They both left the dock and walked up the road that led away from the river. The guards kept us chained to the barge, the hot sun bearing down and with no water. I sat still, watching the black men finish up the loading. One of them caught my eye as he held a ladle from a bucket to his lips and took a drink. His gaze seemed to say that he cared not whether I lived or died. In an instant, I felt as if I meant nothing to him. Still staring at me, he flung the rest of the water into the river, looked away, and with the others, ambled up the road toward the fields.

Again, I pulled on the chain that bound me to the barge.

Persimmons came walking back past the slaves and gathered the guards together. He did not look happy as he spoke. I heard only the words *canvas tents* and him complaining about there not being enough building materials to do the job properly. He glanced at us and shook his head, then told the guards to gather us together. We were unchained from the barge, reconnected to each other, and lined up on the dock. The guards carried clubs and wore a pistol each at the belt. Mr. Roy held a bullwhip loosely coiled in his right hand and stood staring at me.

"I seen you before, through the fence. Couldn't figure it out 'til now," he said.

I nodded, offering no words.

"Look on yer face, hell, you'd think ya gave a shit."

I knew to keep my mouth shut. He let the whip uncurl and

dropped his hand, ready to strike.

"Asked you a question, boy, you give a shit 'bout that dead Negro?"

I turned and looked him in the eye. A mix of rage and fear simmered in him, barely in control, just below the surface.

If I answered truthfully . . .

"No," I said, lying.

"Mr. Roy, I need you to gather at the rear, sir, so we can get these here prisoners bedded for the night. We're up 'fore dawn an' working," said Mr. Persimmons.

Roy stood beside me a few more seconds, his hand squeezing and un-squeezing the handle of the whip, perhaps sensing that I lied. He gave Persimmons a long look of contempt. I turned away from him. Taking slow, deliberate steps, he preceded to the rear of our chain gang. I could feel his presence behind me, as if his stare bore two holes through the back of my head. We left the dock and were marched up the road toward the Big House.

If I was not wearing chains, I might eventually kill this arsehole.

CHAPTER 9

Our gang of five was the first into the swamp, to find dry, hard ground, rises that could be bridged to. An old Indian trail left out of the last sugarcane field some forty acres east of the Mississippi, to disappear into a tangle of cypress trees, Spanish moss, and alligators sunken in black water, their eyes shining just above the waterline. There was no wind, no faint breeze to cool the swelter, only the oppressive heat of the day. The swamp air stunk of death.

We walked on the footpath while the guards attempted to ride horses carrying scatterguns laid across their saddles. As the trail narrowed, less than a mile into the swamp, the horses had to be abandoned. Mr. Roy brought up the rear, with me walking just ahead of him. Persimmons led us down the path, taking notes. Not a word was spoken with no talking allowed amongst us prisoners.

With the barrel of the gun, Roy nudged me forward and said, "You're the first to go."

Not sure what he meant, I ignored him. He nudged me again, harder. "I'm talking to you, boy."

I stopped, allowing the rest of the party to move on.

"I'm talking to you, boy," he said again.

I spoke over my shoulder. "Don't know what ya mean, Mr. Roy." I was in chains, bound at my hands. If I gave him any provocation that I would do him harm, he might have shot me.

He leaned into my backside, with the gun pressed against

me. His hot breath on my neck smelled of onions and whiskey. "Oh, two or three of you always die out here, you be the first."

I stayed still and said, "I'll only die if you can kill me."

He laughed and backed away. Persimmons hollered for us to catch up with the rest of the gang.

The path disappeared, leaving a small bank of earth for all of us to gather on. The swamp, a dark shade of overhanging trees and glittering sunlight reflecting off the surface of the water, offered what seemed a wall, a swirl of green, gray, and black, impenetrable, unyielding, leaving no way to judge its depth, its danger.

"Need someone to . . ." Persimmons paused, looked down, then out across to a tiny rise, an island. ". . . see how shallow this is."

No one volunteered. The other guard, name of Kershaw, pointed to one of us. "Trudeau, I say Trudeau goes."

The prisoner's face turned pale and he began shaking his head. "I don't swim too good, sir."

Mr. Roy laughed, then said, "Hell, boy, you don't need to swim. You slip into a hole in the mud where a tree used to be, cain't get out an' drown, or a gator gets you. Either or . . . swimmin' won't save you."

Persimmons nodded in agreement. Kershaw pointed his scattergun at Trudeau. "Go on, boy, show us how deep that water is."

"At least take the chains off of him," I said.

Persimmons and the two guards looked at me as if I was crazy and did not respond.

Trudeau trembled as he stepped into the mud, water filling in around his shoes. He slogged in up to his knees, turned around, and grinned at the rest of us, as if he was surprised that he had yet to drown.

"See, ain't so bad," said Kershaw, "now, go on."

About ten feet out, the water reached his waist. He stumbled, but did not fall, as if he hit a stump. Twenty feet out and he was two-thirds of the way across to the rise. Three more steps and only his head and shoulders showed. Closing my eyes, I wiped sweat away from my face with a sleeve. When I opened them, Trudeau was gone.

"Where do he go?" Persimmons asked.

"Did a gator git him?" Mr. Roy asked, laughing.

An arm raised up out of the water, the chain shackled to Trudeau's wrist taut, as if he was trying to pull himself loose from a snag. His head broke the surface, enough for him to take a quick breath, then he disappeared again beneath the water.

"Somebody needs to go help him," I said.

Everyone turned to me. More thrashing could be heard from Trudeau, then quiet.

I held out my hands and rattled the chains. "Take these goddamn things off!"

A few seconds passed. No one moved.

"Take them off," Persimmons said, staring at Roy.

"I ain't gonna take those chains off," Roy said, caught by surprise.

Persimmons stepped up to him. "Take them off now; I won't have one of my workers drown 'cause of your bullheadedness."

Roy hesitated.

"*Now,* or else he drowns!"

Roy pulled a key from his belt and slowly unlocked the shackles. The chains had not hit the ground before I plunged in.

The water felt like sludge. Halfway between the shore and where I thought Trudeau might be, I stood, my hair and beard covered in a thick matte of rotting leaves and roots. I pushed off and swam to where I last saw the drowning man, took a quick breath, and dove down, widening my arms to try and catch a piece of him. The water was so thick I could not see. Something

56

brushed against my leg. A chain, then an arm. I pulled on his hand and the chain went taut, keeping me from bringing him to the surface. Several feet down, I found it tangled in a root and yanked once, then twice. The chain broke free. I reached the surface gasping for air, Trudeau's body limp and heavy. A yard or two from the rise, I tried standing and sank into mud up to the tops of my boots. I rolled him back into the water and one at a time, pulled my feet free, then carried him to dry land.

"Is he alive?" Persimmons hollered.

I hit Trudeau several times between his shoulders. He sputtered to life, vomiting swamp water.

"Yes, he's alive."

"Good, then stand up and see if you can find the trail."

I made sure Trudeau still breathed, then turned toward where the Amite River might be, searching for traces of a path to lead us through that god-awful place.

"The trail's visible." I paused to squint through a line of trees that were perhaps a hundred yards ahead. "Beyond, it looks like an opening that could be a river."

"Good, good, just as I thought," said Persimmons. "Now, come on back, we have work to do."

Trudeau glanced at me. He looked as if he was trying to understand what just happened. "I . . . I am thankful."

I nodded and pointed toward the shore we had to swim to. "I'll hold you; you don't hold me. If you panic, we'll both drown, hear?"

Something compelled me to glance again across the swamp toward the river. A flicker of movement caught my eye. Thirty yards away, on the next rise, a man stood staring at me, dressed in white, brown, and black feathers, holding a tomahawk against his chest. The lower half of his face was painted yellow. I blinked and he was gone, leaving only sunlight shimmering through the trees. A chill ran up my spine. For a few more seconds, I watched for any other movement and saw none. Persimmons yelled at us to make haste. Trudeau and I entered the water. Within minutes, we were again with our gang.

"Lost your boots," Roy said, laughing.

I nodded, allowing him to lock the shackles to my wrists.

"We'll get you some shoes. Can't have a man working barefoot, now, can we?" He laughed again. "Might get yer toes cut off. Or bitten by a moccasin."

I stared out across the swamp. "Did ya see him?"

"Who?" asked Persimmons.

"The Indian," I said.

"Ain't no Indians 'round here no more," said Kershaw. "They all moved south, near Terrebonne."

"Felt him whilst I was in the water," Trudeau said.

All of us stared at him.

"Tried to save me."

We turned to face the cypress trees and glittering, black water.

Trudeau sighed and said, "Felt like Jesus tryin' to save me . . ."

Without another word, Mr. Persimmons led us out of the swamp, back to the Hydras plantation, rusting chains and all.

CHAPTER 10

I sank the pole a couple of inches into the muck where I thought the water was deepest. Trudeau steadied the flat boat with another pole so Persimmons could take a reading with his transit, or whatever the device was called.

"Hold steady. What mark do you have at the surface of the water?" he asked.

"Seven and a half, sir," I said.

"Figure it's the deepest?"

I glanced at Trudeau. We floated above the very spot where the day before I had saved him from drowning.

"Yes," I hollered.

"Move on toward the rise and make sure. The pilings must be cut accurately."

Trudeau pushed us closer to the shoreline. I jammed the pole back into the mud. It read five feet, then three feet. We reached the rise; I stepped on land, avoiding the mud as best I could and held the boat for Trudeau. He hesitated, then jumped. From across the water, I heard Roy speak to Persimmons but could not make out what he said. The scattergun he held, if shot, would not come close to harming Trudeau and me. And certainly not his bullwhip. For a brief second, I thought, *Hell, we could pull this boat over to the other side an' be off.* I again glanced at Trudeau as he mumbled to himself, his eyes darting from the water we had just crossed, back to Roy and Persimmons, then beyond us to the next rise. *He ain't one to get lost with, especially with a pack a dogs following us.*

"We're coming across," Persimmons yelled. "The two of you go on."

We dragged the boat through the grass and in between the cypress trees to the water's edge. From behind us, I heard a splash, then "Damn, Roy, hold steady!" Smiling to myself, I gave Trudeau a wink and motioned toward the opposite shore.

The rest of the afternoon was spent measuring the depth of the waters between the three or four rises until we picked up the trail again. Only once did Trudeau fall into the water. I thought I would have to rescue him again before he came sputtering to the surface. I pulled him back onto the boat.

"Praise Jesus," he cried, dripping wet.

I remained silent, sitting cross-legged, listening to the crows chatter amongst themselves, watching them flitter from one tree to the next, swooping toward each other, a sky dance and song. The Lakota counted the crow as sacred; I felt blessed to be shown what lay beyond my petty troubles.

We waited for Persimmons to secure his device. Trudeau paid no attention to the crows or anything else that surrounded us.

"Zeb?"

I was not much interested in conversation.

"Zeb, are you a follower of Jesus?"

I took a few long seconds to decide if I wanted to answer. I had been asked this before by a few different folks, and I always seemed to disappoint them.

"No," I said.

"Why not? You must be a God-fearing man."

"There ain't no god I fear."

"You're not afraid of going to hell without knowin' Jesus?"

"The way I figure, the man's been dead for some time now. How am I goin' to know a dead man?" I knew it was a mistake as soon as I asked the question.

"He's very much alive in my heart. As long as this is true, I know I'll enter the gates of heaven, to live a pure life, forever." He paused. "Don't you want that, Zeb?"

I watched the crows continue to swoop and circle each other through the blue skies of late afternoon. Once upon a time, my brother and I would follow their lead on our ponies, chasing them across the prairie, circling back and around until, finally, they just flew away, as if they had more important things to do than to fly above, entertaining mere humans.

"All this," I said, stretching my hands out to the swamp, "is my heaven . . . and my hell."

Trudeau stared at me. "But . . . all this is temporary."

"Yep, sure is."

I turned away from him to face Persimmons and Roy, ready to take more measurements.

The prison camp consisted of four tents arranged two by two, their openings facing each other with no exits in back, five men each in three, with the guards and Persimmons in the fourth. Trudeau and I shared the tent that sat across from them along with three other fellows named Carson, Betts, and Sinclair. After two days and nights, the stink of five prisoners, our bodies and clothes soaked with sweat and swamp water, filled the tent. The stench seeped through everything, down into our bones. Once we left, it would take many months to wash it all away.

We were afforded a water bucket to wash our hands and faces, filled from a well that sat between our outpost at the edge of the sugarcane field and the slave quarters. As we came from working in the swamp, the plantation's slaves drifted in from the fields, stopping first to wash, then to sit at their communal tables for supper. As with the slaves at Groce's plantation, these folks lowered their heads in prayer, then began to eat in silence. Our table was in a square that the layout of our tents provided.

We ate the same food as the black folk, beef or chicken, and potatoes, served by a young slave girl. No one said a prayer, except for Trudeau.

His eyes seemed to always show a look of constant terror, unless he was praying. He would then close them, his face softening, and a sense of bliss came over him. He prayed anywhere, at any time, until one of the other prisoners threw something, food, a glob of mud or a stick, hitting him in the head. Once, Roy snuck up and screamed into his ear, "If a gator don't kill ya, my whip will, an' God ain't gonna do a goddamn thing 'bout that! Now, get yer ass back to the woodpile." The look of terror returned, with him muttering how Jesus must have saved him for good reason.

This time, at supper, Roy said, "Ain't nobody going to answer your stupid prayers. You're nothing but a goddamn criminal, and not a good one at that. Hell, ya couldn't even kill the poor bastard right, shoulda hit him harder. And shoulda killed the girl too. Mighta gotten away with it all." Persimmons and the rest of the guards acted as if they heard nothing and we continued to eat in silence. It appeared that I was the only one who did not know what Roy spoke of.

Later, I asked Trudeau about his story. He hesitated for a few, long seconds, then said he had met the girl in a one-room schoolhouse back in St. Charles Parish, where he grew up. A teacher, a man from Mississippi, caught them behind the building one afternoon when all the other students had gone home. I asked what they were caught doing. His face turned crimson and he hung his head. He would not say, except that he was bad, *real* bad. Then he looked up and told me, as if confessing for the first time. "The teacher came up on us. I held her mouth shut, but she bit my hand and screamed. She run off. I was scared so I grabbed a log from the woodpile and hit him in the head." He stopped and lowered his eyes. "Was an accident," he insisted, over and over. It took three days for the man to die, his head swelling up twice its size. The girl claimed Trudeau was raping her. She was twelve, he was seventeen. He went to prison for the murder and had been there for six years and would be for life. He found Jesus through a cellmate two years before, and in his mind, was redeemed for his trespasses. As long as he lived, Trudeau swore he would never harm another soul. It seemed the word had gotten around the prison, about his troubles and losing his will to fight. Thus, Roy's constant attacks, harassment from the other prisoners, and his slow decline into madness.

"Praise Jesus," Trudeau whispered.

For three or four days, Trudeau and I worked with Persimmons, laying out a path through the swamp to the Amite River. The map he used was not so accurate. The surveying allowed for a true understanding of our task. Most of the road would be three bridges connected to the four rises with a widening of the existing trail. In some low places that were only mud, we were to build what Persimmons called a corduroy road, logs laid sideways, tight in a row then covered in long planks. On several plain pieces of paper, he rendered the road, designing the various aspects of the bridges in detail along with measurements to build by. I was most impressed and said so. He glanced up from his work, gave a brief smile, and carried on. *Hell, he does in fact know what he's doin'.*

The rest of the chain gang ventured out to cut down cypress trees, drag them back to the sugarcane field, and load them onto wagons. Two plantations upriver, at the Hermitage, a sawmill cleaned and cut the logs according to Persimmon's measurements, then split some of the wood into boards. A few days later, the components of the bridges began rolling up from the pier, each piece marked with numbers and letters Persimmons had provided in his drawings. Huge puzzles to be built, then connected to each other.

We were finishing up the survey, standing on the bank of the Amite River looking back toward Persimmons, when Trudeau stiffened.

"The Indian," he said.

I turned to where he pointed. Downriver, only a few strides away if there was dry land, stood the Indian, clutching the same tomahawk at his chest. He walked slowly toward us, as if he walked on the water, lowering the tomahawk to hang from his left hand. He cupped his right hand to his mouth and screamed, *"Oooweya!"*

Before my eyes, he disappeared.

"Oh, God, Oh, God! It's Jesus, come back as an Injun!" said Trudeau, shaking. *"Take me, take me, oh, Lord, please . . . take me from here!"*

"What's all the ruckus?" asked Persimmons.

"Jesus, I saw Jesus!" hollered Trudeau. "Dressed in feathers."

"Creed, what's he talking about?"

"The Indian, we both saw him this time," I said, staring at the still water on which he stood seconds before.

"Come on, we're done for the day." He paused. "And leave the Indian be."

The whole way back to the plantation, Trudeau shook his head muttering, *"Injun Jesus . . . Injun Jesus."*

At camp, there was a frenzy. A prisoner by the name of Lucius lay unconscious on the wooden supper table, his right leg cracked open, bone splintered through skin and mud-caked clothes. Blood dripped from the table to seep into the ground. A short, round woman stood on a stool leaning over the injuries, and with a knife, stripped away the cloth, exposing torn skin. From a pouch slung across her shoulder, she retrieved a small bottle, uncorked it with her teeth, and handed it to the guard holding Lucius down. "Three drops, three drops only," she said, and went back to cleaning the wounds with a wet cloth. Then, to no one in particular, she asked, "Somebody get me a saw. Now, don't matter what kind." None of us moved. The woman turned to face Persimmons, standing next to me. "Sir, he most certainly will die if he don't lose this leg." She glanced at me with black eyes, her chocolate skin shining with sweat. Persimmons told Kershaw to go and fetch a fine-tooth saw. The woman went back to work trying to save Lucius's life. A man I had not seen before, dressed in high boots, plaid shirt, and suspenders, watched all that was going on from under a wide-brimmed, black hat. He seemed to not miss a thing.

"How'd this happen?" I asked Carson.

He spoke low, giving a slight nod to Roy. "The bastard told Lucius to go on ahead and clear some brush. As soon as he disappeared, Roy ordered these other fellas to finish cutting a tree. We was cutting two or three at a time. The tree fell on the ole boy. We had to pull him from the mud. Damn near drowned. Hell, Mr. Roy just told us to leave him there. Couldn't do that, now could we?" He continued staring at Roy.

"Who's the woman?"

"She's like a doctor, but ain't. One of the slaves."

I nodded to the man. "Who's he?"

"The overseer, come to keep an eye on her," said Carter.

Kershaw brought a saw. Lucius still lay unconscious when she began to cut, first using a knife, then the saw. It took only a few minutes. I thought of Padgett, a friend who had lost part of a leg during the Goliad massacre, and all the troubles we had trying to keep him alive. I wondered how Padgett fared.

Two hours later, Lucius died.

The healer left, only after doing all she could to stop the bleeding. She could not. Lucius did not wake but for speaking gibberish, then became still. Finally, a blanket was laid over him. Soon after, at dusk, the body was removed, the table scrubbed. We sat in silence eating our supper by lamplight. I tried not to think about the bloodstained wood.

"The damn slave killed the bastard," Roy said.

No one acknowledged him.

"Jesus wears feathers."

Everyone stared at Trudeau. The look in his eyes had changed to a gleam of confidence, an absolute sureness of what he spoke about.

"Zeb saw him too."

I glanced around, shrugged, and took another bite of chicken.

"I say we find the bitch an' give her a good beatin'. Hell, I'll do it myself," Roy said, laying his whip on the table.

Persimmons set down his fork and turned to him. "If you go near her, you go back to Baton Rouge and have to explain to the warden how a tree you ordered cut fell on a prisoner you sent in front of. Now, sit there and keep your mouth shut, that's an order."

"Jesus has feathers."

"Will you shut up!" Roy hollered.

"Lucius is light," Trudeau announced, staring at Roy. "And you killed him. The tree didn't kill him, the woman didn't kill him, *you killed him.*"

Roy stood, snatched up the whip, and tried hitting Trudeau in the face with the butt of the handle. Trudeau simply leaned back. Roy swung again, closer. I grabbed the thong a foot or so from the handle. Roy yanked, I held on. We stood for a second, the whip taut. He pulled again, hard. I let go. He stumbled backward over the bench and hit the ground. He struggled to get up, slipping a couple of times. When he finally did stand, his hands were covered in blood-soaked mud. Everyone laughed, including the other guards. It was then clear that Roy was nothing more than a bullyrag, not to be feared, trusted, or respected.

Persimmons stood. "Roy, sit down now! You have done quite enough damage for one day."

Trudeau sat straight in his chair and said, "You killed Lucius."

"Keep quiet now!" Persimmons said, giving him a stern look.

Trudeau closed his eyes, bowed his head in silence, and whispered, *"Jesus wears feathers . . . Praise Jesus."*

CHAPTER 11

A boy stands next to a man, maybe his father, maybe the one who raises the boy and not his father. There is a resemblance, though the boy is darker. He stands like the man, with one foot crossed over the other, hands on both hips. They wear smiles, but not quite smiles, as if they know a secret that cannot be told to anyone, to be kept to themselves always. Snowcapped mountains rise up behind them; the sun breaks through clouds the color of cotton. They stand on a sandy shore of the bluest of rivers. A blue that can only be found in dreams. The boy frowns and glances up at the man, saying something I cannot hear. The man reaches down, touches the boy's shoulder, and answers him. They both look at me and again smile.

Trudeau shook me.

The morning woke with caws of egrets mixed with the fading drone of insects from the night. Though no longer asleep, I kept my eyes closed for as long as I could. *The dream.* I had not dreamt in a long while or had dreamed but could not remember. I did not seem to recognize the boy and the man, yet they were somehow familiar. I knew the mountains they stood against, the Grand Tetons, for I had traveled through them with my brother.

My brother, Jonathan. I had not thought of him for some time, perhaps on purpose, or maybe for the fact that lately I had been quite busy defending my life. If he was there with me, he would have laughed and shaken his head.

"Zebadiah, always findin' trouble," Jonathan might have said, had he still been alive.

Oh, how I missed him.

Trudeau shook me again. "Zeb, Mr. Roy will be coming soon. You're late three times in a week."

My first thought was *how the hell did he know it had been a week*? From his cot, where the heavy, iron ball lay, the chain taut around his ankle, Trudeau was able to reach my cot enough to hover over my face.

The light of the morning crept into the tent, enough to see by. I felt something move. I slowly sat up, staring at what lay between my legs. The snake tried uncurling itself. A young moccasin's poison could kill me quicker than an adult would, especially if she struck where I thought she might be aiming at. Trudeau still leaned down next to my cot. "Shhh," I whispered, and nodded toward my crotch. Trudeau gasped and jerked away. The snake struck at his hand. I snatched it behind its head, the body wreathing around my wrist, and swung my legs to the floor. In one swift motion, I bit the head off, spat it to the ground, and flung the carcass out of the tent. Trudeau stood staring down at the snake head as its jaws slowly opened and shut, perhaps unwilling to believe what I had just done.

"A baby snake, you'd be dying now," I said.

Carson, Betts, and Sinclair stood next to their cots. Betts leaned over to pick up the head. Carson pulled him back. "The damn thing can still bite, you dolt."

Outside came a commotion as others gathered around the still twisting headless moccasin.

"I'll be damned," Roy said as he entered the tent with Kershaw following. "Who did this?" he asked and looked straight at me.

"It's . . . it's a miracle," said Trudeau.

"He bit the head right off!" exclaimed Sinclair.

I sat calmly on my cot, then stood to face Roy.

"You did this?" he asked.

69

"Don't know how the hell a snake like that could end up on my cot," I said.

Roy's face turned a shade red. "Don't know what ya mean." His hand lay on the whip hung loose from his belt.

"Suppose if someone wanted me dead . . ."

"You sayin' I aim to kill ya?"

"Either you or the snake. Both I reckon." I glanced around the tent. "Now, I figure the damn thing didn't crawl into my lap all by itself."

Sinclair and Betts turned to Roy, then away from us both. Betts mumbled, "I thought it was to be a joke."

"Uh-huh," I said.

"Was Jesus that give ya the lightnin' to catch that snake, *hallelujah!*" hollered Trudeau. *"Hallelujah!"* He started dancing a jig, raising his hands into the air, wiggling his fingers, stomping the damp earth into mud. *"Praise Jesus . . . praise Jesus . . . praise Jesus,"* he said. Roy grabbed his arm. He tore away, stumbling over his leg chains. *"Praise Jesus,"* Trudeau cried one more time as he lay on the ground, squeezing his hand, blood seeping from a small puncture.

"Shut up!" Roy screamed, pulling the whip from his belt. He uncurled it and raised his arm to strike. I wrenched the whip from his hand and threw it out of the tent to land next to the headless snake. He attempted to hit me, but I blocked him. His eyes narrowed, filled with hatred and fear. I stood waiting for his next move, ready to hurt him if I had to.

Persimmons entered the tent saying, "What the hell is going on here?"

"If you're goin' to kill me, you best do better," I said, and sat back down on my cot, finished with the fight.

Kershaw pulled his club and offered it to Roy. He snatched it up and said, "Twice you have disgraced me." In one swipe, he

knocked me in the side of my head.
The world went black.

knocked me in the side of my head.
The world went black.

CHAPTER 12

I could not breathe for the heat. Daylight shone evenly through the slats of the door, the alternating shadows offering no relief but for the lack of sun burning on my naked skin. For the afternoon, I had been locked in this wooden coffin, a rectangular box buried in the ground up to the door, exposed to anyone who happened by, slave and slave owner alike. My head felt like it was split wide open.

A few feet away, Trudeau lay in a similar box. His cries and moans reminded me of the insane prisoner who Willie Dan murdered back in New Orleans. Every hour or so, someone beat on the door with a stick, telling him to shut up, else something far worse than a few days and nights locked up might befall him. He would stop for a few moments, then the whimpering began with *"Oh Jesus, oh Jesus . . ."*

Persimmons spoke with someone standing near us. "Both these men are good workers. I need them back tomorrow morning."

"As you wish, sir. While they're here, they will be treated in kind as to the severity of their crimes. Haven't had to use these boxes since I've taken ownership. I treat my slaves good, they obey," said the man, his shadow falling across me. "This one is Creed. He is also a religious man?"

"No, sir, more akin to the Indian," said Persimmons.

"How do you know?"

"He speaks reverently of your Indian hiding in the swamp."

"There are no Indians 'round here, sir. Least none alive. My father-in-law, Mr. Hampton, made sure of it."

"Well, sir, both these men claimed to have seen one."

Silence fell between them. Then Persimmons said, "Thank you for your time with this matter. I must get back, lest your road won't be built."

Persimmons walked away; the other man kneeled beside the box. "Mr. Creed, I have been biding my time, wanting to meet you. I am truly shocked that this would be the circumstance. I hear you threatened the life of a guard after biting off the head of a snake, a moccasin. Sir, is this true?"

"Who are you?" I asked.

"It must be true then. Quite an amazing feat, that you are still alive." He paused, perhaps shaking his head. "I'm so sorry for my rudeness, sir, for my lack of a formal introduction. My name is John S. Preston and I am the proprietor and master of this here plantation where you have found yourself."

He leaned over so I could see his face. A man of maybe thirty, with brown hair and sideburns grown down his cheeks. I could not tell the color of his eyes for the sun shone behind his head. I detected a calm assuredness in his words, a man of culture and respect for others.

I said nothing.

After a few seconds, he said, "Sir, I understand how you may not feel like talkin'. And that you feel you have been wronged; that someone else's will has been imposed upon you. However, I must let you know, Mr. Creed, this situation you find yourself in is quite temporary, a show of sorts to some that you are worthy." He paused. "You have mettle, sir, proven during the great revolution. You will survive this evening. Come tomorrow, most certainly a new day will dawn."

And he was gone.

What the hell did he mean, I have mettle. Why would anyone here care whether I lived or died. Though I did sense that somehow, my misfortune was turning, if only I survived the night . . .

The sun fell past the trees; shadows lay across the small plot of land our coffins were buried in. I slept some. Pain shot through my mouth into the skin of my face, my nose and eyes. My teeth hurt. Though my tongue was numb, I tasted poison. How foolish I was to think that I might be immune to its effect.

Trudeau's voice rose and fell. Sometimes he spoke in full sentences, most times not. By twilight, he was quiet. Then, "My hand's black . . . crust. By the morning, it will be gone, swallowed by the snake."

The moccasin must have struck him. *Damn, I wasn't quick enough,* I had a dreadful feeling. Then there came a voice, separate from mine, detached, somewhere outside my head. *Poor, old Trudeau, he will finally meet his feather-covered Jesus.*

Darkness pooled in the box I lay in.

I dreamed.

The woman who tried saving Lucius introduces herself. "Lindy Lou Green, my slave name. My true name is Lusa Oho Ashe; Black Woman of the Moon." The evening is lit by a swirl of fireflies. An extravagance of light shining through the dark. Am I to die tonight? I ask.

"No," she says. "These ain't for you."

How relieved I am. Though, if it is my time, I would gladly follow their path.

We sit on the porch of the main house, drinking tea served by a young, white slave girl. On the lawn, dogs of all shapes and sizes lie about scratching and sniffing. Occasionally, there comes a growl and a bark.

"You know why all these dogs are here, Zebadiah?"

I shake my head.

" 'Cause we don't beat 'em. We treat 'em nice," she says. "We don't force them into boxes buried in the ground."

I follow her in taking another sip of tea. We sit in silence. For how long: days, months, years? I cannot tell for the sun never shines.

"Dogs make the best slaves, obedient, trustworthy, loyal. Don't you agree, Zebadiah?"

I try to speak but cannot and touch my lips. The tip of my finger is burned.

"The serpent wants her poison back," she says. "It was not meant for you and must be spit out." She hands me an old, green-colored copper spittoon.

I place the cup of tea on the table, lean over, and open my mouth. The whole of my guts retches out of my throat. For hours I vomit the foulest of venom, poisons I have held in my bones for forever. The last drops fill up the spittoon to its brim. I lean back in the chair feeling as light as a feather, as if I might float away into the night. The dogs are quiet. All of them stare at me, their eyes as bright as the fireflies.

From the edge of the swamp, a movement in the cypress trees gives way to the Indian, dressed in white, brown, and black feathers, the lower half of his face painted yellow. He walks slowly through the pack of dogs; each one howls as he passes. Mournful, yet defiant voices rise, an Indian and Negro chant in harmony. The Indian comes onto the porch.

"Offer him your poison."

He kneels before me. I hold out the spittoon as if it were a chalice. He closes his eyes and drinks, then bows and says, "Thank you," in perfect English.

The Indian retreats into the swamp. Trudeau follows surrounded by fireflies. The entire swamp is lit, as if he entered heaven.

I feel sad for I will miss my friend.

Praise Jesus.

"The poison is gone, the taste of it on your tongue remains forever," says Lindy Lou.

The house has disappeared, I stand in a field of cut sugarcane. I smell ancient earth and eternal sweat. Dogs surround me; some carry babies, some hold machetes in their hands.

I woke to the creak of the door as it was being lifted open. The overseer reached in and grabbed my hand to help me out of the box. The bright, early morning sun cut through the trees. Standing buck naked, the poison gone, I felt that, indeed, a brand-new day had dawned.

Persimmons and Roy watched as two black men pulled Trudeau's body from the box.

"Snake got him after all," Roy said with a sneer. "Like I say, least a couple of ya die out here. Creed, you got lucky."

I stepped up to Roy, close. He and Persimmons stared at the scars on my chest, the dent in my shoulder where Baumgartner shot me, Rudy's scar on my cheek, the scar on my thigh left by the cut of Brody's knife. Roy reached for his bullwhip; I snatched it away and threw it into the box.

"You're nothin' but a gutless bully, 'cept ya get men killed, an' never doin' the killin' yourself." I paused and shook my head. Then, "There will be no fireflies when you die, only darkness."

He stared at me with a look of fear and surprise. "Fireflies?"

"If I ever see you again, I will kill you . . . and you'll find out."

I turned to Persimmons. "You will build a fine road, sir. I hope one day to walk on it."

With a blanket draped over my shoulders, the overseer pointed to a footpath leading up to the main house. "Please follow me, sir; Master Preston is expecting you."

CHAPTER 13

Given the dire set of circumstances I had found myself in, a leisurely walk up to the Big House, wrapped only in a blanket, was certainly appealing. Especially after the day and night I had just experienced. I was glad to be alive. Despite the morning brilliance of the sun shining, I still felt the cool luminescence of fireflies and a subtle taste of the serpent's poison left on my tongue. No matter what was about to happen, my life could not become worse, or better.

I did not know the overseer's name; however, everyone we passed, slave or white, called out a hearty, *Good morning, Mister.*

The footpath wandered past warehouses full of sugarcane with men, women, and children, all of them slaves, cutting the stalks to pieces ten or so inches long. These were shoveled into wagons, then driven to the river and loaded onto the barges I had seen earlier. One building held a small mill to work the cane into sugar, with a press manned by muscular, half-naked, young black men to squeeze the juice from the cane. Mister pointed to the barrels, half liquid, half crystalized into solid sugar. "Sold to the steamboats and bargemen stoppin' on their way to New Orleans, needin' a little sweetness," he said, laughing. "We'll be buildin' a grander mill to take care of *all* our cuts, don't have to share profits with nobody."

At the press, the two men stopped for a second to stare at me, as if they were seeing a ghost. Mister hollered to get them back to moving, without a threat or violence. He carried no whip or any other weapon. They lowered their heads, pushed the worn, wooden handles, and continued to squeeze the sugar-cane.

I followed him past the blacksmith shop. An aproned old man and his young apprentice, their dark faces smudged with even darker soot, hammered out red-hot, iron rods, to be made, I presumed, into a variety of tools, scathes, machetes . . . They both paused to look up. The man leaned into the boy and whispered something. The boy grew fearful, then whispered back, and they both stood staring. Again, the overseer motioned for them to get back to work. I supposed a filthy, white man covered in only a blanket might be strange to see in the morning light. At that moment, I was unconcerned about anyone's opinion of me.

We emerged from the buildings onto open grass, to stand before a garden of brilliant, white jasmine, pink roses, and lilac, all lying below three or four blooming magnolia trees. And beyond, the magnificent red brick façade of the Big House. Mister saw my surprise and said, "Hell, this is the backside, wait 'til you see the front." And with that, he guided me to a long, low building to our right. On the porch sat a rocking chair. A clear carafe of coffee and one cup lay on a small, square table. Next to the table, stood the small, round woman who had attempted to save Lucius's life. The same woman who appeared so vivid in my dream.

"Lindy, this here is Zebadiah Creed. He's come from prison and is now Master's special guest. We need a bath an' clean clothes, then some food, ya hear?"

"Lindy Lou Green," I said.

She smiled. "Ah yes, we do know each other. Why . . . ?"

Mister looked at the both of us and shook his head, cutting off her words. "Now don't ask no questions, Lindy, just do as I say, an' have him ready for supper, hear? I'm off to mind the fields." He turned on his heel and walked off.

"Coffee?" she asked.

I could only nod.

She poured me a cup and I graciously accepted, taking a sip. I had not tasted anything like this. The face I made must have shown my surprise. "Nuts?"

"Chicory, Zebadiah."

I felt it might take a while for me to get used to this peculiar brew, though I gulped the coffee down anyway.

Lindy offered the rocking chair. "Would you like to sit?"

Coffee and a rocking chair! What could I have done to deserve this?

I carefully sat down, closed my eyes and leaned back, then rocked forward to stay still. I listened to the hammer of the blacksmith pounding in rhythm with the crunching squeeze of sugarcane; further afield, the swoosh and slice of blades cutting cane. Far off in the distance came the blasting whistle of a riverboat as it passed the plantation. I heard the cheerful chatter and smelled the sweet aroma wafting off meat and vegetables as the women and girls prepared the noonday meal for the rest of their fellow slaves. All in time with the other.

I opened my eyes. Lindy stood about the same height as I sat, staring at me with deep, black eyes. "You're welcome," she said.

Almost in tears, I felt as if she knew my plight exactly.

"How do I deserve this?" I asked.

"Bein' yourself."

She offered to pour me another cup. "You survived the night, the poison."

I nodded and took a sip. The chicory was growing on me. "I had a dream, a vision." I hesitated to tell her more. Yet, deep inside myself, I knew to trust her.

"A dream can be as real as waking life," she said, her eyes

shining black.

"An Indian, the one I saw in the swamp. I watched Trudeau walk after him with fireflies all around. Just like my brother." I wiped my eyes. "With dogs howling . . . You were there."

She smiled, as if what I shared was no surprise. "Master Creed, Houma runs in my blood, alongside my African ancestors. I know the man you speak of." She hesitated, glancing around to ensure our privacy, as if to tell me more might be a mistake. "He is my father."

"So, he's real?"

She did not answer and was quiet for a few, long seconds. I felt that I might never know the truth. Then she said, "Good dogs make better masters."

My head swirled, for she explained as much in the dream.

I again felt the pulse of the plantation. Yet, there now seemed a slight shade on the day, as if invisible clouds dimmed the sun. I stared at Lindy Lou Green, her face plump, yet with high cheekbones, her skin awash with a reddish, golden sheen. Her eyes pierced my soul, much like Willie Dan's, but in an almost saintly way.

"Zebadiah, you show the shine, sir."

I did not know what she meant by this. She must have seen my confusion.

"Is why you saw my father."

I thought of Trudeau. He saw the Indian, same as me. An apparition, or a real man?

"Is he alive?"

She turned away and did not answer, as if she was listening to someone else on the porch whispering to her. Then, "You bit off the head of the snake?"

"Yes, I thought I would save my friend's life."

"Yet, he died. And you tasted the serpent's poison?"

Was this a question? I felt she knew the answer.

"In my dream, you said, that I would taste it forever."

She nodded, with the slightest of grins.

"Zebadiah, Master Preston will ask something of you. This will be the hardest decision you'll ever make."

The clear, blue sky dimmed ever so slightly more, the invisible clouds darkening.

"A storm's a coming," said Lindy Lou Green.

I closed my eyes, leaned back in the rocker, and for a few seconds, tried to relieve my mind of my approaching predicament.

CHAPTER 14

After a bath and hair trim, Lindy offered a new set of clothes. The deep, velvet jacket fit snug against the white frill shirt and black tie I wore, with high-waisted pants. The more often I wore these kinds of clothes, the more comfortable I felt. The boots fit perfect. I had never seen a pair made from alligator hide. *I really like these. Hell, I could walk through the swamp up to the tops an' not get my feet wet.* Again, I gazed at myself in a mirror. All I recognized was my own gray eyes and the scar on my cheek cut by Rudy Dupree.

Mister came back from the fields and accosted Lindy. "You'd better go and talk to old Worley, he ain't doin' much a nothin'. Claims his leg don't work. I asked him to show me why. When he pulled down his britches, ain't nothin' wrong 'cept a knob on his knee. See if that salve'll take the pain away." He looked at me and nodded his approval. "Good, good. The master will be enthused. Now, be off, an' get Worley's leg to workin' an' get him back to the fields."

Lindy glanced at me and at the overseer, then said, "Yes, Mister. I'll get Worley's knobby ole knee to swinging in no time." As Mister turned away, she raised an eyebrow, trusting me with her dig.

Lindy left and I was again alone with Mister. "Now, I need her, mind you, but sometimes she's just too smart for her own good. If it was anybody 'sides Master Preston, she might be long gone down the river."

She's certainly smarter than you, I wanted to say, but did not indicate any approval or disapproval of his statement. I felt I needed to tread a fine line with these folks, else I might find myself back in the swamp and either Roy or me dead; or both.

I lounged on the porch most of the day, snoozing in the rocking chair to the sounds of the plantation. Off in the distance, muffled by cypress trees and black water, I heard the chop of axes as prisoners cut down those trees. *Any time now, Persimmons and that bastard Roy will come along, snatch me up, and I'll be off to the swamp.*

It did not happen.

By late afternoon, I was getting antsy, and hungry. The clothes I wore were not suited for sitting about in the sweltering heat of a long, summer day. But I dared not leave the rocker. Lindy had not come back, nor the overseer. Left alone, I wondered how I had gotten to this place. *Why* was more the question. Why was I there? To fulfill a moral correction to my soul? Hell, everything I had done up to that point, I could justify. *Well, almost everything. Except for that fella I burned up in the beaver's den.* I still felt bad about that. Though there was nothing to do about him, his screams still haunted me.

It was an accident, or so I justified.

Lindy arrived back as the sun touched the trees. A day ago, I lay in a box buried in the ground with a raving lunatic lying next to me; both of us stricken with snake venom. And then there I was gazing at this rotund shaman who came to me in my dream.

"Come with me, Zebadiah Creed," she said, nodding toward the Big House.

We walked through the garden, past the jasmine and roses, under the magnolia trees just beginning to blossom, to the back door. The red bricks were faded and old, washed with years of rain and heat. I brushed a brick with the tips of my fingers as we passed through the door. I felt its age, sadness . . . and pain.

Lindy stopped and stared at me. "You truly do have the shine, Zebadiah Creed. You got a choice on how ya use it, always remember that, sir."

I nodded, knowing she was right.

We entered the kitchen, with servants scurrying about preparing the evening supper. There seemed to be an extravagance to this meal, a tension in the room to cook the food just right with one older woman calling out to do this and that. As we walked through, everyone paused a second to stare, allowing us through to the swinging doors with not a whisper among them. The head cook nodded ever so slightly to Lindy and me. I felt excited, bewildered, and certainly had no idea what to expect that might be waiting behind those doors. Lindy tapped slightly, the kitchen still quiet. From the other side came the voice of a woman saying for us to enter. The doors swung open and in an instant, the kitchen folk returned to their frenzy.

To my left, a staircase swirled up from the dark, brown floor of the hallway, its white steps and red carpet curving toward the second story to disappear into the ceiling. Under a brilliantly lit crystal chandelier stood a young woman with auburn hair, her beige dress sweeping across the sky-blue rug that lay from the door where we stood to the pane-glass front doors of the house. Standing directly behind her was John S. Preston.

She asked, "Mister Zebadiah Creed, I presume?"

"Yes, dear, I told you his name already," Preston said.

"I want to make sure he is the right Zebadiah Creed."

"There is only one, my dear, only one."

I did not know what to say. Behind me, the door swung shut and Lindy Lou was gone. I stood alone before the owners of the Hydras plantation.

"He looks marvelous," she said, smiling, as if she was winking at me.

"Yes, a man of prowess, courage, and . . ." He stepped to the side of his wife, ". . . insight."

"Hmm, does he know what I am thinking?" Her smile eased to a grin, mischievous.

"I do not know, Caroline. Why don't you ask him, my dear?"

"Mister Creed, may I call you Zebadiah?"

"Yes, ma'am."

"He speaks!" she said. "Come shake hands, Zebadiah."

A few steps forward and I stood in front of them both. She was taller than him by an inch. Yet, they both looked equal in stature.

I reached out with my right hand; she offered her left. I bowed, gently grasping her fingers, raising the back of her hand to my lips. I let go and stood up straight. They both stared at me with slight grins.

Preston turned to his wife. "He certainly has manners."

"Yes, he does," she said, twirling away toward an open door. "Come, Zebadiah Creed, and meet our other guests."

We followed, with Preston allowing me to go first.

The room was cool and dimly lit. A parlor of sorts, with several comfort chairs arrayed in a half circle facing a fireplace centered on the wall. Above the mantel hung a tapestry similar to the one that hung in the warden's office, a hunt for a single Negro. A small fire burned, yet, I felt no heat. Broussard stood by the grate; Katharine Brody stood next to him. I entered the room; they both smiled, as if greeting an old friend.

"Ah, *Monsieur* Creed, we finally meet outside of . . . your peculiar circumstances," said Broussard.

CHAPTER 15

I should not have been shocked. Two plantation owners, masters of slaves, businessmen interested in only power and money, together under the roof of such an extravagant house. That these two should be friends made perfect sense. I also should not have been surprised to see Katharine Brody standing next to Broussard, Brody's death giving license for an open romance. A part of me wondered if our imagined amorous meeting in New Orleans might be still intact.

I stood still, stone cold, waiting. Behind me, I heard the closing of a book.

"Mr. Creed, so good that you survived San Jacinto to join us this evening."

I turned and, sitting in a chair near a wall filled with books, sat a man I had only met once. I did not remember his name. However, I recollected from where I knew him. Groce's plantation, the night Lamar Groce beat the young boy for falling asleep. I remembered not liking him at all.

"Dr. Anson Jones," he said, and stood, offering his hand. I reluctantly extended mine and we shook, his palm moist.

"Groce's plantation, with General Houston," I offered.

"Yes, I was instrumental in pushing him forward to fight. Do you recall, sir?"

"I recall him not needin' to be spurred on by anyone."

He shrugged. "The reason why he attacked is immaterial. The fact that Santa Anna was overrun and defeated is the most important aspect of our . . . . cause."

"What cause, sir?"

Jones looked past me. I swiveled around to find Broussard standing directly behind. "Yes, the cause," he said.

Mrs. Preston rang a small handbell and announced, "Dinner is served."

We lined out of the parlor, down the hall past a couple of closed doors, and into the dining room. My thoughts spun as to why I was there with these folks. One man, who took tremendous trouble to attempt to have me kidnapped by a one-eyed bounty hunter, whom I shot and killed. Then finally kidnapped; and then betrayed by my good friend Grainger for a bag of coins, all to see my charge of the murder of Benjamin Brody dismissed. And to find out in prison that he himself had set up Brody's death by the pistol of Willie Dan, a murderous prisoner who happened to be in the cell next to mine. Now, to suspect that Brody's own wife may have been complicit.

And what of John S. Preston and his wife? It seemed by his talk, that Preston had been expecting me to come to Hydras plantation all along, to allow me to toil as a prisoner for a time, then invite me as a treasured guest up to the Big House and to dinner. And there was Dr. Anson Jones. A nefarious man straight back from Texas, intimate with General Houston in a way most folks were not allowed to be. My left hand began to shake. I casually looped a finger into my jacket pocket. I would not offer any more advantage to these folks than they already had.

Mrs. Preston showed me to a chair next to Jones, across from Katharine Brody with Broussard beside her. Preston sat at one end of the table; his wife sat down at the other. As large as the table was, spanning the entire length of the dining room, four chairs lay empty, two on each side, between myself and Mrs. Preston, as if there were other guests to be expected. Lavish was not the word to use to describe the table settings. Opulent was more proper. The centerpiece, a silver vase two feet tall, exploded with colorful flowers and plants, some from the garden I had just walked through. White jasmine, pink roses, purple lilacs, intertwined through thin branches cut from a magnolia tree, its blossoms intact. And through all of this were strewn cattails from the swamp and dried sawgrass from the Gulf Coast. The sterling silverware and crystal glasses set on a white linen cloth twinkled by chandelier, lighting up the entire table. I glanced at Mrs. Preston as she watched me. I should not have been surprised by such richness as this was not my first time to sit at a dinner like this. However, I felt that I would never become accustomed to this much wealth.

Mrs. Preston rang the bell again; the door swung open with six servants entering carrying food. A tray of sliced, roast beef, another tray of brazened pork shoulders, four whole chickens, and an assortment of vegetables: roasted carrots, fried potatoes, sweet yams, and summer squash. The aromas were overwhelming for I had not eaten this well in quite some time. Again, I glanced at Mrs. Preston. A look of bemusement still crossed her face.

"You are unaccustomed to such good food, Mr. Creed?" she asked.

"Ma'am, lately, I'm unaccustomed to anything that ain't moldy and waterlogged." I paused and thought for a second. "Except for what we ate cooked and served by your slaves. There's somethin' about their food that is comforting."

She nodded and smiled. "I am glad to hear that our folks are eating well."

"They are perhaps the best fed on the whole Lower Mississippi," offered Preston. "Now, those working for Claude across the river, well, sir, he does not take good care of his property like he should, like we do here at Hydras. And it's a shame, for they would not rebel near as much, and would be happy, just like our folk."

Dr. Jones nodded. "Yes, sir, a well-fed Negro will cut twice as much cane and carry three times his weight in cuts to the mill. Fact is, add a little sugar in their milk once in a while, not all the time mind you, but once in a while, an' they'll outperform the next four plantations up and down the river. Will certainly be happier than Claude's."

"I say add a little fear to their sugar. Aye, Mr. Creed?" asked Broussard.

I had not expected to become part of their conversation. Again, I paused before I spoke. Then, "I offer no opinion on such matters as I don't own nobody, sir."

"But if you did," said Mrs. Preston.

"I would not."

Silence prevailed except for the clinking of glasses as wine was poured and food was served. When our plates were full and the servants had returned to the kitchen, Mrs. Preston said, "Shall we pray?"

I did not want to make a show of my lack of faith in their God, so I bowed my head along with them.

"Dear Lord," Preston offered. "Protect us from the devil's hand, putrid smell, and disease come out of the swamp, and give us strength to carry out your wishes, a bountiful crop here at Hydras plantation."

"Amen," said Jones, along with Broussard, Preston, and his wife. Katharine Brody muttered an amen under her breath, and I said nothing.

For a while, we ate in silence, then "Mr. Creed, how does one bite the head off a moccasin and live to tell about it?" asked Preston.

I looked around the table. Everyone stared at me, as if I had a magical tale to tell. "As quick as ya can," I simply said.

Broussard was the first to laugh, a nasally Frenchman's laugh.

After everyone stopped, he said, "Yet, you nearly died in the hot box and still did not save your friend."

I said, "You're right, I did not save him; yet that should not have stopped me from tryin', sir."

"So, you feel that it is worth risking your own life for others?" asked Mrs. Preston.

"Mostly, depending on who it is."

Preston asked, "Would you consider risking your life for a cause you believed in?"

There again were those words. "Depends on the cause, sir."

"You fought for the creation of the Texas Republic, to be free from the Mexican tyranny," Jones said. "Did you not support their cause?"

I sat quiet. I had not yet eaten any of my food. I cut a slice of beef into pieces, then sat my knife and fork down. They all waited for my response. Finally, "I supported my friends not gettin' killed, sir." I lowered my head and took a bite of the meat. It was perfectly roasted.

We all commenced to eating.

I could not help but keep glancing at Broussard and Katharine Brody. They did not seem to be intimate as they had hardly spoken to one another since we sat down. My feelings toward Broussard had not grown better, or worse. I wondered how a man could be so callus and cold, only about the business, then turn to feigning friendship. I might have hurt him if I had the chance, for all he had put me through. *Probably wouldn't kill him though, just take his scalp.*

"How is your wound?" I asked Katharine. "It's been eight or nine months, should've healed up by now."

They looked up from their plates. She hesitated, glancing at Broussard. He lowered his head and took a bite of chicken.

"I am fine, Mr. Creed," she said. "How about yourself? I seem to remember that my late husband sliced you open, and

Juliette had to sew you back up, as she did me. Her healing fingers have touched us both."

"Healed up just fine," I said, mimicking her words. "Bothers me some when I walk a long way. Or climb on an' off a somethin'." I raised my eyebrows ever so slightly.

She gave me a sheepish smile, then took another bite, pausing to let the carrot rest against her lips before she gave a hearty crunch, all the while staring at me. I glanced around the table. Only Mrs. Preston seemed to notice, giving us both a knowing grin.

"How is Grainger, have you heard, Mr. Creed?" asked Jones.

I was not expecting a question like that, at this dinner table. I ignored him.

He asked again, with Broussard chiming in. "Yes, tell us, have you heard from your friend?"

I glared at him, as if he were suddenly goading me. "Last I saw of Grainger, I was in chains on the pier an' him sailin' off, back to Texas with a bag of coins worth five hundred dollars, handed to him by you." My face burned. I felt everyone's presence aimed at me. I did not want to appear angry, yet I was seething. My left hand began to shake again. I shoved it under the table. I could not wait until this dinner was over to find out what these folks' true intentions for me being there with them entailed. I wondered if Katharine Brody knew that she sat next to the man who ordered her husband's execution.

I gulped down some wine and asked, "A question for you, Mr. Broussard. How did Benjamin Brody truly die?"

The quick glances around the table were sharp to go with stern faces. Looks of guilt from the men and sadness from the two ladies. No one said a word.

"I heard a rumor," I said.

Broussard gave me a defiant stare and asked, "And what might that be, sir?"

"That he was shot in the face at his home by a paid assassin . . . sir."

Katharine gave a slight whimper, then glared at me. "If this talk about my late husband continues, I will leave this table. Benjamin is gone with no need to bring along such tragedy to this evening's fine meal and company."

"I agree, no more talk about the past, only the future. And what a glorious future to behold," said John S. Preston.

Silence.

There came a knock at the door. He stood and answered, quietly talking to whomever was there. He shut the door and announced, "Our other guests just landed at the dock and will be up shortly to join us."

Katharine still stared at me, now along with Broussard. He looked as if he might send me back to the swamp, or outright kill me. She had no knowledge of Brody's death, except that he was dead, murdered in their home. She seemed to not want to know the truth.

We finished eating, with me cleaning my plate twice. I was stuffed as a pig. Mrs. Preston rang the bell again, smiled, and said "Dessert!"

In walked two servants carrying a pie and a cake each and set them on the table. I smelled cherry and rhubarb; the cakes were strawberry and cinnamon. I asked for a piece of each. The slave serving me leaned in to place the dessert on my plate. I looked up. As I realized I knew her, my heart stopped beating.

Broussard continued to stare at me as she served him. He said, "Thank you, Margo, that is all."

She looked at me square with the saddest of eyes, as if she felt she was not so far away from death and that it was my fault. As Margo left the room, Broussard gave me a wink.

I did not pick up my fork, my belly in knots. I felt as if I might be sick.

"Monsieur Creed, you look pale, sir. As if you've seen a ghost," said Broussard.

With nowhere to go, I sat with my shaking hands in my lap. No one seemed to notice but Mrs. Preston.

"Why won't you eat your pie and cake, Mr. Creed?"

"I . . . I'm so full I just can't eat no more."

Everyone else finished their dessert. Preston pushed himself away from the table and sighed. "Gentlemen, I have recently procured a batch of the best Cuban cigars to be found anywhere in Louisiana. Shall we retire to smoke and chat?" He looked at me. "Mr. Creed, we welcome you as our honored guest, sir."

I still had no real idea as to why I was truly there. With Broussard subtly parading Margo in front of me, I did not feel at all comforted by Preston's formalities. I held my hands together to will away the shakes.

I'm about to find out.

CHAPTER 16

There were two doors down the hall from the dining room. Preston pulled a key from his jacket and unlocked one of them. The door swung open with a whoosh of warm, stale air. I stood behind him with Jones behind me. I stayed clear of Broussard as I could not trust myself to not harm him. Katharine and Mrs. Preston remained in the dining room, pulling their chairs close to talk in private, the servants clearing the table in silence. I did not see Margo.

A servant entered and lit a dozen or more candles, lighting up the walls and spare furnishings, eight chairs in a semicircle. Two of the walls were filled with books from floor to ceiling; the other two walls were covered with murals. In the corner, between the murals, on a dais, stood a lectern. I thought it was an odd way to set up a room, shaping it like a diamond rather than a square or rectangle. I stared at the murals. One seemed to tell the story of a people and their movement to America, white folk dominating the Indians and Negroes in chains tending fields of cotton and sugarcane, or being killed. The other mural was very much a call to arms, the men I fought with in Texas portrayed as saviors. A map in the background included Texas along with parts of Mexico, the southern American states, Spanish Florida, and the Caribbean Islands. Where the two murals came together, there hung a single star. The more I stared, the more I understood, *Order of the Lone Star, The Cause.*

Jones stepped up beside me. "Now you see?"

I did not say a word.

A knock came. Preston walked to one of the doors, opened it, and said, "Gentlemen, our other guests have arrived."

Into the room stepped three men whom I recognized immediately: the warden, the prosecutor, and . . . Willie Dan.

I froze, then reached for a knife at my belt that was not there.

Willie smiled and said, "Hey there, Scalper!" as if he was greeting an old friend.

Everyone turned, to see my reaction. I did not give them their satisfaction. I lowered my arm, stood with my hands at my side, the murals behind me, and simply nodded.

"Ah, it's good to see you two reunited," said Broussard.

Preston locked both doors, then offered brandy and cigars to everyone. I declined the cigar and accepted the brandy. We were all asked to sit. Preston took the step up onto the dais and stood in front of the lectern.

"Gentlemen, first a toast, to the cause, and our new friend." He turned to me and raised his glass; the rest of the men followed suit.

I barely acknowledged them, my eyes only on Willie Dan.

"Now, I know this is quite a surprise to you, Mr. Creed, the dinner and freedom. Look around you, the pieces of your life and the men who shaped them are all here in this very room. We knew of you from the opera, breaking Benjamin's nose and challenging him to a dual, then scalping him to be left alive? I'll just say that we were quite impressed." Preston paused. I sensed that they all agreed. He continued, "You see, Benjamin Brody was a fine businessman, cunning, could sell a batch of beaver furs to anyone, then steal them back with the help of Baumgartner, and resell them to someone else. But when you killed Baumgartner, our man in the operation, Brody lost his way, especially after you took his scalp. He was never the same, and I suppose that was your purpose in leaving him alive. But then, you helped Billy Frieze steal our friend's property—the Negress and her two boys—and our view of you shifted."

I felt his glee at telling my tale, as if he was writing a record to be entered into a book. I glanced at Broussard. He sat stone-faced.

"We thought that you had merely paid a debt to the Negro who helped you kill Amos Baumgartner. I was inclined to think that you were a man of higher principle. And when you joined the Greys to go fight for the cause, well, I was proven right. However, we needed you here more than we needed you in Texas. When Benjamin Brody met his end, well, there was reason to bring you back to become . . ." He glanced around to his fellow conspirators, perhaps looking for agreement, ". . . the assassin you were meant to be."

I sat, with the glass of brandy on my knee, all six of them looking at me. "I ain't no assassin."

Willie laughed. "Only a matter of time, Scalper."

Broussard stood and joined Preston on the dais. "The fur trade is played out. No more beaver to be trapped. Besides, like I said, silk is the new fur, *Monsieur* Creed."

"You have no trade, sir," said the warden.

"You sent me here, why?" I asked.

They all looked around to each other, then the prosecutor said, "You were supposed to have been tried and convicted for the murder of Brody." He smirked. "That goddamn Spanish judge an' Baumgartner's brother got you off and sent you to Baton Rouge for only six months."

Willie Dan sat staring at me. "If they were going to hang ya the next day, you would have left the jail with me."

I took a long drink, turned to Dan, and said, "I shoulda killed you then."

He laughed again. "Exactly, Scal-l-l-per!"

I asked them all, "What do you want from me?"

"Go to New Orleans and assassinate Sam Houston," Preston said.

I was quite sure I heard him wrong. "What did you say?"

"He is very clear, *Monsieur* Creed, we want you to kill the future president of the new Republic of Texas," said Broussard.

I stood and started toward one of the doors.

"I assure you, both are locked, sir."

I twisted the doorknob on one, then the other. I backed against the dusty bookshelves with a thump, the wood creasing my jacket. My head sunk against the foul-smelling books.

Preston cleared his throat. Then, "There is nowhere for you to go, Mr. Creed, so please, come and sit back down. We have many things to discuss with little time."

I stood still.

"Hey, Scalper," Dan said, "this should be no surprise, really."

"Why?" I asked.

"Houston is attempting to break the first piece of the puzzle," said the prosecutor.

The warden chimed in. "He offers up our blood and treasure to the abhorrent abolitionists of the United States."

"What?"

"He will allow our investments to go wasted on the false promise of a true and independent state," said Anson Jones.

I did not move.

"You are closest to him," said Preston. "When he found out you were taken, brought back to New Orleans for Brody's murder, knowing you were innocent, he began a campaign with the judge to secure your freedom."

"His letters were extremely persuasive, as I have read them all," said the prosecutor. "It was enough to lessen your sentence, is what brought you here."

"Ironic, isn't it?" Broussard said, smiling.

"Why?" I asked again. "Why not send the killer, Dan, to just shoot him in the face?"

Willie Dan laughed, hard. "I offer no subtlety. You witnessed this in the jail cell. No, you're the man for the job." Easing up, he said, "Besides, they cannot afford my charge, to kill a man of his stature. You, sir, will do it for free."

I stood silent, the room spinning, the musty books reeking, the smell caught in my throat. The six of them stared at me as if I had an immediate answer.

"What will it be, sir?" asked Preston.

I did not move.

"What will it be, sir?" Broussard repeated.

I could not move. I had killed men before, in battle, in personal fights, burned a man up in a beaver's den. *But I was no assassin!* And . . . to go and kill a friend, a man who, at times, looked upon me with respect when I had little respect for myself.

"I still do not understand," I said.

Jones stood. "Houston can't be trusted. Hell, I had to push him to fight, personally taking the bottle from his hands, his lips, several times. And the occasional woman, well . . . Is he expected to change now that he will more than certainly become president? I shan't think so."

"Not only is he an embarrassment per these behaviors, as we said, Mr. Creed, he does not hold the cause, our cause, in his heart," Preston said.

"What in goddamn hell are you talkin' about . . . what cause, what does that even mean?"

They all stood, turned toward the murals, and clasped hands. Then in unison, said:

"All are one against impure blood,
A golden circle we shall be,
A fortitude against the tides of abolition,
A prosperous land for all the world to see."

My mouth hung open. These grown men, wealthy beyond belief, holding hands and reciting a poem.

They turned back toward me, letting go of their hands.

"What will it be, Mr. Creed?"

I was trapped. If I could get out the door, where would I go? I had no allies, except for Lindy Lou, and she seemed to understand the severity of the question these men were asking me, the deed I was asked to do. *How did she know? What would this act change? How might this assassination possibly change her life?*

My freedom depending on the answer I gave.

"Well, what is your answer?" asked Preston, with a bit of impatience in his voice.

"No," I said. "I will not go and kill my friend."

Willie Dan exclaimed, "I knew it!"

"We will pay you handsomely," said Broussard.

"And you will have your freedom," said the prosecutor.

"You leave the swamp forever," said the warden.

"Then, you can go and kill Grainger for him killing your young friend James," said Willie Dan, smiling. "Just like you planned to do all along."

I stared back at them in defiance.

"No," I said.

They glanced at each other, frowning. Except Willie.

"I told you he would not agree," Jones exclaimed, shaking his head. "At Bernardo plantation, he showed a complete lack of respect to Lamar Groce, walking away from his supper table after being invited as guest of honor."

"He beat the child for falling asleep," I said.

Jones turned back to me. "And deservedly so, Mr. Creed. That child was his to beat, his property." He walked toward me. "As his African slave, bought and paid for . . . his to beat, Mr. Creed. His to kill, if he so desired, Mr. Creed."

"You do not hold our ways of business in light, sir?" Preston asked.

"It is the darkest of black," I said.

Jones stepped in front of me. "You, sir, are worse than an abolitionist. At least they spout their righteousness that springs forth from a rather cracked perspective of God and the Bible. You have no God so your opinion springs from nothing."

"I have also been a slave."

"Then you should have died a slave . . ." He leaned into me, ". . . for that's all you're worth."

I hit him, hard. Blood exploded from his nose. He fell back and I kept pounding his face and head. From behind me I heard two clicks. I kept hitting Jones, now on the floor straddling him, his face a bloody mess. *They will have to kill me to stop.*

The barrel of a pistol was pressed to the back of my head.

"I will blow a hole through your fucking skull, Zebadiah," said Willie Dan.

I stopped, my knuckles bleeding. Jones lay unconscious. He did not hit me once.

I slowly stood. Dan stuck the pistol into my back and pushed me toward a single chair on the dais. "Bind his hands and feet," he said.

Preston grabbed my arms and pulled them behind me. Someone else tied my hands together. I was spun around, lifted up to the chair, and forcefully pushed down. Broussard tried tying my feet and I kicked him in the mouth. Someone struck me on the side of my head, either with a club or the butt of the pistol. I slid back to sit on my hands, my arms pinned behind me. It felt as if both shoulders would crack apart. Broussard finished tying my feet together. I attempted to sit up. All was quiet except for wheezing coming from Jones lying across the floor.

Willie leaned in, close to my ear, and whispered, "He

deserved the ass kickin'.""

Preston, Broussard, the prosecutor, and the warden stood in front of me. The looks on their faces showed their shock at the situation. A few seconds went by that felt like minutes. Broussard pulled a handkerchief from his jacket, wiped his bleeding mouth, and said, "Bring them in, now."

Preston went to the first door, unlocked it, and stepped out into the hallway. In seconds, Lindy Lou appeared escorting in three black folks to the middle of the room, a woman and two young men in chains: Margo and her sons, Abe and Sturgis. Before the door was shut, Lindy glanced around. Seeing me, she did not flinch, as if it were natural to see me tied to a chair sitting below those god-awful murals. I wanted to cry out, to ask her to go and get help. There could not be anyone within a hundred miles to help me, and she knew it.

Lindy shut the door behind her, and except for the clink of chains, the room was silent. Margo stood with her head up staring at us, one at a time. She reached me and, again, all I saw was sadness, as if I had broken her heart. One of the boys said, "Mama?" She immediately shushed him. They shuffled closer to their mother.

Willie Dan circled around behind the family and stood with his back against the bookcase. Broussard paced in front of them, nervous, as if he was the caged animal. The warden and prosecutor turned their chairs around to face the slaves. Jones was seated, still wiping blood from his broken nose.

"So . . . this is it," said Preston, his voice quivering ever so slightly.

Broussard stopped and nodded. "We don't have to do this, *Monsieur* Creed."

"You must pledge to the *cause*, Mr. Creed," said the Warden.

"There will be a lifelong benefit if you go do this, sir," said the prosecutor.

"He needs inspiration," Jones sneered, holding his nose with a handkerchief.

Willie Dan wore a grin and was silent.

Broussard turned to me. "There will be consequences to go with your decision, sir."

Preston had turned pale. "Your choice will decide the future of our great, new republic," he said, his voice sounding a desperate plea.

Staring at Margo and her boys, I shook my head no.

"The deed is upon us," Dan said.

They all turned to him, looking past the family, as if they did not exist.

He smiled. "We must climb down from the fence, gentlemen, and step squarely in the muck."

Broussard lowered his head and nodded. Preston turned to face me.

Willie stepped forward, away from the bookcase.

"Masta, we been good!" whispered Margo, shaking.

The boys and their chains were silent.

Willie Dan paced back and forth, stopping behind Abe, then Sturgis, then Margo, back to Sturgis. Sliding sideways to Margo, he pulled something from his coat I could not see. He reached his arm around ever so gently to grip her shoulder, as if he were giving her a warm embrace. She gasped, her chest heaving forward, held her breath for a second, then exhaled slow, a spot of red appearing on her white servant's shirt. She slumped against Dan, him caressing her, kissing her cheek. He whispered into her ear. Margo's eyes grew wide staring at me. She slipped through his arm and fell to her knees. He pulled the knife from her and held it up, its blade the same color crimson soaking her shirt. He lay her on the floor face up; legs folded beneath her, a small pool of blood seeping from her back. Dan kneeled, wiped the long knife clean with her black skirt, stood, and slid it back into his coat.

The light in Margo's eyes faded to nothing.

No scream pierced my lips. The very core of my being did not believe what my eyes and ears just witnessed, as if I had slipped into another world, of fantasy, of demons and ghosts. I closed my eyes, yet, the instance of this act shone crystal clear in my mind.

The two boys whimpered, their rattling chains shaking me back to the room. They could not look at their mother. I could not look at them.

Death filled the chamber, the house, the plantation.

"We know about your close friend Anna and her father, and where they live up along the Missouri," said Preston.

"And I will go all the way to that shithole and kill her and the good doctor," said Willie Dan, a wide grin spread across his face. "Fact is, Scalper, as well you know, I would enjoy it. Now, do as you're told, go on down to New Orleans and take care of our friend Sam Houston, ya hear?"

I could not cry out, yet tears rolled down my cheeks. I twisted the rope that bound my hands, burning my wrists, then slumped over, those tears dropping onto my knees. I did not hear anyone or anything except the boys' chains as they were led out of the room. And all I could think of . . . the words that screamed from my soul, *this was my fault*!

I looked up; Willie Dan was gone. Preston and Broussard stood before me. Anson Jones, still nursing his broken nose, slouched in a chair. The prosecutor and the warden were nowhere to be seen, as they must have left with Dan. Margo's body still lay on the floor in a pool of blood.

"You will leave tomorrow morning. We have heard that Houston is nearly healed enough to travel back to Texas, so we haven't much time," said Preston.

"Dan has already left for Missouri," Broussard said, glancing over to Margo. "He will stay close to your friends and will receive word when the deed is done . . . or not."

"Broussard will accompany you back to New Orleans. You have one day and night once you arrive," said Preston.

"If you deviate from our plan in any way, we will have you killed, along with your friend and her father. Do you understand, Mr. Creed?"

"He'll kill them anyway," I said.

"No, sir, we don't think so. For all the work he's done for us, well, we find him to be an honorable man," Preston said.

Broussard sighed. "You will have to trust us and him, as we trust you, Mr. Creed."

I sat, still slumped over, my hands numb, my shoulders breaking; the tears on my face dried. "Cut me loose," I whispered, staring at Margo's body.

Preston stepped up behind, and with a knife, slit the rope that bound my hands. I brought them to my lap, rubbing the raw skin at my wrists. He cut the rope tying my feet together and stepped off the dais. All three of them stared at me, Preston still holding the knife in his hand. I stood and stretched, not looking at any one of them. I walked past Margo into the hallway, shutting the door behind me.

CHAPTER 17

At the open window, I sat looking out past the white pillars of the house into darkness. Insects sang in rhythm with the stars. A low fire burned, through the trees to my left, near the slave quarters. Below, out a side door, two men carried something wrapped in cloth, away from the house, into the night. Within minutes, I heard wailing, then crying. Then, abrupt silence. My eyes welled with tears and I turned away from the window.

I had been guided to the bedroom by Mrs. Preston, chatting the whole way up the spiral staircase and down the hallway. I did not hear a word she said. She left me at the door and bid me good night. Alone, I dreaded the dreams to come, if I slept at all.

There came a soft knock. As the door was not locked, I said come in. The knob turned, slender fingers grasped the edge of the door, swinging it open. Katharine Brody stood, a faint silhouette to the hallway's light shining through her nightgown.

"Zebadiah," she whispered. "May I come in?"

I sat upright on the bed, fully clothed with the alligator boots still on my feet. She stepped into the room. I was surprised at what she wore. I knew then for sure that she and Broussard were not intimate. She sat on the bed, crossed her legs, and stared at me for a few, long seconds.

"Yes?" I asked.

"It's that I knew, all along."

"What did you know?"

105

"Who killed my husband."

I turned away from her and sighed. *A confession?*

"Zebadiah, please look at me. I know it was that horrible man who came late tonight . . . and I know what he did to that poor woman."

"Do you know who put him up to it?" I asked, turning back to her.

She slowly nodded. A tear fell down her cheek. She quickly wiped it away. "This is the first tear I've shed for Benjamin."

I trusted her feelings. Again, I felt I was the cause of someone's deep pain.

She looked at my boots. "You would be more comfortable with them off."

I shrugged. "Didn't figure I'd get much sleep tonight anyway."

She stood and walked to my side of the bed.

"Let me help you," she said, and reached for my left boot, took a hold, and slipped it off, easing my foot to the bed. She dropped the boot to the floor and pulled off the right one, dropping it to the floor with a thump. I wiggled my toes. Both feet felt unburdened.

She sat down next to me. "The first I saw you, at the opera, those many months ago, I thought, what a strong man. When you hit Benjamin, most of me hated you. Yet . . ." she bowed her head. "When you saved my life, I . . ." She reached out and stroked my hand. "You . . ."

I drew her in, and we kissed, melting away the bane of all the days and nights I had spent alone, cold, and with no one in the world to touch, to feel.

Katharine lay her head down on my shoulder, our bodies close, holding each other, sleeping.

That night, I did not dream.

CHAPTER 18

Morning came and she was gone. I was still dressed, except for my boots. I slipped them on and stood at the window. The sun shone. Though, as if the invisible clouds filtered the brightness, a dull shine lay upon the land. There was no chopping of trees. There were no harsh voices echoing from the swamp. The fact was, there were no regular, daily sounds like the day before. The whole plantation lay in dead silence. A knock came at the door. I opened it expecting Katharine Brody.

"Our steamboat to New Orleans arrives by ten," said Anson Jones, his nose bandaged and both eyes turned black. "I expect you will be joining us?" he asked, as if I had a choice. He lingered at my door for a few seconds.

"You remind me of Brody, when I busted his nose. Then of course you know what happened after that," I said, looking at the top of his head, his hair short but nice and thick. "Your scalp won't hang from my belt, though it would sure make a good prize."

His face turned red, then stammered, "Just, just be on the boat, if you know what's good for you."

I shut the door in his face. *It would be so easy to kill him,* I thought.

Behind me, from outside the window, I heard singing. At first, slow and mournful, voices sung low and high, harmonies drifting up through the trees surrounding the slave quarters. Rising in tempo, there began a call and response, and once in a while, *praise Jesus.* The single voice a male, strong, deep, resonating through the open window. The singing reached a fever pitch, then stopped. All the plantation was again silent.

I sat at the edge of the bed close to tears. *How could these folks sing like this?* I asked myself. Then came an answer from deep within me. *They are a strong people, stronger than I could ever be.*

A woman began to speak.

"We are saved, for our spirit continues to toil in good faith by Jesus Christ's guiding hand, and by our master's hand. The love they shine upon us gives strength to work another day in the fields," said Lindy Lou.

Then spoke a man I recognized from the night before. "I will read for you from the Bible. *In the sweat of thy face shalt thou eat bread, till thou return unto the ground; for out of it wast thou taken: for dust thou art, and unto dust shalt thou return,* Genesis 3:19."

Preston stopped. Once again, there came silence throughout the plantation.

I wanted to cry out, *You goddamn bastard!*

Another knock at the door. I swung it open, allowing it to slam against the wall. There stood Katharine Brody, unflinched by the bang.

"Mr. Creed, will you escort me downstairs for breakfast?"

For a few, long seconds I stood gazing at her, wanting to hold her, to be held again by her. We had not lain together the night before. And now I desperately wished we had.

I offered her my hand. She took hold and I left the room.

Breakfast was served on the porch, behind the white pillars. At a round table with black, wicker chairs sat Mrs. Preston. I stopped to gaze at towering trees draping over the long road that led straight to the Mississippi River.

"I am so sorry that the both of you must leave so very soon," said Mrs. Preston. "I thought we might become closer friends."

She offered us to have a seat.

A servant came and poured coffee, another brought cornbread and honey with strawberries and blackberries. Both servants did their best to cloud the cold looks they gave to us. I did not know if Mrs. Preston knew about what happened to Margo. Of course, the slaves that served us knew.

We ate in silence, my demeanor not allowing for small talk. Preston walked onto the porch and sat down next to his wife. The servant poured his coffee.

"Another one died last night," he said.

"Who, dear?"

I waited for him to say the name Margo.

"Worley, my dear. The old man had something wrong with his knee and he gained infection. I spoke to Lindy Lou. She said she tried to heal it, but sadly, could not and we had to put him down." Preston paused. "Lost four hundred dollars, at least."

"Hmmm," said Mrs. Preston. "Do you think her touch has lessened?"

"I don't know. That juju of hers, well . . ."

"Put him down like a dog?" I asked.

They both looked at me like I was crazy.

"I feel the loss, Mr. Creed, when any one of my slaves die, sir."

"And what about Margo, *sir*?"

In the bright, morning sun I could see his face turn a shade red.

"Margo?" asked Mrs. Preston. "Who is he speaking of, dear?"

Preston ignored his wife's question and said, "She was not mine."

From beyond the trees, the singing began again.

"Good dogs make better masters, right, Mr. Preston?"

He stood, then I stood, both of us glaring at the other.

"I have work to do," he said finally, turned to Katharine, and held out his hand. She took hold and he bowed. "Always a pleasure, Mrs. Brody. I hope to see you soon in New Orleans."

Preston turned back to me and said, "Safe travels south, Mr. Creed."

With not another word, he spun away and walked into the house.

Mrs. Preston stood. "I do hope for the two of you a . . . continued warm relationship." With an ever so slight smile, she followed her husband through the open, front door.

Katharine and I locked eyes, and for a second or two, there came a sense of understanding, an agreement, that the evening spent together was perfect.

I had nothing to gather for my trip back to New Orleans. I did not own the clothes on my back nor the alligator boots on my feet. They were given to me by Preston. I carried no weapon. Though I had free rein of the plantation the couple of hours before the steamboat arrived, I was very much a prisoner.

I wanted to see Lindy Lou before I left. *She might be holding the other side of the coin in her hand.*

The singing faded the closer I got to the slave quarters. I expected the group of Sunday worshipers gathered together. I was not prepared to see the bodies of Worley and Margo laid out on funeral pyres. No one made the effort to cover up Margo's murder. Another unfortunate death on the Hydras plantation.

I smelled the burning sage Lindy Lou waved over Margo, then Worley. She stepped back and bowed her head, the rest of the slaves doing the same.

"Our love, their love, to know freedom, at last."

One of the men lit each bed of cypress wood they lay on. Soon, the flames engulfed them, the smell of burning flesh fill-

ing the sultry, morning air. Lindy stood alone; her head still
bowed. I joined her.

"You witnessed her death," she said.

"Yes."

"You blame yourself."

I hesitated, then, "Yes."

"The world moves around us, through us, in ways we cannot
understand, Mr. Creed," she said, turning to me. She seemed to
not be one bit angry, sad perhaps, but not angry.

"If only I hadn't . . ."

"You cain't foresee consequences, though we must be held
accountable. Our guilt shows what kind of conscience we carry
about us."

I nodded.

"Do you feel guilty?"

Again, I nodded. Light smoke from the funeral pyre swirled
around us.

"This feeling you carry will guide you to do right. As will the
guilt felt by this nation we live in." She pointed to a spot in the
middle of her forehead. "I have seen it."

"The dream."

This time, she nodded. "Good dogs do make better masters.
Turn yer back on us though, an' we will bite."

Lindy Lou handed me the last of the burning sage and joined
her people.

Again, I stood alone.

I could see Katharine, still on the porch, by herself, leaning
against a pillar, staring at the road to the river, as if she had
nowhere else to be but to wait there for a carriage to take her to
the boat.

On top of the house there sat a platform of sorts, with a
white railing. Broussard stood looking down at me through the
crown of trees. Right below him, attached to wood, was the

broad image of a serpent, very much like the snake whose head I bit off. I had not seen it before because I had not taken the time to look up. Before this, I had no time to take.

With his hands gripping the top rail, Broussard gave the slightest wave with his fingers. Then, as if he noticed something behind him in the distance, he turned and was gone.

From afar, a steamboat whistle blew. It was time to leave the Hydras plantation.

Chapter 19

A four-seated carriage sat in front of the Big House along with a small wagon to carry luggage. I did not know how long Broussard and Katharine had been staying at the plantation, one evening or one week, as they traveled with three large pieces each. The two boys, Abe and Sturgis, no longer in chains, carted them out the front door and onto the wagon. Neither one glanced at me. They were not at their mother's funeral.

Anson Jones carried his own bag. Of them all, I thought he would be the one to have a slave tote his personals around.

Mrs. Preston stood by herself on the porch. "Safe travels, ya'll. You must come again."

Master Preston shook Broussard's and Jones's hands, bowing to Mrs. Brody. "I shall see you soon in New Orleans, my friends."

He bowed slightly to me and said, "Mr. Creed . . . may the *Cause* be with you."

I said nothing.

The ride was short. I sat next to Katharine with Broussard and Jones staring at me the whole way. The two boys along with a driver followed behind in the wagon.

"No matter how this plays out, I will kill the both of you," I said.

They gave each other a quick glance and continued to stare at me. Katharine watched the overhanging trees glide by and did not say a word, as if she heard nothing.

The steamboat looked familiar. At the bow, across the hull, *Diana*. As I walked up the brow, my hands began to shake, then I stopped and looked upriver, all the way to St. Louis and beyond, to the Lower Missouri . . . and to Anna. I lowered my head and walked aboard.

The prosecutor, with his chalky, white face, and the dandy warden met us on the veranda deck. By the light of day, they looked so small.

The two brothers unloaded the luggage, hauled the pieces up the gangway, and disappeared into the bowels of the steamboat.

From the shore came the rattle of another wagon. Kershaw drove onto the landing with Persimmons by his side. In the back, covered with a tarp, lay a body on a wooden pallet. They pulled up to a barge, the same prison barge I was chained to as we floated down from Baton Rouge just a week prior.

Over the noise of the steam pipes and last whistle before getting underway, Broussard hollered, "What happened?"

Kershaw lifted the tarp. Roy's eyes stared blank to the sky; a look of terror creased permanently on his face. Where his right shoulder and arm should have been, there was only a bloody stump.

"Alligator got him," Persimmons hollered back. I was sure I detected a smile.

I felt nothing for the man.

The big wheel began to turn, churning the Mississippi water into mud. From behind his back, Broussard pulled a shiny, silk top hat and presented it to me.

"You'll want to wear this once we reach the city, *Monsieur* Creed. For soon, you will be one of its most distinguished men of action."

We were underway, headed south back to New Orleans. One last time, I hoped. Left alone at the rail, a top hat hung from my fingers, I watched the shore drift past. Around a slight bend, between two oaks, stood the Houma Indian, with a tomahawk hung from his fingers. Lindy Lou's father. I gave a slight bow. He turned and disappeared into the trees.

CHAPTER 20

New Orleans, the Eleventh of June 1836

Her room had not changed in nine months, except that next to the door, a gold and copper water pipe had replaced the porcelain bowl and chamber pot that had lain against the wall. By the morning sun shining through the cracked windowpane, I noticed the dust, as if the implement had not been used for smoking in a long while. The same unlabeled bottle of cognac with two glasses sat on the low table, emptied and refilled many times I assumed, since the last I had been in the room.

Sophie le Roux sat in one of the small chairs, covered her mouth with a silk handkerchief, and coughed. A different sounding cough than Jim Bowie had the last I saw him, dying of consumption at the Alamo. Hers had a slight rattle. Though as she pulled the cloth away from her lips, I could not help but look for blood.

Her weight was down, from the voluptuous, full-bodied woman she once was, to thin, haggard. She did her best to hide inside a thicker petticoat, but I saw it in her arms, ever so slight with skin sagging. Her face, covered thick in makeup, showed a weariness beyond her age.

She brushed her graying hair away from her black eyes and said, "So, what brings my hero back to me?"

Not waiting for her to offer, I leaned down and poured myself a drink, then sat on the bed and stared out the window. The wharf across the street, where I first watched Baumgartner unload furs, was deserted. "Not much business these days?"

"I do not know what you speak of," she said.

"The wharf, your wharf. There are no boats."

"This is why you come here, asking me of boats?"

I could see that she was already irritated.

"Hmm, Sophie, why did I come?" I asked. "You summoned me."

Sighing, she gazed at her hands and fingers, more slender now than when we first met.

Sophie looked up and said, "I am dying, Zebadiah."

The words were not what I expected, for I had thought her impervious to a fairly young death. Yet, I was not in shock. Having known this woman for some time, the way she presented the statement, feigning unabashed honesty, was certainly the kind of performance she would begin with, whether on death's doorstep, or not.

She waited for a response. I offered her none.

"The doctor says I have the cancer."

I could not think of anything to say and continued to stare out the window at the dark swamp that lay across the road. I was wasted and tore up to be sitting with this woman in the first place with what I had to do later in the evening. *Ah, to be in my mountains. My rugged, snowcapped mountains.* I had a far better chance of surviving avalanches, bear and Indian attacks, and disease than the treachery of the folks I found myself entangled with. For by the end of the night, I might be dead.

And at that moment, I was expected to offer some sympathy to the woman who may have tried to kill me nine months before?

I drained the glass. "I'm sorry to hear such sad news," I said, and poured myself another drink.

Her eyes welled up with tears. Wiping them away, she asked, "Why are you back in New Orleans? I thought you would be in Missouri, with that other woman."

Was she jealous of Anna, a woman I had been with for only a few weeks and had not seen in ten months?

"I have been in prison."

"Ah, yes, for the murder of Benjamin Brody."

"No, I did not kill him. A man by the name of Willie Dan killed Brody. Shot him in the face on his own doorstep, or so he says." I stared at her. With the mention of Willie Dan came a spark of recognition she attempted to hide by wiping her eyes again.

"But of course, you knew this," I offered.

She stood and walked to the window shaking her head. "Who were you speaking of?"

I did not answer. She was at least acquainted with Dan. Sophie always knew more than she let on.

"Why are you back in New Orleans?" she again asked.

"To kill a man."

She turned back to me. "Ah, so you are Sam Houston's assassin."

I did not show the complete shock I felt as she said this. Did she truly know all that went on in this godforsaken city? Every movement of her body, every breath she took to speak, I did not trust. Yet, at that moment, on that day, I needed her. Somehow, she knew of my burden. If I denied the truth, she would see through me.

"How do you know this?"

She laughed, coughed again into her hanky, then said, "Ah, *Monsieur* Zeb, my spies are everywhere." Her smug look overcame any doubt I had that she knew my intentions.

"I need your help," I said, surprised at how easily my voice cracked.

"What could a dying, old woman have to offer?"

"Your spies."

Sophie smiled and nodded.

Three stories below, wagons ran on Liberty Street. I heard the jingle of harnesses and wheels slushing through mud made by the early, morning rain. Laughter erupted from the crowded boardwalk with a man answering in creole, then a woman's gentle voice chiming in, sounding like a melody from the opera. A part of me hated the gaiety of these folks, jealous of their seeming lack of dark responsibilities. I was sure that none of them were as put upon as I was to kill a man by the next morning.

"Houston's about healed up enough to travel, so I've been told. Do you know a man by the name of Christy, William H. Christy?" I asked.

Her smile turned to a frown. "*Oui*, Zebadiah. He is a frequent client of mine. I am not too fond of him and his friends."

"Why? What is he about?"

She hesitated, then said, "He is mean to my girls."

"How so?"

Her frown deepened. "The girls he chooses are my two Irish beauties. Yet, in public, *Monsieur* Christy does nothing but insult those most unfortunate *les immigrants* that have come of late to our city. By his talk, he would have them all run out of town on a rail, out of the country and driven into the gulf, back to where they came from across the ocean.

"Except for my girls, of course. Who he loves to fuck, and torment."

I sat for a second, with her gazing out the window, her back still to me. "Why do you send them, then?" I asked.

She turned her head slightly. "He is perhaps the richest of all men in Louisiana, richer than Broussard. He pays well." There was a quiver in her voice, as if she shared only part of the truth. Sophie swiveled around to face me. "On your own, you will be hard-pressed to get into his home, where the general lies."

"This is where your girls can help," I said. "All I need is a knife and a pistol placed somewhere in the house. I will do the rest."

She nodded. "Hmm, *monsieur*. You do plan on killing your friend?"

Glancing down at my alligator boots, I did not answer.

"One of your favorites is now *Monsieur* Christy's."

I looked up.

"Juliette, she is currently his favorite *Fille de Joie*," she said.

Laughter drifted up from the boardwalk, the young woman speaking in tongues, a melody sung in French, then English, in a joyous rush of words. I resented her happiness. I stood next to Sophie and looked down through the cracked windowpane. She was beautiful, wearing a light-blue sundress, twirling a white parasol on her shoulder, walking arm in arm with a handsome, top-hatted man in a tan suit, perhaps a few years older. The farther away they strolled, I was glad, for I did not want to hear her sweetness any longer.

Juliette? I'll be goddamned.

Silence filled the room. I poured another drink, this time offering Sophie her own cognac. She refused and I sat back down on the bed, for some reason, not quite ready to leave her.

"Have you seen him . . . and my daughter?" She hissed the words, with a subtle ferociousness in her tone I had never heard before.

I was taken aback by the sudden turn of the conversation.

"Who do you speak of?" I asked.

"Jean Laffite. Whom you know as . . . Frenchy."

"Yes, only a brief instant before I was wheeled off to prison." For a second or two, I thought not to even ask, then . . . "Have you seen him, or your daughter?"

It was as if she could no longer speak, choked by the coming sobs, afraid of the answer she would have to give me. She simply shook her head and turned, wiping tears from her cheeks. "It would be too hard."

"But you know where they are?"

She nodded.

"I want to meet with Frenchy, you can arrange this?"

A few seconds passed. She again nodded.

I stood and touched her on the shoulder. She shirked my hand away, and did not look up, reminding me of an old, scorned woman. I drained the glass, set it on the table, and walked out the door.

CHAPTER 21

Frenchy stood at the open door. A light, afternoon shower dampened the packed dirt, hardly hampering the folks strolling down Bourbon Street. He wore the same pantaloons, shiny black boots, black belt, and white, satin shirt that he did while standing on Blood Island, near St. Louis some nine months before, sending me down the river. Now, more silver streaked through his black hair, the swirl of his mustache not black at all. His blue eyes, though, were as clear as they were when he had stared down at me the evening we had first met, from the edge of a pit holding two dead wolverines with one man torn to bits and bled to death. I stood down there with a bloody knife in hand, Frenchy's wide eyes expressionless but for the wonder of who the hell I was.

The building he asked to meet in appeared to be abandoned with the front windows boarded up and the side door chained with a large padlock hanging down. A cold, brick fireplace took up most of the back. A torn bellows built into a metal frame stood pointing to where a fire would be. To the side, wrought-iron utensils were laid out haphazard on a bench built to waist height and pushed up next to a leather apron hung on the stone wall. An anvil sat square in front of the fireplace perched atop a wooden block. A blacksmith's hammer lay handle up, as if the master had stepped away for a moment, then back to work. The smell of soot and sweat seeped out of everything. I sat in one of three chairs facing the doorway where Frenchy stood peering out into the street.

"They do not spell my last name correctly, these books," he said. "It is two Fs, one T."

"I don't understand," I said.

"No matter, I am not Frenchy, nor am I Jean Laffite, they both are dead to me. I am . . . John Laflin." He turned to stand before me. "From this day, you will call me by this name, *Monsieur* Creed."

His knife, the long knife Benjamin Brody used to cut him to the heart, was sheathed in his belt. The same plain, wood-handled knife I used to cut Brody on his left cheek, at the opera house the evening I challenged him to the duel. Frenchy, the name I would forever call him in my mind, rested his right hand upon its butt, drumming his fingers, as if he were ready to end the conversation we had just begun.

"Your daughter has grown," I said.

A look of surprise crossed his face, then a slight grin. "*Oui*, Zebadiah, indeed she has."

"She carries her own sword."

"A cutlass it is, *monsieur*, not a sword. A very different blade, and use," he said, as if I should know this. I sensed he thought that I might be poking him a little with a stick, or the point of a cutlass.

"Any new pet wolverines?" I asked.

By the glance he gave me, I knew that he knew I was toying with him.

"Yes, I had one shipped from Minnesota. For a time, he was a playful beast, helping me continue the march of justice within the confines of my own establishment. Then, alas, after the devil chewed through the iron bars of the gate attacking Gerald, I grew tired of its antics, its constant purring, and stabbed it through the heart. As I watched you do to my favorite *Pepe*." Frenchy grew a smile on his face. "Quite the technique I learned, quick and efficient."

I did not expect the compliment and suspected that he was now toying with me. I smiled and said nothing.

"You returned to New Orleans to ask about my daughter and my pet? I should think you be headed north to Missouri, Zebadiah."

I wondered about this question. Did he also know why I was back in this shithole of a city?

Without waiting for my reaction, he asked, "You did not kill Benjamin Brody?"

"No, I did not."

He pulled the knife from his belt and held it to a slat of sunlight that suddenly appeared. "His blood does not touch this blade?"

"Only by the cut I gave him on his left cheek. I used my brother's knife to scalp him." I could tell that he was not pleased.

He turned back to the door. "He is dead now, is all that matters."

The sun broke through the clouds and from where I sat, I could see steam rising up from the damp street. Frenchy's appearance had changed since I last saw him in St. Louis, not so much shorter, but all around smaller. A few folks paused to stare when they saw him. Everyone else walked on by.

"To some, I am merely a stranger standing in the doorway of an abandoned blacksmith shop. To others . . ." He stopped to tip his hat to a young passerby. "I am but a ghost no longer to be feared. Twelve years and forgotten."

I felt sad for him feeling this way, for at one time, fear and power were his most beloved companions.

"Are you afraid of me, Zebadiah?"

Still with his back to me, I shook my head, surprised by the question.

"Speak up, do you still fear me?" he asked, his tone harsh.

I could not tell whether I was about to speak the truth or lie. Then I sighed and said, "No, I suppose I don't."

He stepped away from the door and again stood before me, his angry eyes locked with mine.

I felt as if he knew I uttered a lie. Yet, as soon as the words were spoken, in my heart I knew the truth. I no longer feared him.

His eyes softened into confusion, maybe expecting me to say something different. Then with steadfastness, he stated, "Good then, you have finally grown into a man."

I kept his gaze, wanting to understand what he was saying.

"You survived Goliad," he said.

"Yes."

"How did you survive?"

"I ran, sir."

"You ran to keep your soul alive."

"Yes," I said.

"Your fear saved you."

"I suppose . . ."

For the first time in quite a while I thought of James. I then thought of Grainger and my blood began to boil. "There was another whom I saved from death."

"As I, *monsieur*, as I."

He looked to the ceiling and raised both hands above, addressing the whole world. "I lost everything I built, a kingdom; sea power I held with a thousand different ships; the fear in the eyes of men I plundered, the fear of the men who sailed my ships; the contempt held for me by Spain and England. The honor of being a true, American hero . . . I sank it all off the coast of Veracruz, to hide away in Frenchy's Emporium, in St. Louie."

"Why?" I asked.

He looked back down at me. "For the young girl who now

wears a cutlass at her hip."

"Hmm . . ." I understood.

"You and I have faced death and turned away, *Monsieur* Creed, and are better men for it."

I felt compelled to finish my story. "The boy I saved was later shot by my supposed friend, the betrayer who received money from the bounty on my head. He deserves to die, by my hand."

He returned his gaze to me. "So, you could keep this boy from dying by the rifles of many, yet by one man's pistol, you could not?"

I glared at him. "How do you know?"

"Your tale is no secret, nor is the traitor and his whereabouts a secret."

"Is he here in New Orleans?" I asked, with an immediate pit in my gut. *I could go this afternoon and . . .*

Frenchy shook his head. "Sadly, no, *monsieur*, he is back in Texas, on his ranch. You will have to go there to kill him."

The sad events of the last month or so had led me to place the priority of killing Willie Dan before I killed Grainger. "After my business is complete here in the city, I must travel north . . . before heading west."

"Hmm, you have time for this . . . *Monsieur* Creed."

I was not sure what he meant.

A shadow fell across the room from the doorway. Frenchy stepped beside me with his knife drawn. I laid a hand on the loaded pistol at my belt and as I stood, swiveled to face the door. An oak cane appeared, its golden handle gripped by a chocolate-skinned hand sweeping any invisible dust and cobwebs aside. A purple feather showed, then a beaver top hat as Olgens Pierre stepped inside the blacksmith shop.

"You look like you're 'bout ready to attack something, or somebody," he said. "How you going to kill this ole ghost?"

CHAPTER 22

The last I saw Olgens Pierre he had sailed away to Haiti from Barataria with Margo, Abe, and Sturgis ten months before. I thought I would never see him again.

Yet, there he stood, straight and tall, his dress a perfect fit, immaculate. He removed the top hat, set it on the handle of the cane, and laid them against the wall just inside the door. Clasping his hands together in front of himself, he said, "It is good to see you, my friend."

Frenchy stepped toward Olgens, still holding his plain-handled knife. "Aye," he said. "I should cut you from ear to ear, *my friend.*"

Olgens opened his arms, welcoming the threat. "You can try. You have failed in every other attempt."

One step more and the old friends stood face to face with Olgens nearly a half a head taller than Frenchy. They stared at one another in silence. Olgens slowly reached out and slipped the knife from Frenchy's fingers, leaned in, and wrapped his arms around the pirate's shoulders. He offered me the knife and said, "It's good to embrace you, Jean."

I knew then they were far closer friends than I would ever know.

Olgens held Frenchy at arm's length. "You have aged well!"

Frenchy shook him off and turned toward me. I handed him back his knife. Tears filled his eyes. Then to Olgens he said, "My name is John. From now on, you call me John."

Olgens shrugged and walked on into the middle of the shop. "Whatever name you choose to go by." Then, "Do we have drinks to celebrate our reunion?"

But for the knife, he had yet to acknowledge my presence as I had not wanted to intrude in their reintroductions. Now, he offered a bow and his hand. "Zebadiah Creed. It is good that you are alive, sir."

We shook. "Why is everybody so damned surprised that I'm alive?" I asked.

They both smiled at each other and shrugged. "Because you are a man of nine lives," said Olgens.

Frenchy went to a cabinet under the bench. He pulled a bottle and three glasses and poured drinks. Three chairs, three glasses. This meeting was well prepared for.

Olgens and I took our drinks. "Shall we toast?" he asked.

"To a life of freedom, friendship, and family," Olgens said.

As I gulped down the rum, I nearly choked. *Did he not know about Margo?*

Olgens must have noticed. He winked at Frenchy. "Why the sad face, Zebadiah? This moment is for celebrating."

Frenchy's face fell and he looked away. He glanced my way, then walked back to the bench and poured himself another drink.

Olgens stared at me. "Has something happened?"

"Let us sit," said Frenchy.

We formed a triangle with our chairs and sat down.

"Why are you here in New Orleans?" Frenchy asked.

Both of us looked at the old pirate.

"I ask Olgens first," he said.

"I am embarrassed to say."

Frenchy and I waited.

"I've come to take back Margo and our sons from that bastard Broussard." He looked down at his hands. The right one seemed to be recently healed with fresh scars across its knuckles. "He came to my home in Haiti with armed men, in the dead of night, outnumbering my guards, killing all but two." He paused, sighing deeply. "I was tied to a chair and beaten. He said he was reclaiming his property. Margo and the boys were taken from their beds, placed in chains, and driven away before dawn." He raised his head. "I have come to steal them back and kill Broussard."

I caught a glance from Frenchy. *Did he know?* I hung my head, stood, walked to the bench, and poured another drink. I carried the bottle back to our chairs and set it on the floor in the center of the triangle, then gulped the drink down. Not having drunk much those last few months my head began to swim.

I leaned back and said, "I know where they are."

"Where? I have men waiting. A whole army. We'll go now!" He began to get up from the chair but as he gazed at my face, he stopped and slowly sat back down.

I could not hide my guilt and shame. My eyes welled with tears. I reached for the bottle. Frenchy snatched it away, took Oglens's glass, refilled it, and handed it back to him.

Olgens drank the rum, bent over, and laid the glass gently on the floor next to his chair.

He sat straight and whispered, "Tell me where they are, Zebadiah."

After a few long seconds the words formed in my mind. "Abe and Sturgis are here, in New Orleans, with Broussard. Margo is . . . is dead, killed, murdered."

"What?"

"She was killed by a man name of Willie Dan on a plantation near Baton Rouge." I was shocked at how I could suddenly speak so frankly.

Olgens sat with a blank stare and turned to Frenchy. "Is this true?"

Frenchy's nod was ever so slight.

Olgens groaned, wrapping his arms around his gut. He began to rock back and forth. Tears streamed down his face. He tried to speak but words would not come. He sat with his eyes squeezed tight, holding himself.

Finally, "Margo and I married last year. She was my wife."

As if the very sun knew to hide its face, a dark cloud broke, pouring rain down with a roar onto the roof of the abandoned blacksmith shop. Outside along Bourbon Street, folks scattered to find shelter. Water dripped from the ceiling to pool randomly on the uneven floor. Olgens stood. Frenchy and I stood. As if we did not exist, he strode to the door. Stopped by sheets of rain, he turned and stepped around us toward the fireplace. I glanced at Frenchy, then heard the head of the hammer scrape across the top of the anvil. I twisted around to see Olgens raise the hammer high above his head and, with a swoosh, slam it against the anvil. He again raised the hammer. He screamed as if his soul was dying and swung down. With a crack, the handle split in two. The hammer's head bounced off the pitted surface, crashed into the wall, and dropped to the floor with a thud. From the ceiling, black soot showered down around us.

In silence, Olgens held the broken handle loose in his hand. Frenchy stepped to him, reached down, and pried it from his fingers, as Olgens did with Frenchy's knife. He laid it on the anvil and held his friend, whispering in his ear. I did not hear the words, but Olgens relaxed in Frenchy's arms and was guided back to his chair. He sat slumped, then straightened up, wiping tears from his cheeks. He narrowed his eyes, turned to me, and in a whisper asked, "Where is Broussard and my boys?"

The three of us sat for another hour or so. The rain eased; the sunlight of the late afternoon did not return. I gave an explanation of what had happened since I left Texas, my prison stay, the trial, building the road through the swamp, my forthcoming assassination of Sam Houston.

Olgens insisted on great details about Margo's murder and, who the hell was Willie Dan.

"You have been their *gudgeon* for a long while, my friend," Frenchy said to me.

Olgens asked, "Did you not sense that you were being used to perpetuate these evil men's plans?" He was back to his stoic self, yet, the look in his eyes showed that he wanted so much more from me, to give him a deeper understanding of why she had to die.

I felt embarrassed, humiliated, and a betrayer of friends. I slowly shook my head.

"Where is this Willie Dan now?" Frenchy asked, sniffing. Then, "I have heard of him. Somewhere along the river, I have heard his name whispered."

"He's gone to Missouri to kill Anna and her father . . . if I don't kill Houston."

Olgens asked, "How will he know that you have done the deed?"

I hesitated, trying to find the right words. "A network of spies that runs from the lowest of road agents to the highest of functionaries of the government. This secret Order of the Lone Star was mentioned by a Texian an' ranchero the name of Don Padilla as far west as Victoria, Texas. Hell, he helped write the Texas Republic's constitution until the others, the plantation owners, insisted on slavery bein' the biggest part of it. Now that I look back, the whole goddamn revolution was paid for by this confederation. If they're able to do that, then surely they can send word upriver to their paid assassin before I can reach him."

Olgens and Frenchy sat pondering this information. Again, I was ashamed to know this about these rogues and how far I had come with them and their plans.

Frenchy stood and stretched, looked down at me, and smiled. "Well, *monsieur,* we must act tonight, as you have suggested. Then get you upriver faster than these *connards* can relay the truth we are about to set in motion."

CHAPTER 23

The lamplighter stretched his arms up, holding the long pole steady with both hands. The wick of the lamp was lit in an instant and the young man shuffled on. Within minutes, the whole of Girod Street was lit for the evening.

I stood across from William Christy's house, in the shadow of a dark hedge, away from the pool of light caused by the lamp closest to me. I did not want to be seen by the two men standing on the porch. A few minutes earlier, in the fading twilight, I walked past the house. The guards glared at me with disdain, as if they gave everyone who strolled by this look to threaten them to stay away. Not wanting to make myself obvious, I tipped my hat and sauntered back across the street. But not before noticing the two pistols in each one's belt and the stock of rifles laid against one wall.

General Houston was indeed well protected.

The house was three stories with balconies surrounding the second and third. From my brief conversation with Juliette, I found out that Houston was convalescing on the second floor, mainly in the middle sitting room facing the street. During his stay, he had occasionally been seen on the balcony waving to well-wishers. This evening there were none, perhaps because of the rain, or perhaps because of the guards' constant glares and their heavy armament.

I knew Juliette to be inside. Saoirse, the other girl whom Christy harbored, had just left the street and walked down a side path to the back of the house. The two men on the porch obviously knew the young woman for they let her pass. We were told there would be guards on the second floor back balcony with, I was sure, as many guns as there were on the front porch.

From my left sounded horse's hooves and the wheels of a carriage. It stopped in front of the house. From where I stood, I could not see who exited. As the guest's boots hit the steps, one of the guards said, "Good evening, sir."

The voice I heard respond was unmistakable. The front door opened, and Broussard walked in.

The carriage stayed put, blocking my view.

I crossed the street, walked around the carriage, and approached the porch. Broussard's driver had joined the two guards.

At the first step, all three men pulled pistols. I raised my hands.

"Go on about your business, for you have none here," said the one blocking my way.

"My business is indeed here, friend."

"I know of no visitors due this evening," he said. Then, "You passed us a while ago, why did you not stop?"

"I was waiting on Master Broussard to arrive, sir."

"Who are you here to see?"

"The general, sir."

All three looked at each other, then the man in front of me asked, "And what is your name?"

"Zebadiah, Zebadiah Creed," I said.

He placed his pistol in his belt and went inside.

I stood motionless with the second guard and driver, the street deserted. Both their pistols were still pointed my way.

The front door opened. Broussard stepped out onto the porch. "Ah, *Monsieur* Creed, you have arrived." He nodded to the men. "Search him."

I lowered my hands and opened my jacket. The clothes I wore were given to me by Sophie, stylish for the day, yet warm for a summer evening. Or perhaps because the deed I was about to attempt raised my temperature, for I was sweating.

The guard checked all my pockets and patted down my legs. "You seem nervous," he said.

"Excited to see my old friend is all."

"Not even a penknife, sir."

Broussard beckoned for me to join him and extended his hand. As I walked up the steps, I saw someone standing just inside the door whom I did not know, though by his dress, he clearly appeared to be a man of means. I stood frozen for a long second looking Broussard square in the eye, and slowly raised my hand. *You goddamn bastard.* We shook, his fingers gripping mine. He glanced down at our clasped hands, then to the silk top hat I wore, and smiled.

"Ah, Zebadiah Creed." He let go and stepped aside. "I introduce to you, William H. Christy."

Christy examined me up and down. "So, this is the famous survivor of Goliad . . . And hero of San Jacinto." He did not offer to shake. Instead, he bowed, welcoming me into his home, and said, "May I take your hat, sir?"

CHAPTER 24

Christy escorted me up a wide staircase, the guard behind me with Broussard following him. Before Christy entered the sitting room, he pulled me aside. In a quiet voice, he said, "The general is still in recovery. He's just now walking but cannot yet deliver himself down the stairs." He glanced past me to Broussard and frowned. Yet, as he spoke, the look in his eyes gave away a true concern for his friend, General Houston. "I'm afraid he will always limp with a cane."

Christy gently knocked, then swung the door open.

Houston appeared asleep, slumped in a chair facing the open doors to the balcony. On a table next to him sat a bottle of whiskey and glass. One oil lamp lit the room. His left foot was wrapped in bandages and propped on a stool. He looked heavier than he did the last I saw him, lying under a tree just off the battlefield of San Jacinto, the evening of our victory against the Mexican armies. He had turned his back on Grainger and me after ordering us to go and find Santa Anna. The next morning, I was kidnapped and stolen away to New Orleans and my young friend James shot in the gut by Grainger.

There, in the dim lamplight of a room above Girod Street in New Orleans, I stood over the invalid general and wondered how much he knew of my current plight.

Christy leaned down and shook Houston awake. With a couple of tries, he lifted his head and opened his eyes. It took a few seconds for him to recognize me. He glanced at Christy,

136

then Broussard and back to me, his entire face showing surprise, as if he saw a ghost.

Christy nodded and said, "I believe you two are friends."

Houston tried to stand but could not and slipped back into the chair. He sat up as straight as he could with both feet on the floor and reached for his crutches laid against the table. He waved off help from any of us and finally stood on his own, wincing as he placed pressure on his injured foot. He turned to me and offered his hand.

"Zebadiah Creed, I thought you were in prison, or dead."

I smiled and said, "Neither one, sir."

Our handshake was strong, as it should have been between two friends who had experienced what we had lived through.

He wavered. I reached out and took ahold of his shoulders and steadied him. The closer I got, I smelled the whiskey and his eyes were bloodshot. He looked to the chair and with a whoosh, sat back down, the crutches landing on the floor. He closed his eyes, then opened them to stare at me, as if he could not believe I still stood before him.

"Why are you here?" he asked.

I looked past him to Broussard, who now hung in the shadows of the back of the room. I had no true answer to give.

"I'm here to see my old friend to safety," I said.

There came a knock. Broussard opened the door and there stood Anson Jones. As he stepped into the room, I thought, *another witness to the murder.*

Who's there?" Houston asked, turning to see who had entered.

Jones answered, "It's just me, Sam . . . Dr. Anson." He nodded to Broussard, as if confirming the secret they held between them.

Houston looked confused. "Where have you been? I haven't seen you since damn near the day I arrived here in this voodoo city . . ." Then, to no one in particular. "How long have I been here?"

"Sir, I had important business to attend to upriver, for the cause." Again, Jones glanced at Broussard. "For the Republic of Texas."

"Hmm, well, my physician claims I have a few more weeks of healing before I go back." He glanced at me. "Now that Zebadiah's here, I'm sure that with the two of you accompanying me, along with my guards, it will be sooner."

I did not say a word.

After a few long seconds, Houston asked, "Zeb, you will be going back to Texas with me? There's much work to be done and you'll be a great asset to the building of our new nation." He hesitated. "Besides . . . you must resolve this issue you have with Grainger."

He said the words almost as if they were a question, that he was not quite sure of the story told to him about me by someone who may have only wanted half the truth known.

There came a slight rap at the door. Christy looked surprised, as if he did not expect anyone else. He pulled the door open. Juliette stood in the hallway next to the guard and curtsied. As Christy started to shut the door on her, she said, "I was told to . . ." She held out a rectangular box wrapped with ribbon and tied into a bow.

Christy seemed instantly impatient. "Well, spit it out, girl."

Juliette stammered, ". . . bring Mister Creed this gift."

"From who?" Christy asked.

She nodded to Broussard.

Christy seemed startled by her answer but did not say anything more and let her enter the room.

Hearing her voice, Houston perked up in his chair. "Is that my darling Juliette?"

She looked around the room without acknowledging me.

Houston turned in his chair and stared at her, as if he should be the one she went to.

Christy nodded toward me. "Well, there he is, girl. Give him the gift."

She stepped forward and presented the box. Broussard stayed in the shadows with Jones by his side. I accepted it and bowed. Juliette glanced up once, not at all letting on that we might know each other. She curtsied and backed away.

Houston reached out and grabbed her by the wrist and guided her closer to his chair. He offered her his lap. She hesitated and instead of looking at Christy for help, she again glanced at me. It was obvious that she had succumbed to the general's advances before, yet right then she appeared to want nothing to do with him. Christy grabbed her other wrist and pulled her away. "She must go now, there will be time for that later," he said and escorted her to the door. She looked at me one last time, and with an almost imperceptible nod, walked out of the room. I hoped no one noticed.

"Well, open it," said Broussard.

I had forgotten about the gift I held in my hands.

I pulled on the bow and let the ribbon fall to the floor. Everyone in the room stared at the box. I lifted the lid, slid it back, and immediately recognized the knife's handle. I looked up. Broussard's eyes shone so bright in the shadows I thought they might burn holes through to my soul.

"Grainger gave it to me before he went back to Texas," he said.

The Bowie knife lay on a bed of dark, blue silk cloth. Even in the dim lamplight, its wide blade appeared to glow, illuminating the inside of the box. Broussard continued to stare at me.

"Whatcha got there, son?" Houston asked.

I picked the knife up by its handle and held it in front of me, running my thumb down its blade. The entire Texas War came flooding back. The first time I met Jim Bowie during the Grass Fight, with Grainger, and the first battle to drive the Mexicans from San Antonio; the last I saw Bowie, with him already dying of consumption, three days before the fall of the Alamo. It was then that I gained possession of the knife. I killed one man and scalped another with that blade, and foolishly thought that by trading it for the safe passage of nearly four hundred Texas prisoners, I might save their lives from slaughter. I was wrong.

And now, I was expected to murder my friend General Sam Houston with the knife I held in my hand. I laid the box down, opened my jacket, and slid it in my belt. From the corner of my eye, I saw Broussard nod.

"Hey, it's Bowie's knife. I recognize it from San Jacinto. You still have that scalp you took off the Mexican soldier?" Houston asked, sitting up. He certainly felt better than when I first came into the room. Whatever whiskey he drank earlier was wearing off.

Christy went to the table, poured a drink, handed it to Houston, and said, "Noticed your pain, sir."

The general lowered his head as if he suddenly were asleep, then slowly waved off the glass.

I understood why they needed to keep Houston sedated, because of his injury. I also knew that with him being drunk, it would be far easier for me to assassinate him there in his room, in front of Christy, Broussard, and now Anson Jones as witnesses.

Houston raised his head up and said, "Everybody out, except Zebadiah. I need to speak with him privately."

No one moved.

"Out. Now!" Houston yelled.

Jones was first to the door, then Christy. Broussard held it open and nodded, as if telling me to go on and get it over with. He pulled the door shut. Houston and I were alone.

A frown creased his face and he asked, "Why have you truly come here, Zebadiah?"

His eyes were brighter than a few seconds before, when Christy hovered over him. He sat up a little straighter in the chair, his shoulders back. He seemed more in command of himself. Sam Houston was a much smarter drunk than who he led on to be.

I stood at the open doors of the balcony and remained silent. With the back of my hand, I wiped my brow.

"Well, why are you here?" he asked.

Across the street, a man stepped into the pool of light illuminated by the lamp I had earlier avoided, looked up at me, and nodded. The carriage in front of the house had been moved for him to be seen from the porch. The instant one of the guards hollered *who goes there,* the man walked onto the dark street toward the house, pulled a pistol, and fired, *shhh-boom!* The blast broke the evening silence of the neighborhood. One of the guards fired back, missing the lone man. Two others stepped onto the street and fired their pistols toward the porch. From the back of the house, I heard shots. Christy's home was being invaded.

I spun around to face Houston and said, "I have come to assassinate you."

He sat frozen, his face turned to the color of chalk. Then, from under the chair's cushion, he retrieved a small pistol, pulled the hammer back, and aimed it at my chest.

"You'll have to be quicker than this powder an' ball," he said, leveling his eyes on me. "I've killed better men than you on a whim."

He trusted the idea that I was about to kill him.

"I was never going to do it," I said, shaking my head, and carefully opened my jacket. With two fingers, I lifted the knife from my belt and laid it on the table next to the whiskey bottle, then raised my hands.

From inside the house came more pistol shots and a woman's scream.

The battle downstairs lasted only a couple of minutes, with men shouting, "No, No, No . . . !" then silenced with the crack of pistol shots. One man's muffled cries drifted up with the smell, then the smoke of gunpowder seeping through the closed door, filling the room with a subtle haze. Then, all was quiet. Houston had laid the pistol in his lap when he heard the woman's scream, whispering, *Juliette?* He tried getting up from the chair without his crutches but could not. He picked them off the floor and rose to his feet. There came noise on the stairs, boots stomping up to the second floor along with a softer set of footsteps. Houston raised the small pistol, ready to shoot whoever walked through the door. I placed the knife back in my belt and stepped aside. Two men walked down the hall to stop outside the room. The door was unlatched and swung open. Broussard shuffled in, his hands tied, his face brutally beaten with blood smeared over a broken nose and dripping onto his white shirt. The point of a cutlass was pressed to his back. When both men were in the room, the door was left ajar.

Houston lowered his pistol, then wavered between the two, not knowing who to point at.

"Olgens will be along soon," said Frenchy. "He's gone to get his boys."

CHAPTER 25

Olgens's men must have replaced Broussard's guards for all I heard from the front porch were orders for the gathering folks on the street to move along, go back to their homes, that they had no interest here. The crowd quickly dispersed, and the neighborhood was again quiet. As far as I could see, there was no law come to investigate the takeover of the house.

Houston had homed in on Frenchy with his gun.

"Sir, he is our ally. It was Broussard here that thought he could coerce me into murdering you," I said. "Because you are my friend, he was not successful."

"And what of Christy and Jones? And my guards?" Houston asked, stepping in front of Broussard.

"*Général* Houston! I am so . . . so . . . happy to finally make your acquaintance, sir." The few times I had been in the presence of Frenchy conversing with other men, I had never witnessed him being tongue-tied like he was at that moment. Realizing Broussard stood between himself and Houston, he drove the conspirator to his knees by slamming the butt end of the cutlass down on a shoulder. Broussard yelped in pain. Frenchy pulled the plain-handled knife and held it to his throat. "One more squeal and I let Zebadiah cut off your lips," he said nodding toward me.

"Christy and Jones?" Houston again asked, staring down at the beaten man kneeling before him.

"Ah, *Général*, they are all safe from death. For now," said

Frenchy. "Until we find how they play into the plot to kill you."

Houston's face again turned white, then red with anger. He began to wobble, stopped himself, and stood firm on both feet. "Christy and Jones, now!"

I heard the rattle of a sword at the door. In the dark hallway stood Frenchy's daughter, Sapphire.

No, the rattle of a cutlass . . .

She entered the room. Frenchy motioned for her to lean close and whispered something. Sapphire whispered back, staring at me with her black eyes. With one, last word to her father, she left, again, leaving the door ajar.

"She will bring the men you request," Frenchy said, "I'm afraid only two of your guards have survived."

Houston still stood in front of Broussard, for the moment looking bewildered. Then his face turned to stone and his eyes grew cold. I had seen this in him one time before, as we were about to slaughter the whole of Santa Anna's army. With a struggle, he knelt down to meet Broussard face to face.

"What have you done?" Houston asked.

The confederate said nothing. On his knees, Houston shuffled closer. "I asked, *what have you done?*"

Frenchy kicked Broussard square on his right shoulder. With a groan, he toppled to the floor. Frenchy bent down, grabbed a handful of hair, and pulled the beaten man's head up to face Houston. "*Monsieur* Broussard, I suggest you answer the *Général's* question."

Broussard slowly caught his breath and said, "You will betray us, sir."

"How do you mean?" Houston asked, still kneeling. Again, he winced in pain. I slid his chair over and helped him to his feet so he could then sit and face Broussard.

"Thank you, Zebadiah."

Broussard looked up and glared at me. I offered him no

response and disappeared to the back of the room.

"Again, I ask, what do you mean, betray us. I don't know you . . . except by name."

Broussard opened his mouth, licked his swollen lips, and said, "You know my deeds, for you defeated the Mexicans. It was partly my money that allowed you to be successful. It was I who purchased the guns and powder. It was my idea to secure the cannons and I paid for their delivery. So, *Général*, though we had never met until this evening, you know my actions well, sir." He sneered and lowered his head.

"Who else?"

Broussard did not answer.

"Who else lies at the heart of this conspiracy?" Houston asked. "Anson Jones? My friend William Christy?" He glanced at me with his cold eyes. "Zebadiah Creed?"

"Who else?" he growled.

Broussard raised his head to meet Houston eye to eye and said, "Jones understands the value of an honorable cause, to remain independent, to maintain our way of life. God's way of life."

Houston seemed confused. He again looked up at me.

"The creation of a world order of slave countries, keepin' folks in chains forever, flying the lone star flag," I said. "John Preston of the Hydras plantation, Dr. Anson Jones, and him are involved . . . along with the prosecutor of my trial here in New Orleans and the warden of the prison I was thrown into. How many hundreds more? I do not know. Oh, and of course their assassin Willie Dan who's gone off to kill my friend Anna Keynes up on the Missouri, if I don't kill you." I felt out of breath. That to say the words, to explain the whole plot, drained me of every bit of feelings I had left, except for anger. Through my teeth, I said, "Up at the plantation, near Baton Rouge, this piece a shit ordered Willie Dan to murder a slave woman name of Margo, right in front of her boys, with Jones as a witness. Just to prove to me they would do anything for their goddamn, piece a shit cause.

"She was Olgens Pierre's wife."

"Did you say that Mr. Pierre has gone to get *the boys*?" Houston asked Frenchy, again appearing confused.

"*Oui, Général,* they are Margo's sons and witnesses to her murder." He raised Broussard's head up, showing two black eyes, busted lips, and bruises. "Did not take long to find out where they were."

"Hmm . . ." Houston said, staring at Broussard.

The room was quiet, as was the entire house and street, as if the world hung on his next words. Then, "You will be taken back to Texas, tried for the failed attempt at taking my life, and hung beside your fellow conspirator Anson Jones."

Frenchy glanced at me, then back to Houston, and said, "With all due respect, *Général, Monsieur* Creed and I have an idea what this particular situation may be more suited for."

Houston again ordered, *"Bring me Christy and Jones."*

There came a slight tap on the open door and the rattle of a cutlass.

"*Oui, Général,* they are here," Frenchy said.

CHAPTER 26

Olgens walked behind Sapphire as she led Christy and Jones to stand before Houston. Once in the room, he held a pistol on them both. I could not help but notice the blood covering his boots and hems of his pants. The rest of his dress was immaculate, as always. He glanced about until he found me and smiled.

"My boys were not so far away," he said, "they are safe." He sighed, with his shoulders drooping. He then straightened into a brace as he laid eyes on Broussard. The dried blood covering his face and Olgens's boots might have been the same blood.

Houston first addressed Christy. "Are you a part of this conspiracy?"

Christy, who appeared enraged, his face as red as the blood on Olgens's boots, said, "They killed three of my guards and two of yours." He glanced at Broussard. "What he did, killing nothing but a slave? This reaction, to say the least, is unconscionable." Nearly in tears, he stared at Houston. "Of course I was not a part of such a thing. I could not be, for I was here with you, as your friend and caretaker," Christy pleaded, his life hanging on his old friend trusting every word he said. Houston softened his eyes. I was sure he was doing everything in his power to believe him.

Broussard sniffed and said, *"Don't believe him!* It is his house we stand in now offering up this place freely . . ."

I did not expect Christy to move so quick to hit him. One

more spot on Broussard's face began to swell. I knew then that he was to take the brunt of guilt for this conspiracy.

Frenchy pulled his knife again, pointed it at Broussard, and with his fingers to his lips said, *"Shhhh."*

Houston turned to his battlefield doctor. "What about it, Jones?" he asked, spitting the words out of his mouth. "Creed says that you were conspiring in the very room where that poor woman was murdered, is this true?"

Anson Jones did not look up.

"Answer me!" Houston demanded.

Jones nodded.

"Answer me out loud, you goddamn traitor, yes or no!"

Jones stared at the general's pistol aimed at his gut and said, "Yes, I betrayed you."

"A bold bastard you are," Houston swore, "to admit this to my face, yet not even look me in the eye, you *son of a bitch!*" He laid the pistol on the table, lifted one of his crutches, leaned forward, and swiped Jones across his head. He winced but withstood the attack. Houston hit him again, this time in the ear. He yelped, brushed the crutch aside, and stepped away. With the point of his cutlass, Frenchy urged him back to his place. Houston hit Jones one more time, making his ear bleed.

Exhausted, Houston let out a cry, as if he were about to break, and slumped back into his chair. "We were in battle together," he exclaimed, to no one in particular.

There came silence for a few seconds. So quiet I thought I could hear everyone's beating hearts.

"We have a way toward justice," Olgens offered. "And a plan to take get you back to Texas, tonight."

Houston stared at Olgens and asked, "Now who are you?"

"Olgens Pierre, at your service, sir. I am the husband of Margo."

Houston reached for the bottle and poured himself a drink.

"And who is she?"

"My wife," Olgens said, pointing to Broussard. "Murdered by this man's authority." He pointed to Jones. "In the presence of this man, and witnessed by my friend Zebadiah Creed. We have a plan, sir, to mete out justice, all around this room."

"The trial has begun, *Monsieur Général*," said Frenchy.

One of Houston's two guards stepped from the hallway through the door.

"Ah, Joseph, thank God you survived," Houston said, then waved his hand toward Jones and Broussard. "Leave Christy and lock these two in the next bedroom. If they try and escape, kill them both."

"Yes, sir," he said, and with the help of Frenchy and his daughter, each with their cutlass, the conspirators were led away. With a click, the door was locked, and the guard passed through to the balcony to prevent their escape to the outside.

Sapphire stood next to her father. "Who is she?" Houston asked, acting as if this was the first he noticed her.

"She is my lovely daughter, *monsieur*," said Frenchy.

"And what is your name, girl?"

She glanced at her father. He nodded and said, "Her name is Sapphire, sir. Named after such a precious jewel as one has ever seen."

"You're mighty young to be wielding that sword."

Before Frenchy could say a word, I said, "Sir, it's not a sword, it's a cutlass . . . sir."

I noticed a glimmer of a smile from Frenchy as he slid his weapon into its scabbard.

"Sir, I don't believe we have formally met," Houston said.

Frenchy stood before him. "*Général*, I am called many names, some deserved, some not. Though you may know me as Frenchy from St. Louie, as our friend Zebadiah does. Or you may know me as our mutual friend, the *Général* Andrew Jackson does. He calls me Jean, Jean Laffite."

"I knew it!" Houston said. "There's something about you that I recognized; have we met, sir?"

"I do not believe so, though my reputation, ill or otherwise, proceeds me."

"Hmmm," said Houston.

"This evening, I am not Jean Laffite. Will you be so kind as to address me as John Laflin, *monsieur*? That is now my name. Perhaps another alias to hide behind, or a way to walk the Earth unnoticed."

Houston thought about this for a few seconds, then smiled and nodded. "Based on the legendary exploits of the hero pirate Jean Laffite and the tales of his death so many years ago, I understand the necessity of anonymity, sir." He bowed his head in respect. "I too sometimes wish to simply disappear."

"Tonight, you shall, sir," answered Olgens Pierre. He then said to Sapphire, "My dear, be so kind as to bring back to us Broussard."

I smiled to myself and thought, *finally, justice is about to be served.*

CHAPTER 27

Broussard grunted, as if he wanted to remind us that he was still in the room.

We stopped talking and looked down at him. He sat cross-legged in the middle of the floor with his hands tied. The blood had dried on his face. He had a broken nose, two black eyes, and possibly a broken shoulder where Frenchy had hit him with the handle of his cutlass. It seemed as if Broussard was ready to be done with all the discussion about his fate.

"I shall not survive the night, so just shoot me and be finished," he said.

"Oh, this will come to a head," said Houston. "It might not be as quick as you would like."

Everyone offered a nervous laugh but me. I turned my back on them all and stood at the open doors to the balcony. It must have been close to midnight for folks had extinguished the lights of the neighborhood homes. The streetlamps burned on. The slightest of breezes brushed my cheek, a bare relief from a stifling, summer evening's heat, and then was gone. I listened to my friends argue about what to do with this man, this wealthy plantation owner, a man of means, power, and influence. What were the repercussions of a vigilante punishment? For, at that moment, this was what we were, a vigilante mob of powerful men in our own right. The winner and hero of the Texas revolution, the most famous pirate of all America, the wealthiest landowner in Haiti, and me, a wanderer and witness to the murder of a slave. I understood frontier justice, more so than these men bickering about what to do. In my eyes, a man was equal to another, no matter what. I had lived my life by this law. The fact that I shared the room and this horrendous situation with men of differing points of view—men who were my friends—did not change my view of the outcome and fate of Broussard.

"Hang him and be done with it," I said through gritted teeth.

I felt all their stares fall upon me. I slowly turned to face them, laid a hand on my knife's handle, and said, "I have witnessed senseless brutality by the order of this man. I've been in his snare for many months now. I've killed a man because of him. I've been bartered about in the court and nearly hung because of him." I felt my face burn, tightening against my skull. My heart pounded. I spat out the words. "And my time with this situation is far from over, for now I must go north and find the most gleeful goddamn murderer I have ever known and kill him before he kills the woman I love."

I paused to catch my breath, then calmly added, "All I ask for is his scalp."

Their silence matched the silence of the late hour. Frenchy gave the same look he gave when I killed his wolverine all those months before, a mix of awe and fear. Houston had closed his eyes, feigning himself asleep in his chair. Christy stared at me, probably thinking I was insane. Olgens smiled and nodded in agreement. Sapphire's black eyes gleamed bright, as if she had already seen the deed done in her mind.

"You . . . you can't scalp me, that would be entirely uncivilized," said Broussard, sitting up straight.

"But what about the body?" Christy asked. "Will the act be done here? What about my neighbors? They have already witnessed the takeover of my home. A man hung on my property will certainly tarnish my standing in the community. And again,

I ask, what about the body?"

Olgens laughed, then said, "We will be quiet, you can count on that."

"Yes, we will do it in stealth," said Frenchy, "and *Monsieur* Broussard will disappear, as if he decided to simply go away . . . forever."

Houston opened his eyes. "I will be your witness, Mr. Creed. We all shall be. It seems that Mr. Broussard here certainly deserves his just rewards, as do you."

I pulled my knife and took a step forward. Broussard tried getting up but could not. I stood above him.

"No, no, you were never meant to hang," he confessed. "We . . . Willie Dan thought it best you go free, that he could somehow tempt you to do our bidding, because he thought you were like him. And, and when you wouldn't leave the jail. . . . We *had* to change plans! You see, Houston has to . . ." His eyes were wild, spinning back and forth between us all. They narrowed onto Olgens. "She was mine, bought and paid for, to do with as I pleased!" he growled, then screamed, *"Margo was mine, mine you fucking coon!"*

Before Broussard could scream again, Frenchy stepped behind him, forced open his jaw, and crammed a handkerchief into his mouth.

"You will leave him alive for me, won't you?" Olgens asked, his eyes black as the darkest nights of my dreams.

Christy slowly closed the balcony doors.

Frenchy offered to me Broussard.

When I reached out, he swiveled his head around, his ass squirming on the carpet. I smelled piss. Frenchy interlocked his fingers across Broussard's face and held a knee to the back of his neck. They both looked at me, with Broussard's eyes pleading. Frenchy's eyes gleamed with anticipation.

My heart no longer beat heavy in my chest. My hands did

not shake. I was as calm as when I first killed a man. I smoothed his thinning hair. "Shhhh," I said, grabbing a fistful, and cut into his scalp a perfect circle.

CHAPTER 28

The first floor of Christy's home was a battlefield. I recognized two of Broussard's guards laid out dead with four others in the hallway to the front door. Blood pooled in patches on the carpet of the parlor. Powder smoke lingered in the air as all the windows had been shuttered. We descended into a chaotic jumble of furniture. Five men lounged about wiping and reloading pistols. Their distinctive clothes and color of skin gave away where they came from. When they saw Olgens, the Haitians all snapped to attention with no hesitation. In French, he ordered one of them to go and find a rope. Without question, the man disappeared through the kitchen. The other four stood ready.

Were there more of his army? I wondered. Or were these five the only ones to take control and kill all of the men lying in the hall? I sensed there may be more dead upstairs. I glanced at Olgens with a sense of renewed respect.

Joseph escorted Christy and Jones down the stairs, leaving Christy to survey the damage and taking Jones on into the kitchen. Houston had an easier time coming down the stairs than did Broussard, for I helped him with his crutches. Frenchy walked Broussard to the first landing, then gave him a shove. Broussard tumbled down the rest of the stairs to crumple into a heap with a whimper. There came a gasp from Olgens's men when they saw the circle cut out of the top of Broussard's head. The four of them began to laugh. One asked how he could possibly still be alive. I pulled the knife and bloody scalp from my belt. One remarked, in French, *"Very clean, monsieur, very clean."*

I stared down at Broussard and yanked the handkerchief out of his mouth. He was indeed alive, barely.

He lifted his head and sputtered, "The truth will be told, for the cause, and it will travel the river, north with hurricane speed, to *Monsieur* Dan . . . and he will kill your friends."

I towered over him, shocked that he was so coherent. "Ain't no truth told tonight. Not on your behalf, anyway," I said, "Your cause as you call it will lose. A friend of mine says, 'Good dogs make better masters. Turn your back on us though, and we will bite.' " I held up his scalp. "Consider yourself bitten."

I placed the scalp and knife back in my belt, then spied the silk hat he had given to me hanging in the hallway. I walked over and snatched it off its hook. By the parlor entry, I noticed a much smaller body, covered in linen cloth. My heart stopped. I cried out, *"Juliette?"*

"I am here, Zebadiah."

I turned and there she stood, near the stairs with Houston. I rushed to her. I wanted to lift her up and into my arms. Instead, she held out the knife and pistol I had asked her to hide, and curtsied. I gazed at her for a few seconds, then realized I had not hidden my disappointment, so I smiled and took a step back. She had chosen Houston, then. He leaned on her, his arm around her waist.

"Glad you're alive," she said.

"Me too." I spun the hat in my hands by its brim, looking down.

"Saoirse was my friend," Juliette said, staring at the wrapped body. Houston nodded in agreement and held her closer in comfort.

Broussard sat upright with his elbows leaning against the bottom stair, his eyes closed, groaning. *He won't last much longer,* I thought, and positioned the hat on top of his head. He winced as I gave it a couple of taps. "I won't be needin' this where I'm goin'," I said.

I secured the extra weapons in my belt. With Juliette, we gathered up Houston and helped him toward the kitchen. Christy stood by the door, a look of shock on his face.

"What . . . shall I do with the bodies?" he asked.

Houston stopped and said to his friend, "I was warned. We were warned."

Christy's look changed to confusion.

Houston said. "Our friend George Boyd sent the sword and his note of warning, that there were conspiracies that might lead to my demise . . ."

Christy shrugged. "I thought it all talk."

"Talk is where it begins," Houston said, his glare hardening as he locked onto Christy. They stood for a few more seconds, Houston perhaps wondering if Christy could somehow be every bit the partner with Broussard and the others. Or maybe he was thinking that they might never meet again. He sighed. "You may keep the sword as a token of our friendship. It's upstairs with the rest of my belongings I cannot take with me back to Texas."

"Time to go," I said.

Christy offered his hand. "Farewell, Samuel."

"Thank you," Houston said, gripping Christy's hand in return. "I hope to see you at the inauguration?" He paused for a reaction from his friend.

"Yes, yes, of course," Christy said, returning his attention to the dead bodies lying in the doorway.

We walked on through the kitchen to the back of the house.

In a small, attached room, Anson Jones sat tied to a chair. He had not been beaten, except for Houston's wallop to his ear. I eased the general into the chair across from him and stepped away.

"Get me a drink, will you, Zebadiah?" Houston asked. "Juliette can stay."

I hesitated, then said, "Yes, sir," and went to find a bottle. When I returned a few moments later, Jones had been untied and was helping Houston out of his chair.

"Mr. Jones will be accompanying me back to Texas," he said, "a free man."

I was shocked and showed it. "Sir?"

How could he trust this goddamn traitor, this scallywag, this assistant murderer?

Houston looked me in the eye and said, "Please, don't ask any questions."

I took a deep breath and said no more.

Sapphire and Frenchy stood outside the open door. "We must go, now *monsieur,* else we get caught in the moonlight."

Houston, with the help of Jones and Juliette, stepped down to the gravel path that led through a grove of trees just beyond the house. I followed, with two of Olgens's men behind us, their pistols pulled in case of trouble. But for our boots scraping the gravel, it was deathly silent.

Halfway to the trees, I heard what sounded like a kick to the pants. We all turned to see Broussard fall, then jerk upward, silhouetted by the glow of a lamp at the second floor. His neck must have broken. One hand that had clutched at the rope flailed and then swung with the rest of his body. Somehow, the silk top hat remained attached to his head. All I could hear was the creak of the railing on which the rope was tied. At the third story balcony, I could just make out Olgens Pierre standing with his arms crossed. A glimmer in the shape of a woman appeared beside him. *Margo?* I stared at the apparition, hoping for his sake she was with him. I wiped my eyes, and she was gone.

"We must go, *now, we meet at Sophie's!*" Frenchy whispered.

Within seconds of entering the woods, the lights from

Christy's house disappeared.

I walked behind as Juliette and Jones helped General Houston make his way through the early morning darkness.

CHAPTER 29

Sophie's downstairs parlor smelled of iodine and whiskey.

Olgens Pierre and I stood together where we first met, with Sophie again pouring us scotch. She had brought a bucket of water behind the bar to wash Broussard's blood off our hands. This act we could not have possibly imagined performing all those months before as we discussed Margo, and her sons' enslavement, and plotted how they might be freed.

Frenchy stood with us and raised his glass. "May the bastard rot in hell!"

We drained our whiskey in silence.

"Now down to business," Frenchy said. "Word is being circulated amongst Broussard's minions that Le Général has indeed been murdered. This prevarication will travel far enough ahead of our friend here," he nodded to me, "to give him time to find the assassin, before they are beset by the truth. Me and ma fille will escort him through to St Louie. Général Houston will be spirited away in secret, over land, to Texas, leaving here before the light of day."

I was not sure who he was talking to, sharing our plans out loud. We were the ones who made them. Perhaps he was making sure we were all in agreement. Or maybe, after all the excitement and a few drinks, he just needed to hear himself talk.

General Houston sat on a red velvet, high-backed divan, a glass of bourbon in his hand, his head laid back and eyes closed. A look of pain creased his face. Juliette sat on the matching stool with his foot in her lap, re-dressing his injury with fresh iodine and cotton bandages, as it seemed she had done many times before.

"You are my sweet," he said.

She smiled and continued wrapping his ankle.

"Juliette will be joining Mr. Jones and myself on our travels back to Texas," Houston said to us all.

Silence again filled the room for several seconds, until, "It is time she goes out on her own," Sophie said, frowning, "Good to finally be rid of her." She held to the bar as if she might fall. Sapphire stepped up and allowed Sophie to gently lean against her.

The rest of us turned to Juliette, still sitting on the footstool. She glanced at the general and again smiled. Houston offered her his hand and she joined him on the divan.

Juliette caught my eye. She gave me a wistful look, as if she already missed what we might have shared together. A slight nod was my only reaction. To add sadness and regret to my evening's emotional toll was almost too much for me to bear.

"I will stay here with my *mère*," Sapphire said.

Those were the first words I heard her utter in New Orleans. Frenchy whirled around and stared at his daughter and ex-mistress.

As he was about to say something, Sapphire continued. "*Maman* is sick, and I wish to care for her." She wiped a tear from her cheek and stood up straight, staring at her father, as if she dared him to say something otherwise.

"You don't know her," Frenchy said, slamming his glass on the bar. "She is conniving, a . . . a witch she is," he stuttered, the words trailing off.

His expression cracked, betraying a breaking heart. He lowered his head, as if he knew there was to be no arguing.

What he thought best for her, or how he felt about losing his daughter to the mother from whom he spirited her away, no longer mattered. He looked them both up and down. Sophie stood the best she could, countering her disease, leaning on her daughter. Sapphire held strong, eyes like black diamonds, her head high with a hand on the handle of her cutlass, as if revealing her pride in being both her father's and mother's daughter.

"I have raised you up as well as I could, and now . . . I see," said Frenchy. He then turned to me and said, "Our boat leaves at daybreak from wharf twelve."

He stepped away from the bar, bowed to Sophie, and walked out the front door.

Soon, I bid mother and daughter good night and Sapphire helped Sophie upstairs and to bed.

General Houston and Juliette retired to her room, I presumed, to prepare for their long journey.

Olgens and I stood alone at the bar, in silence, finishing our scotch. We both were wrung out, and with our own long journeys still ahead, toasted.

"To family . . ." Olgens paused, the words caught in his throat.

". . . and friends," I said, and we drank up.

I stepped out to piss. When I came back inside, Olgens was gone.

The bastard didn't even say goodbye.

I sat down on the divan and laid my head back. "Whew, what a goddamn day," I whispered and closed my eyes. Smelling Juliette's faint scent of lilac, I fell fast asleep.

At dawn, I escorted Houston, Juliette, and Anson Jones to the outside, kitchen door where a fully provisioned wagon waited. Both of Houston's guards stood ready. Jones climbed into the back of the wagon. If it were me, he would be hanging alongside Broussard. I hoped to never see him again, the traitor.

Houston put out his hand. "Thank you, for saving my life . . ." He stopped, then pulled me into his embrace. "You are a great warrior, Zebadiah Creed," he whispered. "Do not forget it, son." He pushed me away and squeezed my arm. "After your business north, you will come to Texas. You also have business to take care of there."

I nodded, my eyes welling with tears. This man I would deeply miss.

Juliette stood before me. "Take care, Zebadiah," she said.

We held each other for a few, quiet seconds. She reached up and kissed me softly on the cheek, broke away from arms that did not want to release her, and joined Houston.

His one hand clutched the handle of a crutch, his other held Juliette. "Did you enjoy the biscuits?" he asked.

I stared at them both and shrugged, not knowing what he was talking about.

"The biscuits, while you were in jail," said Juliette.

For a second, I thought back to how good they tasted, licking crumbs from my filthy fingers, sustaining me in one of my darkest times.

"Ah . . ." I said, again nodding. "Of course, it was you all along."

I should not have been surprised.

With a knowing glance to one another, they climbed into the back of the covered wagon, drew the canvas shut, and rode off westward.

The steamboat was smaller than the others strewn along the wharf, with a full paddle wheel stretching across its stern.

"The fastest," Frenchy said proudly as I stepped aboard. "We shall be in St. Louie in a week."

The wharf was deserted but for a couple of the steamers being loaded with cargo, good that no one came near ours. Of course, they would have been thwarted by Frenchy's two armed men at the brow. I was concerned about the show of force, for it being daylight. I mentioned this to Frenchy. He shrugged and said he owned the wharf we were tied to. I relaxed a little. The less delays the better, I was anxious to get on up the river.

He guided me through the main sitting and dining cabins and out to the bow, bragging the whole way about how many races his steamer had won up and down the Mississippi, that it could not be beat. We stepped to the front rail. There before us, a small schooner was tied alongside the wharf. On the open deck stood Olgens and his boys, Abe and Sturgis.

"I say," he hollered, "a beautiful morning to be underway, headed home. What do you say, Mr. Creed?"

I smiled and hollered back, "It is indeed so, Mr. Pierre! I was sure you left without a goodbye."

"Ah, Zebadiah, I would not be so rude." Then, "Come visit us in Haiti?" he offered.

"That I will."

He gathered the two boys in his arms and said, "We thank you, sir."

Together, all three of them bowed.

I stepped away from the rail and returned their bow.

"Jean, it was good to see you," Olgens said to Frenchy.

"I tell you, my name is John, John Laflin!"

"Yes, yes, whatever your name is today. Remember, you will always owe me, and I will always owe you," Olgens said.

Frenchy bowed to his old friend.

The sailors threw their lines, allowing the schooner to catch the current of the river south.

I gave one, final wave goodbye.

The steamer's last warning bell rang, and the big wheel began to spin, churning the muddy water of the Mississippi into brown sludge.

I said to Frenchy, "I have a question, where shall I sleep? I am just damn tired."

He beckoned me to follow him.

"Ain't no stops along the way?"

Frenchy nodded. Then with the grin of someone who always knows a little more than those around him, he said, " 'Tis *your* journey, *Monsieur* Creed. I am only along for the ride, my friend, only along for the ride."

Around the bend, at the same wharf where I landed some weeks before, where Grainger collected from Broussard the bounty on my head, Sophie and Sapphire stood, both wearing yellow dresses. Frenchy offered a wave. The daughter waved back, the mother did not.

CHAPTER 30

North to St. Louis, Midsummer 1836

The water of the Mississippi sparkles as fresh as a mountain spring. Along the shore, the fingers of willow trees brush ripples made by our keelboat. My brother, Jonathan, stands at the bow guiding us through island marshes sprinkled across the breadth of the mightiest of rivers. I man the rudder. I hold a clear mind and clean heart. I am at ease with the world.

As the late, afternoon sun shines upon us, a wave lifts up the bow and down into a slight trough. There comes another and another, until the river is filled with waves, swamping the islands, and beginning to swamp our empty keelboat. Jonathan glances back to me and says, "What the hell, Zeb." He then points upriver to a steamboat, its paddle wheel spinning faster than could ever be possible, sending a four-foot-high wake toward both shores. I think, if we could somehow catch the steamer, right up to the wheel's draft, we might reach calmer waters and follow the boat all the way to the Missouri. The closer we get, the more I try to read the name written across the stern. At the back rail, above the thrashing paddles, there stands two men staring down at us, one wearing a cutlass at his side, the other . . .

I woke up.

At first, I thought I might be at Sophie's, alone on her soft featherbed, under silk sheets, the gentle rain drizzling down the cracked window above the dark and empty Liberty Street. Then I felt the rumble of the boiler pushing steam to the boat's swift-turning paddle wheel. Thunder rumbled in the distance. The cabin lit up with every lightning strike, revealing a basin on the bulkhead with a towel hung to dry, open shelves to lay my knife and new clothes on, and Broussard's scalp. A small table beside my bunk supported an oil lamp. I could write letters on a compact desk, if I so chose. These things of luxury were absent on the steamboat *Diana,* that time so long before, traveling the opposite route south to New Orleans. I closed my eyes again and took a couple of deep breaths. With nothing to do but lie in the dark and listen to the rain beat against the porthole, the streaks of lightning growing fewer and fewer, and feeling protected from those aiming to kill me for the first time in a long while, I tried to relax. I could not.

We passed the Hydras plantation the afternoon before. From the starboard rail, for a brief moment, I saw the pillars and porch of the house, up the road beyond the giant oaks. But for the prisoner's barge, the dock was empty. I wondered how Persimmons and his road gang were coming along. *They surely must be two-thirds finished by now.* A part of me wanted to walk the length of it, marveling at the design and handiwork. I swore I smelled Margo's funeral pyre burning and thought of Lindy Lou and her dogs howling in my dream. She said I had a decision to make that would affect many, many folks. *Had that choice been made?*

I cringed at the whistle blown by the captain, acknowledging our passing by.

Three mornings before, we left New Orleans. I hoped to never return. Yet, to leave under what great circumstances the future might bring, I could not fathom. I was not concerned with the consequences of my actions. I knew that I would find

Willie Dan before he found Anna.

I saw Anna last in a dream, as I lay sleeping in the dirt outside the chapel at the Presidio La Bahía, better known as Goliad. She carried my child. I woke that morning only to escape slaughter by Santa Anna's order. James Lee and I watched a hundred unarmed men shot down where they stood. James and I escaped by jumping into a river and floating away. That evening, from a mile's distance, we smelled the dead, nearly four hundred bodies stacked up like cordwood, set to fire. We heard later that some never burned and that for nearly a month, they were left to rot in the sun with the crows and vultures feasting on them. I had long since passed those poor souls by.

I did not know why I went to Texas, there was nothing proven by my going. I held nothing but contempt for my experiences, except, perhaps, for my saving James from slaughter. I could not stop him from dying by the shot of my betrayer, the blood on Grainger's hands thereby seeping onto my hands as well. I found myself wringing my fingers together, as if they were someone else's beyond my control.

I stood and gazed out the porthole, but for the rain on the glass, I saw nothing. I dressed, stepped into the corridor, and headed to the veranda deck. I found a chair and sat. I could not tell what time it was, though it felt like early morning, just before sunrise. The rain had slowed. The sultry air smelled of fresh water, black earth, and death. Yet, I saw nothing of the shoreline, no matter how sharply I peered through the darkness.

I could not relax in my cabin with Broussard's scalp lying there stinking. Even if all the men in that room four nights before had implored me to stop, I would not have. And if my reputation preceded me, well, then, when the bastard was found hanging from Christy's balcony, all who saw his missing scalp might know who did this and say my name in fear and disgust. Scalper. This was what I wanted. Maybe this was what I needed to reconcile with my demons buried so deep that only another killer like Willie Dan could recognize them. Yet, I also felt a sense of respite from my higher conscience. I did not feel at all guilty for what I did. I had taken scalps before.

This was who I was. I had killed others for their scalps, but I did not kill Broussard.

Again, I thought of Anna. *Would she know me?* Would she recognize my plight those long months after I walked away, to seek revenge for my brother's murder, leaving her alone to care for her dying father? I surely was not the same man, for I could never wash the stain of blood off my hands, nor remedy the memories of killing the men that stepped before me in a fight. Fights I chose. No one forced me to walk toward them with pistols and knives drawn. *Would she notice and turn me away? Would she even remember me?*

Still, as I pondered these things, I felt no shame for what I had done. Or what I was about to do once I found Willie Dan.

From behind me, I heard boot steps on the deck. I instantly reached for my knife and it was not there.

"My favorite time of day. The dark before the dawn," said Frenchy, now standing beside me. "You have taken my chair, Zebadiah."

I started up and he waved his hand for me to stay seated.

"What are you thinking, Zebadiah?"

I took a while to answer, then, "What lays behind me. And what lies ahead."

"Ah, a pondering of one's fate. Have you reached an understanding?"

"I am only certain about what lays behind."

"Do you know the first time I came up the Mississippi, a baby cradled in my arms, with nothing left to own but the child's blanket and my cutlass, I felt relieved . . . and terrified. As frightened as I was in battle on board ship." He took a breath. "The time my brother and I plundered our first prize, then watched the ocean swallow it whole, leaving only bubbles on the water to be swept away by waves, killing all on board. I did not know then that my future, in all its worth and shame, would lead me to share this morning with you."

I was becoming more and more Frenchy's confidant. Sometimes, though, I had no idea what he might be aiming at in his talk.

He continued. "You ponder your future as if it is necessary to fulfill the past. What murderous things we've done to survive. We have a choice to leave our lives buried. Trouble being, there will always be someone to come and dig the dirt away and expose the bones."

We fell into silence. The eastern shore had become ever so slightly visible, a brush of gray as we swept past. Weeping willows emerged at the water's edge with silhouetted pines farther up the bank. The rain had stopped. I felt the steamboat's paddles churning the muddy water of the Mississippi. If I sat too much longer, I might have been lulled back to sleep. I stood and we both stepped to the rail.

Frenchy again spoke. "I asked you once, 'Who are you, Zebadiah?' And as I recall, you claimed to be a savage. Is this still true, my friend?"

I was taken aback by the sudden question, for I had not thought of that night many months before in St. Louis, at Frenchy's Emporium, in his study with his bodyguard, Gerard, the first time I met Sapphire. He had asked me that question after reading *The Last of the Mohicans*, him weeping at a passage describing babies and their mothers being bashed to death by the Huron. I took a long time to answer. He waited.

"I didn't claim to be savage at the time," I said.

"Ah, yes, I remember, you claimed to be a warrior. A savage is different?"

"Yes," I said.

"The acts are the same, driven only by disparate points of view. You had wanted to fight Rudy, who I am sure you would have killed as you watched him die slowly. I simply cut off his head and was done with him. Either way, my friend, he is dead, justice and vengeance served at once. Which is the savagery?"

Rudy had died instantly, almost mercifully. I am sure I would not have been so swift as I would have relished seeing the life drain from his cold-blooded eyes.

"In Texas," I said, "at the last battle, the first Mexican that shot at me, I shot dead. The second, I smashed his face with my rifle. As he pleaded for mercy, I scalped him and let him lie. A few minutes later, I refused to shoot a man standing before me, his hands raised in the air. A proud Texan stepped up an' shot his head clean off. Well, back at camp, I was the coward for not killing the soldier with his hands raised. Later in the night, they all hollered out, *'Who scalped the Mexican?'* The answer came back, *'The damn savage, Zebadiah Creed.'* "

Frenchy stared out at the lush, green shoreline, lost in thought. With his voice soft, as if he were speaking to himself, he said, "I remember every sunrise and sunset I have ever witnessed, by land and by sea. Not one comes close to being the same as another. I can never change them into anything but what they are, *magnifiquement tragique.*"

He seemed not to expect a response but continued to gaze at the morning light shining through the trees. I provided none.

"We shall arrive at Natchez by dusk . . . to pick up wood," he said and strolled away, leaving me alone at the rail to face the coming day.

CHAPTER 31

Natchez had certainly grown since I saw it last. With no wharf just nine months before, three-quarters of new construction lay before us. Two other steamers took up most of the berths, but our captain found enough space to squeeze into. The late afternoon sun began to dip into the trees across the river.

As we pulled in, I commented to Frenchy, nodding to the shoreline, "Sure is flat over yonder in Arkansas compared to the bluffs below Natchez."

He peered at me sideways. "We have yet to reach the Arkansas border. Still a few more miles of Louisiana to go." His glance told me I should have known this.

This far south and without a map, I thought the water and shore looked all the same. "Hell, sure looks like Arkansas trees to me."

Frenchy rolled his eyes and said nothing more about my lacking a sense for geography.

Our captain blew his whistle one last time, and lines were thrown, tied to shiny, new bollards, mooring us.

Crewmen lowered the two gangplanks and scores of men began loading wooden boxes, all the same size, onto the steamer. An overseer directed which ones went into its specific hold, either forward or aft. I thought they were slaves at first as most wore rags. But they were just filthy, not dark-skinned. Some wore no shoes. A putrid smell wafted up to us. A stench of decay. A stink I remembered.

It had come from a place north of Natchez. Abandoned by my friend Billy Frieze, I spent one night of indiscretion in the tangled forest of the Devil's Punchbowl, home to a rotting church surrounded by a camp full of reeking miscreants who devoted themselves to a man willing to kill any one of them at his leisure. I cringed at the smell.

Frenchy stood beside me nodding, as if he was quite satisfied with the laborious progress of the loading. As evening settled, the loading party followed the last of the boxes aboard. Only one man stood on the wharf.

"Greetings," John Murrell hollered from below.

I shuddered at seeing the murderer staring up at us with a wide, gaping smile, his eyes glistening.

"I thought I threw you in the river, tied to a chair?" he called, obviously recognizing me.

"Pushed myself in," I said.

"An' ya didn't drown?"

"Ropes come loose," I answered.

He did not appear to be too surprised, shrugged, and said, "Maybe next time, I fill your belly full a rocks, huh?"

I shook my head, glaring down at him. "Maybe I'd cut your throat first."

Murrell laughed. "Ah, just fuckin' with you."

Frenchy asked, "So, you two know each other?"

"You could say that." I spit over the side of the boat.

No one spoke for a few seconds. Murrell began shuffling his feet, glancing up at us, as if he were anxious to get the night going.

Finally, "Come aboard, come aboard, Johnny . . ." Frenchy offered. ". . . and we shall reacquaint ourselves with a drink in hand as old friends should do." He glanced at me. "*Monsieur* Creed shall join us?"

Murrell strolled up the gangplank and disappeared into the boat.

"This is why we stopped?" I asked. "Where's the wood to fuel the boiler?"

Frenchy grinned and stroked his mustache. "Ah, I said we pick up wood. I did not say what for, now did I?"

Without a word, I backed away from him and headed to my cabin. I would certainly not have a drink with that son of a bitch without at least one knife at my belt. And maybe a loaded pistol or two.

From below, in the hold of the steamboat, I heard muffled scrapes and thuds, then quiet. *If this new cargo slows us down in any way . . .* I thought, now feeling pissed at Frenchy for stopping in the first place. For wood boxes, not fuel wood. *What the hell is in those boxes? And why did those stinking scallywags come aboard. Must be a dozen, at least.* I shook my head and stuffed a pistol in my belt.

With a lone whistle echoing against the bluffs below Natchez, we were again underway.

The chandelier lit the dining cabin with three descending, ever widening rings of a hundred candles burning, each dripping wax into cups the shape of seashells. Its crystal prisms hung like drops of water, throwing multicolored sparkles against the bulkheads. Thin, opaque figurines, one for each candle, cast bluish shadows to the room, a hundred horses with fishtails glimmering underwater. I had not seen anything like it. The old, seagoing Frenchy must have had a hand in designing this glowing fixture.

Three cups and a bottle of rum adorned the table where we sat. Tiny drops of wax from the candles above us splashed onto the black tablecloth and dried in splotches. I looked up once, then glanced at Frenchy. He seemed not to notice the flaw of his seashell cups being too small to catch all the hot wax with the gentle swaying of the steamboat.

"How have you been?" Murrell asked. Both Frenchy and I stared at him. He smiled enough to show the gap from his missing two front teeth.

"Hmmm . . . I am well," said Frenchy, with a casual lilt to his voice.

Murrell turned his head. "And you?"

I had not expected formal niceties to begin our conversation. Frankly, I had no idea what to expect from this evening. I nodded, saying nothing.

"Devil got yer tongue?" Murrell asked.

I swirled my rum, watching a blob of wax spin in my cup, took a long drink, and casually said, "I am also well." Though the look I gave him told him different.

"Hmmm," he said, staring at me with his watery eyes.

I had to ask. "I wondered last time we met; what the hell's wrong with your eyes? Always seems like yer cryin."

Murrell leaned forward. "I got poison in my tears, don'tcha know."

Silence.

Murrell opened his coat to show the handle of a knife, shook out a handkerchief from an inside pocket, and dabbed the corners of both his eyes. "There will be no tears shed this night," he said.

A drop of wax splashed onto the table. Frenchy glanced up at the chandelier, then at Murrell, and smiled.

From deep within the bowels of the steamer rose singing, human voices. Their ethereal melody, note for note perfect and muffled by wooden bulkheads and water, sent a chill up my back. I had heard this song twice, once on the Missouri many months before, hummed by Rudy Dupree, as he freed Jonathan and me from a sandbar I had plowed us into, thus starting the events leading me to sit at that table. The other time I heard the tune was at the Devil's Punchbowl, sung by Murrell's murderous gang of thieves. The same men occupying the holds below us.

The singing stopped. But for the grumble of the boiler, the spin of the paddle wheel, and the tinkling of the chandelier above our heads, we sat in silence.

Murrell had closed his eyes and cocked his head to listen, then without any prompting, said, "My church burned down."

"If I remember, Johnny, wasn't much of a church to begin with," said Frenchy.

Again, Murrell addressed me. "Do you agree? It sure seems like you liked my little chapel, an' all it's . . . offerings. Food, shelter fer the night." He raised his eyebrows and smiled.

"Ya called me a liar, then tied me to a chair."

"If I remember, durin' the dark night under the stars, you had some mighty sweet comp'ny. Bein' tied up didn't stop ya from risin' to the occasion. If ya know what I mean," he said, leering at me.

My head was suddenly swirling. What he spoke of, I had sworn was part of a dream, not real. Yet, I could not deny what might have happened between me and his girl, Honey, with him somehow knowing.

"Now, here is a tale I have not heard," said Frenchy.

I waited, took another drink, and said, "Your church had a goddamn hole in the roof."

"Ah, Mr. Creed, to let the darkness out an' the ole sunshine in, to accommodate transgressors such as ourselves." He wore a full smile, a yapping, black hole. "Sinners an' . . . an' whores."

"We went for a card game, an' ya killed your own man, shot a ball straight into his head. Claimed I lied . . ." I nodded to Frenchy. ". . . about our friendship. Well, that was about the only thing I didn't lie about that night."

"At the time, we were friends?" asked Frenchy.

"I saved you from bein' run through by Christina, your favorite *Fille de joie*. Quite the friendly gesture."

"Well," said Frenchy, "spouting off that someone you just meet is your friend." He raised his hands to the chandelier, as if appealing to heaven. "No matter the *gesture,* I suppose this might make you think we are friends."

I could not tell if he was playing with me, or serious.

"I have killed men who have assumed as much," he said, then winked.

The singing started again, this time louder, surrounding us, as if the tones of the musical notes seeped into the very bones of the boat.

Murrell noticed my hand shaking a bit and smiled. "Don'tcha love my men's singing? They may stink like shit, but they sound like songbirds."

Frenchy snapped his fingers, breaking the spell. An old, razor-thin black man dressed in whites stepped into the cabin. He said, "Dinner is served, sir."

Three young servants entered through the kitchen door carrying plates with silver domes covering them and set one in front of each of us. Frenchy nodded and with a single whoosh, the covers were lifted.

"Bon appétit," he said.

The smeared jelly on the lamb chop glistened by candlelight, the exposed, charred bone arching up, inviting itself to be grasped by hungry hands. Murrell did not hesitate to be the first and tore off a bite.

Frenchy glanced at my plate and nodded, inviting me to begin eating before him. The steaming lamb cut like butter. I took a bite with my fork. The sweet jelly mixed with a bit of charred meat dissolved in my mouth. I closed my eyes and could not think of anything better that I had eaten.

Frenchy took his first bite and with a mouthful, said, "An old slave's recipe."

"Reminds me of the goat I served ya that night, huh, Mr. Creed?"

I held back a sneer. The greens, carrots, and potatoes tasted as if seasoned by the saltwater of the gulf. With each bite, I fell deeper into a trance, wiping my plate clean with sliced sourdough, leaving only a gnawed bone to be taken away. If I ate any dripped wax, I did not notice.

Murrell finished minutes before me. We both sat and watched Frenchy slowly devour his meal.

The servants cleared the plates, served coffee, and offered cigars with an ashtray placed on the table.

The singing had stopped sometime during our meal and did not start up again.

"So, what are you going to do now?" Frenchy asked Murrell.

Murrell wiped tears from the corners of his eyes with the same napkin he used to wipe his mouth and smiled. "I go and speak the good word of Jesus Christ to those sinners in Rodney."

Frenchy smiled, as if he might suspect the real reason why a marauding band of murderers and thieves would be interested in spreading the gospel.

"*Oui, monsieur,* and what shall these folk provide for you in return?"

Murrell closed his eyes and said, "Horses are what we need for I intend to spread the good word 'long the Natchez Trace clean to Nashville. Shake hands with Ole Hickory himself."

"If you steal a town's horses, you steal its soul," said Frenchy.

"True, but these folk ain't got no soul to begin with. Is why I'm goin' there in the first place."

Frenchy simply nodded, as if in agreement, and poured another round of rum.

Silence again sat with us as we smoked and drank.

The longer I stayed with these two men, I wondered, *What the hell am I doin' here?*

I said, "Thank you for the supper. I shall now retire."

I crushed my cigar and tried pushing my chair back to stand.

Murrell's boot blocked one of the legs. "You ain't goin' nowhere . . . 'til we finish our coffee and smokes, as gentlemen."

I pushed harder.

Murrell pointed a small pistol at me. "Sit the fuck down, Scalper."

"Seems there's some reckoning to take place, *oui, Monsieur* Creed?" said Frenchy.

I glanced at Frenchy, wearing a smug look on his face. I thought, *here we go*, and squared up with Murrell. "So be it," I whispered.

"Speak up, man, fer one such ass as yourself, ya might own up to yer forgiveness if you're so bein'. I doubt it's that, fer you're riled." He smiled. "Or is it cowardice?"

I was seething, with bitter resentment and humiliation. Yet, I did not welcome this fight. I shook my head. "Now, *Johnny,* I have no spark against you."

"No, yer sore, at me fer throwin' ya off a that cliff now ain'tcha. Now ya come to dinner, yer coat bulgin' with weapons. Just like ya showed at my church, tryin' to kill me."

"We went there to play a game of cards."

"Now, if I rightly remember, ya don't play cards, said so yerself."

I was done talking. I forced the chair back and slowly stood, opening my coat to reveal a pistol and a knife. I looked down at him and said, "Where I come from, if a man stands before ya with a fair beef offering a fair fight, and you don't take him up on it, then that ain't nothin' but bein' a coward himself." I nodded to Frenchy and frowned. "And *with such a good friend* as witness."

Murrell let out a whistle, almost like a bird chirping. In seconds, both doors to the outside and kitchen swung open. The cabin filled with six of his men to line the bulkheads at attention, surrounding us. He held his pistol and stood close to face me.

"Ah, Zeb, I bring my own witnesses," he said.

I heard a hammer's click, and a chuckle. Frenchy sat with a smile, one hand stroking his long mustache. With the other, he held a pistol pointed straight at Murrell.

The clanks and rattle of pistols being pulled filled the cabin.

"Now, my friends, a true, how you say, standoff?" Frenchy glanced around at Murrell's stinking miscreants. "If I kill your messiah here, and I will put a ball right through him, what will you do without your brave preacher?"

The couple I saw lowered their pistols a bit, staring at their leader.

Murrell glanced at his men and shook his head, as if calling them off. Then turned to Frenchy, and with his eyes leaking tears down his cheeks, shrugged and said, "So, shoot me."

With one hand, I shoved his pistol down just as he pulled the trigger. With the other, hit him hard in the mouth with the butt of my knife. The ball splintered the wood of the deck between my legs and smoke of the shot filled the space between us. Before I could hit him again, he slammed the side of my face with the barrel of his pistol. It stung, but I kept my bearings, and hit him again, breaking his nose with a crunch. I dodged the blade of his knife, escaping the slice to my belly. Blood from his nose spread across his face. The pistol fell from his hand, but he held onto the knife, wiping his eyes with a sleeve. I took another step back, flipping my blade to point toward him. We faced each other.

Slightly hunched and already out of breath, he smiled and took another swipe at me. I cut him across the back of the hand. He yelped, his knife slipping from his fingers. I whirled closer and swept his legs out from under him. We both stumbled to the floor, and with a knee rammed into his groin, I placed the tip of my knife to his throat.

"Ain't no tears shed tonight," I said, and began to slowly push the blade into his skin.

"Do not kill him!" Frenchy hollered. *"And do not scalp him!"*

I stopped but held the knife at Murrell's gullet. Still smiling, he said, "Look around, my friend, and see what you inherit." He stared at me, swallowed, and slowly drew his smile into a frown. He closed his eyes, his face relaxing to almost shine with contentment, as if he wanted me to cut his throat. "Go ahead," he whispered.

I glanced about the cabin. The men that lined the bulkheads blended with shadows the light of the chandelier could not touch. All I saw were their eyes and the glint of their pistols and knives. The smell in the cabin had turned sickly sweet, a hunger for blood. I held my knife steady, its blade again resting under his chin. I took a shallow breath and coughed, as if breathing smoke and stink, and closed my eyes. The shadows of his tribe bore down upon my very soul.

"Cut him, like Rudy did you, and let him live," said Frenchy, pointing his pistol at me.

Murrell smiled without a flinch as I sliced into his left cheek by a shallow inch. None of his loyal followers attempted to stop me.

I stood above him and offered a hand up. He accepted and we both sat back down in our chairs, wrung out. He waved his men away and they filed out, the doors shut behind them. Our heavy breathing and the tinkling of crystalline waterdrops were the only sounds in the cabin. Frenchy put his pistol away and poured the three of us a drink.

"To friendship," he said, raising his cup and smiling like the devil.

The skinny, old servant brought wet, white towels for Murrell to clean his mess of a face. Frenchy pointed to the deck. The old man bent down and wiped up blood and tears. Murrell and Frenchy sat, seeming to talk business. But for Murrell's cheek and him nursing a busted nose and cut hand, they acted as if the incident never happened. I poured myself more rum, wincing as I touched my swollen cheek where the pistol struck me. Murrell continued to mumble, more and more incoherent. He closed his eyes, leaned back his head, and covered his face with the towel. Within seconds it was soaked red. He stopped speaking, then, fell sideways to the deck with a thump, and lay there. Frenchy snapped his fingers and the servants lifted him back to the chair, replacing the towel over his face. Murrell lowered his head, chin to chest, as if asleep, the bloody towel falling to the table. A hot drop of wax splotched into his hair. He did not notice.

"He might need to be stitched up," I said. "He's lost some blood."

Frenchy stroked his mustache. "*Oui,* you cut him good. He knows you forever now, as well as his men." Then he laughed and said, "You like breaking noses."

I stared at Murrell and shrugged. "Easy target . . ."

We both took a drink.

"He knows about Willie Dan," I said.

"*Oui* . . . everyone knows of Willie Dan."

"No, he knows what I am about, here on the river."

"Maybe. It is no secret, Zebadiah."

Again, silence, but for Murrell's guttural breathing through his mouth.

Frenchy nodded to him and asked, "If you kill this man,

182

what do you think will happen?"

I shrugged. "I'd go on up the river, same as I'm doin' now."

"They will follow, his tribe, the shadow . . . claim you as the new leader. If you do not claim *them*, they will hunt you down and kill you. Is why he fought so weak. Maybe he is tired of being the messiah of these lost souls."

He snapped his fingers twice and his servants took Murrell away without a fuss, I presumed, to get patched up.

I finished my rum, bowed, and bid Frenchy a good evening.

Sometime before sunup, I woke to a quiet boat, the paddle wheel still. I dressed and went to the veranda. We lay at the shore with the forward gangplank out. There was no town or village, only enough bare, open ground to disembark. From the innards of the steamer came Murrell's men, the wood boxes left behind. Murrell was the last to leave, his face bandaged across his cheek and nose, his hand wrapped. Without a backward glance, he and his Devil's Punchbowl bandits disappeared into the predawn black of the forest.

With the gangplank drawn and the paddle wheel again spinning, we headed to the middle of the wide Mississippi and north, on to St. Louis, Missouri.

Chapter 32

The next three days, I saw Frenchy twice, only in passing, and with not another conversation between us until we reached St. Louis. For two evenings, I supped in my cabin. I found a book, *Don Quixote*. The crazy, old man could not stand by and watch his world torn to tatters. Yet, he himself caused much of the tears. After several chapters read, I set the book down, thinking I had nothing in common with those that went against this old man, that he had every right to slay the beasts that troubled him.

The farther upriver we plowed, I became listless, wandering the steamboat. Soon, I became obsessed with one thing, I suppose to take my mind off the real reason I headed north. I wanted to know what was in those damn wooden boxes stored below decks.

Frenchy's skeleton crew kept his steamboat running at full speed, with his personal servants providing the best service I had experienced since . . . well, I could not remember any better to this point in my life. If I wanted breakfast with eggs, bacon, and biscuits at 11, all I had to do was ask. If I became hungry at midnight, the same. However, each time I wandered down to where the boxes were stored, I was turned back by two men armed to the teeth, one of Frenchy's and one of Murrell's. *Were they full of guns? Surely not, what would Frenchy need with so many? Furs maybe? Though they would be stored in bundles and not wood boxes, and certainly not taken north up the Mississippi, but*

184

across the great Atlantic to be made into top hats. Gold and silver perhaps, from Frenchy's pirate bounty? Ah yes . . . that must be it, treasure to be buried somewhere along the river. Not even attempts at casual conversation would turn the guards' heads away from their duty to protect the valuable property that lay in the holds of the steamboat.

The bruise on my face grew, turning my right eye black and blue. I did not notice it until the morning after the fight, washing my face in the cabin basin below a small mirror. The morning we tied up to the wharf at St. Louis, I could barely see out of that eye.

Frenchy and I again stood on the veranda, portside, overlooking the crowded wharf. Cargo lay scattered about, seeming haphazard, owned by certain individuals or companies for temporary storage. To accommodate the massive amount of goods flowing on and off the barges, keelboats, and steamers, most folks doing the heavy lifting were slaves. As it was the last time I arrived at St. Louis, all of them wore rags and no chains. Some of them sang as they worked with overseers standing quietly to the side, arms crossed and bullwhips at their belts. As soon as our gangplanks were laid, six armed men with three pistols each at their belts walked down to the wharf to stand guard, three at each gangplank. Gerard, whom I called Grizzly when we first met months before, came strolling up to the boat to stand before us.

"Morning, sir," he said, and bowed to Frenchy. "Glad to see you home safe." He nodded to me. "Mr. Creed, welcome back to St. Louis, sir."

I said, "Good to see you again, Gerard."

"All's well in New Orleans, sir?" he asked.

"*Oui,* as to be expected," Frenchy answered.

Gerard's glance swept the rails of the steamboat. "Are you alone, sir?"

"I am indeed."

Since I clearly accompanied him, I knew I was not part of this conversation.

"The girl stayed with her mother," said Frenchy.

Gerard nodded, looked down as if disappointed, then back to his boss. "Very good, sir." He motioned to one gangplank, then the other. "Shall we get started?"

Two covered wagons approached the steamer, the crowd making way for them as if they held more importance than others. One stopped forward and one stopped aft, both drivers and passengers as armed as the militia standing on the wharf. The canvas over the backs was pulled aside, and four, young black men stepped down from each wagon, trailed up the gangplanks, and disappeared.

"Those boxes must be holdin' something mighty special," I said.

Frenchy did not answer nor make a comment. Instead, he turned to me and stared at the right side of my head. "I've often wondered. You never told me the story of how you lost the top of your ear."

He surprised me with the question since the healed injury was so slight. Only the very tip was missing. I figured most folks never noticed.

"I was bushwhacked in Texas," I offered. I did not feel compelled to go on.

The first box walked down the forward plank was loaded into the wagon. In plain daylight, I saw no markings as to where they might have come from and where they could be going, though the boxes themselves were exceedingly well made. With this army of security, the items contained must hold something valuable as hell, just as I thought.

I nodded. "What's in them?"

"Who shot your ear?" he asked, ignoring my question.

Taken aback by the question, I answered, "An old, goddamn, one-eyed bounty hunter."

"And him?"

I did not hesitate. "I watched him bleed to death in the middle of a road."

"But not before you let him shoot you."

"At the time, it was four against one. I shot him an' one a his partners. But not before he got a shot off from the rifle he was aimin' at my head."

"And the others?"

"Grainger shot the other two."

"Hmmm . . ." Frenchy said. "So Grainger was indeed your friend. And how did you kill this bounty hunter, *Monsieur* Creed?"

Why did he want to know the particulars, I asked myself, pulling back my coat. "I sliced his leg with this here knife."

"And Grainger?"

"He and I rode on to meet Houston, delivering our message 'bout the plight of them poor fellas at the Alamo." I squared up with him. "Why are you asking me about this now, before we set foot here in St. Louis?"

The second and third boxes were loaded into the wagons. I did not know how many were left.

"I knew the man you killed."

Why was I not surprised?

There came another box pulled from the steamer and placed in a wagon.

"A good man then. He works with me for a while, until . . . he trips past the line of good, to bad. Then all he is good for is killing."

"He was an old man with one eye, is probably why he missed with only a piece a my ear shot."

"He reminds me of you, *Monsieur* Creed."

I shook my head, not understanding. "I ain't a bounty hunter."

"No, you are not . . . for now."

Two days after I killed the one-eyed bastard, I went to where he lay in a ditch, torn up by critters, and buried him with another dead man. I sang a Lakota death song for the two, but I felt no remorse, and I did not feel any while talking with Frenchy.

"He tried to kill me, so I killed him. Simple as that." I glanced at Frenchy. "I sure don't know what the future holds for me, but it ain't bounty huntin'."

"That's what Frank thought, until he was. It's a lonesome death on a road in the middle of a dark forest, doing someone else's dirty deeds," said Frenchy.

I faced him. "An' what about you? You've killed before. You claim to have sent hundreds of sailors to their watery graves. Hell, you chopped off Rudy's head!"

He smiled at this and said, "*Oui, Monsieur* Creed. Rudy stole from me. I catch him and he pays the price."

"What the hell is the difference?"

"Rudy did his own bidding, no one else's," he said. "Who are you after today, and why? Ask yourself this question."

"Are you sayin' that someone else wants Willie Dan dead?"

"Besides our friend Olgens Pierre? I propose there are many that would like to see him killed, *Monsieur* Creed."

The forward wagon was closed up and ready to go, and it appeared that the last box was about to be loaded into the aft wagon. Frenchy whistled for the slaves to stop and lay it down on the wharf.

"Gerard," he hollered, "go and pry the top off so we may show *Monsieur* Creed the contents."

Gerard pulled a large knife from his sheath and worked open the crate. The top slid off. He brushed back hay to reveal rifles, many of them.

"I intend on starting a war, *monsieur.* A war to determine the soul of America. Are you with me, or are you merely someone else's bounty hunter?"

CHAPTER 33

Lower Missouri, Summer 1836

The guns were brand-new percussion cap and ball .50 caliber Hawken rifles. The same rifle Jonathan and I carried downriver, then stolen by Rudy Dupree and Amos Baumgartner. These were not for fighting in battles, but for protection and hunting, favored by all the trappers I knew. Though they could kill a man at near four hundred yards, most just put meat on the fire and a coat around the shoulders.

Frenchy had tried to persuade me to help him with his grand endeavor; though he pretended to be illusive in details, he shared with me the arc of his plans.

"The East fills with the Germans, Irish, and English. They push their way past us, through the mountains, to the coast, to what is Oregon Territory. With them come armies of soldiers. What comes after . . ." He paused to look down. "With that piece-of-shit *President* Jackson's blessing, they push all the Indians out of the East to crowd the plains south of us. This will happen again, and again . . . and again."

I did not want any part of Frenchy's war, no matter who was fighting who. Not after the Alamo, after Goliad. Once in a while, I still smelled the Texas fight in my clothes and glimpsed bloodstains on my hands. One man I could kill, for good reason. Killing strangers I held no grudge against, I had not the stomach for. Those rifles were better off covered in hay and left in their boxes.

I told Frenchy that as much as I understood and sympathized with his mission, I could not help him with his fight, whatever that might be.

I described a little of the dream I'd had the evening of the dinner at Groce's plantation, back in Texas, after meeting the German woman I saved from drowning, and her brother, in the hay barn and how she had survived a brutal rape by the Mexican army only to be left helpless and insane. Refugees from a war brought on by greed and lust for power over folks of different colors and creeds. In the dream, streams of folks rushed to a magnificent tree, climbing to safety. Though I knew the branches would surely break, I could do nothing but stand with my brother and watch.

Now, I had become too anxious, not to battle a general injustice, but to save the only person still dear to me. I could no longer just stand on a steamboat veranda and watch the world pass by. I needed to be in control and ready for anything that I might encounter once I reached Anna. With a good horse, I could make her cabin in two or three days by traveling the road between St. Louis and Boonville, one day shy of paddling there by steamboat. A strong, swift horse was all I needed.

Along with the offer of a horse, saddle, and food for my journey, Frenchy rose early and had pulled one of the rifles out of a box. He presented it to me as I was about to leave for Boonville.

"I do thank you," I said, returning that odd wink he had given to me, *"mon ami . . ."*

Bowing, he said, *"Monsieur* Creed, may your sights be true." Looking up. "If *Monsieur* Dan does not kill you," he offered, "you will be back."

I carried the rifle across my lap along with a full shooting bag given to me by Gerard. I tucked my knife and two loaded pistols in my belt. Filled with excitement and dread, I left that morning.

I was prepared for Willie Dan. I did not know if I was ready to meet Anna.

The road out of St. Louis headed due west and was well traveled with wagons full of some of the very folks Frenchy complained about. Already haggard from their travels, they were a determined lot, carrying all their possessions, as if clinging to the life they would never live again. Later, most of those things would be thrown by the wayside. Some would surely die along the roads and trails to their new lands, by accident, disease, starvation, and even murder, leaving hundreds of grave markers strewn across half the country. I did not particularly feel for these folks one way or another. Their lives were their own to live, as was mine.

Kicking up summer dust, some individuals trotted alone on horseback at a leisurely pace. As I passed, I glanced at everyone to see if by chance Willie Dan rode amongst them, although I was fairly certain he would have already arrived and awaited the news of Houston's death by my hand.

My new Appaloosa pony was a prancer when trying to hold him still. But true to my beckoning, he could run like hell when prodded. I sang to him my Lakota songs as I rode, gently bringing the beast under my spell. Soon, he would glance back at me and nod, as if he now understood the urgency of our journey. I did not know his name, so I called him *Misun*, my little brother.

I made the town of Point Lookoff by late afternoon, though more a village overlooking the broad expanse of the Missouri River and not too far away from where it joined the mighty Mississippi. I had been there a few times with Jonathan. I camped near the water, fed *Misun* the oats given to me by Gerard, struck a small fire, and settled in with a couple of strips of jerky and a cold biscuit. The evening's warmth enveloped my tiny circle of light, with stars a canopy of cool brilliance. The gentle rush of a snowmelt river lulled me to sleep.

I had one dream.

A hand reaches out of darkness, through prison bars, and strokes my filthy hair and beard. I covet the caress of her gentle fingers and close my eyes. Anna says, "My poor Zebadiah, you've come so far . . ." Her hand retreats and all is silent but for the scurry of the rats and snoring from the next cell. Willie Dan yawns and says, "Hey, Scalper, you still here?"

Packed before dawn, and with another biscuit, I rode west.

CHAPTER 34

Crossing the Osage River before dusk as the last ferry customer of the day, I wanted a little more than jerky to chew and ground to sleep on. I had heard from Gerard that there might be a comfortable place to lay my head just up from the shore. With his boat secured at the small pier, the ferryman held a lantern to my face. He did not look into my eyes but stared at the scar on my left cheek.

"Seen this same cut, same place, same . . . mark on a 'nother fella no more'na two week ago, some kinda clan, is it?" He held up his inner wrist to the light. Burned into his skin, a circle surrounding a triangle. "Mine," he said with a smile. "We're scattered across Missouri onto the Great Plains. Mostly ferrymen and such. If I told ya what it meant, then you'da joined us. But you ain't no ferryman, I can tell." He looked me up and down. "By the long gaze in the eyes of the other fella . . ." He nodded to my scar, then met my stare. ". . . and yours, I don't wanna know what the two of ya are part of."

The ferryman lowered the lantern and let me pass. "Said you'd be comin' this a way," he hollered, as I trudged up the riverbank to the road.

I stopped and turned, facing down at him. "How do you know it's me?"

He rubbed a finger diagonal across his left cheek and went back to preparing for his last crossing of the day.

That son of a bitch, I thought, and rode off without a glance back.

A quarter mile farther west, nearly hidden by trees, sat the ramshackle building Gerard had mentioned. Lit by the last light of the day, the short path to the place, too small for wagons, allowed me and my horse, brushing through bushes, to saunter up to a broad porch. To its right, a stable. A man stood at the porch steps wearing an apron, wiping his hands on a towel. Above his head, a sign read "Most Visitors Welcome." I smelled cooking. In particular, I smelled biscuits!

"You had a hard ride today, mister. Dust off your boots an' come join us for supper, will ya?" the innkeeper said, and turned to walk through the front door. He paused and, over his shoulder, said, "Leave your horse with the boy at the stable, then come on inside." He walked on into his establishment, waving for me to join him.

I led *Misun* toward the stable doors. From the early, evening shadows stepped a boy of maybe ten. Without a word, he offered my horse a carrot, stroking the side of his head and neck. I climbed down and dusted myself off. The boy had shining blue eyes and curly, blond hair. He smiled, took the reins, and walked *Misun* through the stable doors. I followed and helped him remove the saddle. By the fading twilight, the boy began to brush the horse, offering a comforting *shh* with every stroke. Along with the rifle, I gathered up my possibles and strolled over to the porch, climbed the steps, and entered the inn.

Three or four lanterns lit up the front room. A bar spread across the back with several bottles and glasses lining shelves built into the wall. To the side, a cook fire blazed with two grills, on one sat a boiling pot, on the other sizzled thick cuts of meat. Directly on the coals sat a cast-iron skillet. Biscuits rose as I watched. A white-haired woman toiled over it all, turning the meat, stirring the pot. With a piece of rag wrapped around her aged, black hand, she reached in and pulled the hot skillet from the fire. The biscuits looked a perfect light brown.

From behind the bar, my host said, "I hope you like raccoon stew."

The last I had eaten a meal such as this, some eight months before, I had shared with Anna.

Six chairs surrounded a long table, filling the center of the room. A vase of freshly cut wildflowers sat in the middle. Plates, silver, and wooden cups were placed at every chair.

On the other side of the room there sat four easy chairs facing a small fireplace. Above the mantel hung a large painting, an idyllic scene of a lone tree at the bend of a slow river. A water stain washed diagonal through the clouds, darkening one half of the sky, as if tearing the painting in two. The more I stared, the more I felt I knew this place.

I shook off the feeling and stepped to the bar. "Drink?" I asked.

The man smiled. "Of course, what will you have?" Before I could answer, he turned, pulled a glass and bottle off the shelf, and said, "You might like this." Pouring the liquor, he smiled again. "Name's Henry King Williams. What's yours, son?"

Maybe twenty years older, he was a large man, with a shaved head and face. I could not tell if he was light-skinned for a black man, or dark-skinned for a white. He moved only with purpose, giving a sense that he had owned this establishment for many, many years.

I stared back at the man who just offered his name, took a drink, and set the glass on the bar. "Zebadiah . . . Zebadiah Creed is my name."

"Zebadiah Creed, hmmm, a strong name," he said, and reached his hand out to shake. His fingers gripped my hand and held on two or three seconds longer than usual. I did not attempt to pull away. With our release, Henry seemed pleased at my response.

I quickly took another drink and glanced to the old woman staring at me as she stirred the pot of raccoon stew. I closed my eyes, the liquor stronger than I expected. I gripped the bar and stared at the bottle. I finished the glass.

Henry asked, "How did you find us, Zeb?"

I closed my eyes again and inhaled a long breath, trying to remember. At the moment, my mind in a fog, I could not tell him for sure.

The room began to heat up. "Frenchy? The ferryman?" I said out loud. "No, no, it was Gerard, Frenchy's man."

"Gerard . . ." he repeated. "Frenchy?"

I heard a clutter at the table behind me and swirled around. The woman had dished out six bowls of stew and laid the sizzling meat onto the plates. All the cups were full. The boy sat in one of the chairs with his hands crossed in front of his food. A single plate stacked full of steaming biscuits sat before him.

Now standing beside me, Henry King Williams touched my arm and waved a hand toward the table. "Shall we sit?"

My insides were spooked, with a tingling from the top of my head, down my back, and out my fingertips.

Henry leaned into me. "Some folks say this here liquor has some strange kick to it. I like it myself, brings lost dreams to mind," he said, guiding me to my chair.

I sat next to the boy, facing the bar. The woman sat at one end of the table, with Henry at the head. "We say a prayer at this inn, for all weary travelers of the road. Shall we bow our heads?" He lowered his eyes. "Lord, we offer ourselves to thee, believers of the faith that we shall be redeemed, here and hereafter, our blood-soaked sins of the road washed clean forever, amen."

Before I could take one bite, there came a gentle knock at the door. The last I experienced late guests, I was tied to a chair and forced to witness Margo's murder. I laid a hand on the Bowie knife.

As if on its own, the door opened. For a few seconds, only the darkness of the evening spilled into the room. I must have blinked for there appeared in the doorway an apparition of a man, not quite there for the night shone through him. I swore I saw fireflies. He moved into the light of the lanterns. I wiped my eyes with a sleeve to see better. Two men stood together inside, with the door now shut. I did not hear it latch.

"Ah, my friends, finally . . . Just in time for supper," Henry said, standing at the head of the table. He offered them a seat. Clad in buckskin, they wore knives at their belts, the handles made of antler.

"Zebadiah Creed, this here is Francis and Fredrick. The Tuck brothers."

They both brushed their hair back, smiled, and nodded. Francis sat across from me, Fredrick next to him.

Henry waved us to eat. Starting with me, the boy offered biscuits all around. I took a bite of one. It tasted like mana from heaven, the butter and bread melting in my mouth. If I died that night, I thought, I'd die a happy man.

I could not help but look at the brothers. Francis being perhaps a couple of years the elder, I thought they might be somewhere in their thirties. Certainly older than myself by ten or so years. They seemed as hungry as I for neither looked up until the bowls of stew were finished. I slurped the last of mine, using another biscuit to wipe the bowl. The sweetness of the stew meat tasted familiar, though it had been a while since the last I had eaten raccoon. The broiled meat tasted like beef. With all of us through with supper, the boy poured us more drink from the same bottle.

"Shall we toast?" Henry asked, breaking the silence, and stood.

The brothers lifted their heads from their clean plates and bowls, the first I saw their eyes, steel-gray eyes. Across Francis's left cheek, by an inch, ran the faintest of scars, seen only by the right angle of light. I quickly glanced at Fredrick. There was none.

They slowly pushed back their chairs, stood as I did, and we raised our cups.

"Friendship and family, may we always be together, in life and in death," Henry proposed.

Neither brother had yet to speak a word. They both nodded and we toasted. The instant our cups touched, I felt a spark in my fingers. I quickly drew mine away and drank. The brothers stared at me, as if they expected me to say something.

"Zebadiah here is a long way from home," said Henry, as we all sat back down. "Shall we welcome him properly to our band of brothers, rogues, and . . . warriors?"

The brothers again nodded.

My head spun, from the swim of the drink, the haze of the room.

"We've crossed paths somewhere," I said. "Maybe Rendez-vous?"

The older brother shrugged.

With the help of the boy, the woman began clearing the table. As she approached the cook fire, the room filled with the sweet smell of a cobbler baking. Atop one of the grills sat a Dutch oven. She lifted the lid. Steam rose to swirl up into the darkness of the rafters above us.

"Ah, dessert is ready," Henry said. "I hope you like huckleber-ries; they grow everywhere this time of year."

The boy set out new bowls with a heaping of piping-hot cob-bler. I closed my eyes and breathed in the aroma. Instantly, I was once again sitting outside our tipi, at the fire, Mother hand-ing Jonathan and me bowls of huckleberry cobbler. We scooped the tasty treat with our fingers, licking the bowl clean. Mother smiled and asked if we wanted more, with both of us nodding yes, of course.

I opened my eyes and glanced around. The brothers and Henry stared at me, their desserts finished. I looked down at my bowl. It was empty.

"Shall we smoke?" Henry asked.

The four of us stood at once with Henry leading us to the chairs at the fireplace. He showed me to one on the end, the two brothers between us. We sat, again without a word. The brothers pulled pipes and tobacco bags from their belts and filled the bowls. Henry drew a long stick from the fire and allowed them to light their pipes. They blew white smoke into the air, filling the room with the aroma of sacred ceremony. I closed my eyes and breathed in the smoke. A vision of my brother, by dim firelight, filling our tipi with the very same white smoke, then passing the pipe on to our father. I opened my eyes and peered closer at the brothers sitting relaxed in their chairs. They had not answered my question of whether we had met before. Fact was, neither had said a word since entering the inn.

"I get a sense that we've met before. Again, perhaps Rendezvous?" I asked, with a nervous break in my voice.

"Do you speak English?" I asked, with a touch of sarcasm. They did not appear to be anything but a couple of white men, maybe French?

"*Parle Français?*" I asked.

They both nodded. Francis said, "*Oui, monsieur, Français et Lakota.*"

Lakota! I knew there was something familiar about them.

Fredrick handed me his pipe. Henry reached out to relight the bowl, the stick still on fire. I breathed in the cool smoke, expanding my chest, letting go of the smoke, allowing it to curl up my nose, and inhaled again. I closed my eyes, drifting back to our tipi, my mother and father. They smiled as I drew another breath. I opened my eyes.

"Zebadiah, where do you come from?" Fredrick asked, in perfect English.

His voice. I knew his voice. I stared at him, unashamed to do so. He now appeared to wear a Lakota war shirt, a bear-claw necklace. At his belt, in the shadows of the chair he sat in, hung a coup ring with two scalps lying upon his thigh. I squeezed my eyes shut, thinking these two men were not real, part of some dream I conjured up. Or the drink had somehow twisted my mind.

I opened them and Fredrick presented me with his knife. By the fire, its elk handle shimmered, the long blade reflecting the flickering light of the lanterns. I took hold and held it up. I felt as if I had held this knife before, used it to scalp, to kill.

"I know this blade," I said, handing it back with a shaking hand.

"All Lakota knives are made the same," said Francis.

"So, you are Lakota?" asked Fredrick.

"Partly raised."

The brothers nodded. Fredrick placed the knife back at his belt.

"I am a Lakota warrior," I said, shocked that I would be so honest with these three strangers. I sat up straighter and rubbed the faded scars of the Sun Dance etched into my chest.

"Of course you are, Zebadiah, as are we," Francis said, nodding to his brother, and he raised his smock to show his scars, faded more than mine, yet unmistakable.

At that moment, I missed Jonathan, deeply. I missed my brother down in the depths of my soul and hung my head. In a flash, I harkened back to the two of us riding the north plains, our ponies' hooves pounding the prairie dirt, side by side racing through the thunder of a thousand buffalo. Our tribe embracing us as their own. I welled up in tears, as if no one sat before me. As if they were not really there.

"My brother died last year," I whispered.

"Why, what happened?"

I took a long time telling our story, the room quiet but for my voice, the smoke of the pipe lingering in the dark rafters. I felt compelled to share with these strangers my truth. My secret.

"He's dead because of me," I choked. "My pride, my conceit . . . my greed."

I finished telling the particulars of our story, the details of his death and how I came to still be living, the fact that I traveled this very road because of him.

Francis glanced at his brother, then leaned toward me, close, and began to softly speak, as if he knew my plight. "This happens . . . though there are many ways life can flow. Our world is not often as we see it, Zebadiah. Ghosts come and go, some living, most not. We choose our way. Who lives and dies we cannot know." He glanced again to Fredrick. "Can we now, brother?"

Fredrick nodded and smiled. Innocence shone all about him.

I closed my eyes, wiping new tears from my face.

I missed my brother so.

"Your brother's wife an' son, where are they now?" Francis asked.

"I suppose they're with the Blackfoot, way up the Missouri, near where it starts. Left 'em last year to go to Rendezvous."

He gave Fredrick a surprised look, then said, "The Blackfoot don't embrace white folk, and you say he took on one of their women?"

I nodded. "In a fight against a band of Flathead, he saved her brother's life. They became friends, blood brothers." I did not want to share too damn much detail, else we would be there all night, me talking and them listening. "They let us trap on their lands. Only white men I knew of who they let, without killing 'em. Is why the company wondered how we were always flush with furs when all the other trappers, well . . . with the beaver playin' out an' all."

"Half-breed amongst the Blackfoot," Fredrick said, sighing. "Worse than a white boy growing up with 'em. At least the white boy knows his place. This boy, he's of the world but not in it. Caught up in between."

The room grew darker, the fires waning. I felt worse than when I began the tale of my brother's life and death, about his wife and young boy left behind.

"You going north, I expect, to find him, let him know about his daddy?" Francis asked.

"Yes," I said finally.

Both brothers nodded in agreement.

Henry stood by the fire and cleared his throat, the spell broken. "Time for sleeping now fellas, the three of you have long rides ahead. Sunup comes early."

The light of the room hung low, the old woman and boy gone. While we talked, I had not noticed three cots laid out, two together near the cook fire, one lay beside the chairs we sat in. I yawned, for I was suddenly as tired as I ever felt in my life.

"Tomorrow brings a new day dawning, right boys? And for now, I bid you good evening," Henry said, then bowed and disappeared behind a cloth beside the bar.

I woke to a rooster crowing, the inn turning gray with the morning, the fires down to embers. I sat up and looked over to my new friends. They were gone; the cots put away. I had slept so soundly I did not wake to their departure. I lay back down and thought of the evening before. These brothers, so similar to Jonathan and me, only older. The one called Francis, with his faint scar on his left cheek, cut far earlier than Rudy could have done. *This legacy must've been happening long before the bastard cut my face,* I thought. The knife. I swore I had held that knife, the weight, the balance so familiar. Maybe it was indeed Jonathan's for I could not remember what had happened to his. This thought made me sit up. *How could this fellow end up with it?* What journey had it taken to reach this man's hand?

I stretched, the morning upon me. They were gone. Which way, I would never know. In my mind, I resolved that I might never see them again. *For this day, I will reach Anna's.*

I pulled on my boots and folded the cot. By the morning light now streaming into the room, I noticed dust and cobwebs. The fires had grown cold, as if they had never been lit. The glass and bottle still sat on the bar, inviting me to take one, last drink.

The porch seemed far more rickety than the evening before, with a small hole broken through one side. *Misun* idled at the hitching post, ready to ride. The boy stood with a hand rubbing the horse's neck.

I felt a brush of my sleeve. Henry stood beside me. "You're headed west," he said.

"Yes."

We shook hands. "Thanks for your hospitality, sir," I said, and pulled what coin I had from my bag and offered it to him.

He accepted the money. "Safe travels, my friend." He handed me a canvas bag. "A couple of pieces of steak to chew on from last night, a biscuit, and cobbler."

I thanked him, climbed onto my horse, and trotted off toward the road.

"Beware, he knows you're coming," Henry hollered. "The man you're after. He knows you're coming."

I stopped and turned in my saddle to ask how he knew, but the innkeeper was gone.

Willie Dan, *the bastard.*

I followed the path to the road and spurred *Misun* on toward Arrow Rock.

CHAPTER 35

I stopped beside the privy. Just down the hill, past the corral full of overgrown thorn bushes, through swaying elm trees, lay the cabin. Juber, the old hound, stood on the porch howling. Anna walked out, shushing the dog. She gazed up the path but did not seem to see me, then shooed Juber back inside and shut the door behind her. I nearly cried out, feeling sudden relief that she lived.

I nudged *Misun* on down the path. As I passed the corral, the door opened, and she stepped back out onto the porch aiming a scattergun at me. With the late, afternoon sun behind me, she squinted to see who rode up to her home.

"Stop right there, mister."

I rode the horse a few feet farther, into the shade of trees. She slowly lowered the gun to cradle in her arms.

"Hello, Anna."

"You've come back," she said, her voice a soft cry, barely spoken above a whisper.

She wore the same black pants and white smock with curly, blond hair hung down to her shoulders. She stood as stunning as the first I saw her, bringing me back from the dead, by her hand and her father's.

I dismounted and walked toward the cabin. The dog Rascal came bounding out the door to jump off the porch and stand barking at my feet, tail wagging, with Juber right behind. A couple of dogs happy to see me. As I leaned over to pet Rascal,

I glanced up at Anna and smiled.

"They remember me."

"Of course, Zebadiah, dogs don't forget, now do they?" She smiled back.

For a few, long seconds, I kneeled with Rascal in my arms, rubbing his ears, stroking his back, him licking my face. How I had missed this dog.

Anna laid the gun inside the door, stepped off the porch, and knelt before me, tussling both dogs' fur. Gazing into my eyes, she said, "You've had a hard ride, Zebadiah. Come inside and sit for a while." As she studied my face, a look of wonder, then sadness crossed hers. She smiled again, her eyes bright as ever.

We both stood. I tied *Misun* to the hitching post, reached for my rifle and shooting bag, and followed Anna and her dogs into the cabin.

I walked through the afternoon sunlight streaming through the front doorway and waited for my eyes to adjust. The supper table sat in the same place in the center of the cabin. The beds had been shuffled around with two sitting close together and curtains drawn between them, as if to shield those lying there from each other. I laid the rifle against the wall next to her scattergun, kept my pistol and knife at my belt, pulled a chair from the table, and sat. Anna's father was nowhere to be seen.

"Where is Dr. Keynes?" I asked.

Anna bent over the fire. "Are you hungry, Zebadiah?"

"Your papa?"

She stood straight, turned to me, and said, "He died, late last year."

"I'm so sorry," I said. "He was a good man."

"Would you like a biscuit, Zebadiah? I have two left from this morning I was saving for a patient of mine. He also loves biscuits."

It seemed she did not want to talk about her father. The day

I left them both I knew he was not long for this world. The loneliness and sorrow she must have known had crept into her eyes.

Then she said, "Zebadiah, but for a few weeks, you didn't know the man he was. The father he was."

Her blunt statement surprised me. "Well, he saved my life."

"We saved your life, the dogs helped save your life," she said.

"Yes, an' I'm so very grateful to you."

"You are not the only life he saved . . ." she said, then, bent back over the fire.

I did not understand her sudden coolness, feeling the need to defend her father. Though she was right, I had not known the doctor long, I hoped the gratitude I offered lent some solace toward her feeling his loss.

I remembered being laid up, recovering from my wounds, unable to move, the both of them tending to my every need. With her backside toward me I had watched her cook, a self-assured, innocent girl I thought I knew. I closed my eyes, the heat and worry of this late afternoon easing, sitting in the same chair I sat in all those months before, nearly healed, her dabbing dogwood salve onto my wounds, the touch of knees together, a gentle kiss on her forehead. That rainy evening, we stood in the middle of the cabin, holding each other as candles burned low, the slow, dark dance of giving in. I opened my eyes and glanced to her bed I had stood over, watching her sleep, feeling the dam nearly break after rejecting her offer for us to lie together.

I closed my eyes again and sat there, remembering the night. Not wanting to disrespect her father, I had said. The real reason . . . afraid I would never leave her to go and avenge my brother's murder.

"You are lost in thought."

I opened my eyes. Anna held out the biscuit.

I nodded and smiled, accepting her offer.

She looked at the knife and pistol, then the rifle at the door. "How long is your visit?" she asked.

The question was a sensible one, for when I left, there were no promises of my return. As far as she might know, I was simply passing through, stopping in to say hello and be on my way. How could I broach the subject of my true reasons for her standing in front of me with an outstretched hand, offering up a biscuit? *When do I tell her I'm there to save her life.* A deadly reason I created.

"At least for the night, if you'll have me," I said.

With the slightest of hesitation, she nodded.

Baked earlier in the day, the biscuit tasted delicious, crunchy yet with butter soaked through. I slowly ate every crumb. The bits that did fall on the floor, Rascal cleaned up. I reached down and stroked his head. *Good to have a dog at my feet.*

Wiping her hands on a towel, Anna sat down across the table. "Where have you been, Zeb?"

I looked away and ever so slightly shook my head. *Where do I start?* I thought. How do my experiences become mere stories, tales to be told across a supper table to a woman I left behind, to go and kill two men that murdered my brother? This, the mere beginning of my tales to be shared. And then to come back nearly a year later.

"I have gone down the river to the sea, on to Texas, and back," I said, more of a declaration.

"Did you find the men you were looking for?"

"Yes."

Frowning, she turned away, as if not wanting to know about their demise. Unless asked, I would not offer her the details.

But then she turned back and asked, "Texas. Hmm, did you go and fight?"

"Yes."

Anna sat straight in the chair and brushed her pants, as if

209

ironing the wrinkles with her hands. "Do you come from there today?"

"No."

"Ah, Zebadiah, you must tell me everything."

I stared at her, trying not to show the hardness of my eyes, that she might see through to the truth.

The story I told began the morning I stepped on the steamboat *Diana* in Boonville headed to St. Louis, the September before, with Fontenelle and Billie Frieze befriending me, or more like me grudgingly befriending Billie. How I met Frenchy and witnessed the sad death of John Brigham by the snarling teeth of two wolverines. The quick and painless death of Rudy Dupree by guillotine. I had to explain how the mechanism worked. Anna seemed stupefied by the cruelty, the brutal act of cutting one's head clean off in the swiftest of manner. She acted even more surprised that I could not answer her question as to how Frenchy came to own a guillotine in the first place.

"Go on," she said, shaking her head.

I did not tell her the tale of my night at John Murrell's broken church, being too embarrassed by the whole incident. I continued on down the river.

"New Orleans?"

"Yes, is where I found Baumgartner, my brother's true murderer."

"What did you do?"

I hesitated, staring down at my hands folded together on the table. "I killed him," I said.

At that moment, I could not look her in the eye. Neither remorse nor shame filled my heart, but a feeling that somehow, after all these months, I had come back only to let her down.

"I should not be surprised," she said.

Then added, again rubbing her hands with the towel as if she had heard enough. "You finished the deed you set out to do,

Zebadiah. There is no more to say."

The rest of my tale, I thought, *to Texas and back might never be told to her.*

"I must go to Arrow Rock in the morning, to care for a recent patient of mine. You are welcome to stay the night and then travel with me." She stood. "Will you be wanting to see your brother's grave before you leave?"

I simply nodded.

"Then we must be quick, Zebadiah Creed, while the sun still shines." She picked up her scattergun and strode onto the porch, leaving me to follow her out the door with the dogs.

The well-worn trail down to Jameson Island offered an easy walk that I did not remember taking the last time I knelt at Jonathan's grave. Then, I needed Anna's help nearly every step of the way. This day, we treaded side by side yet separate, without touching, mostly silent the whole way down. I carried at my belt the loaded pistol and knife, ready for Willie Dan at any time to come busting out of the bushes. I did not know what to say to her other than to watch her step. She glanced at me as if I were the one who she should be saying this to, as she had followed the trail most all of her life. Anna left me with the dogs and walked on ahead.

We reached the island, the thick of the forest, the dogwood tree radiant in its summer splendor. I smelled mint and grew a bit sickened. I held on to a branch steadying myself, flooded with memories of Jonathan and I being shot and tied together to the tree, Rudy swiftly slicing open my left cheek with his long knife, and finally, Baumgartner placing a pistol to my head, then my brother's, and pulling the trigger. With all our possessions, including our beaver pelts and keelboat stolen, I was left for the critters to get at. If not for Rascal and Juber finding me, Dr. Keynes would not have brought me back to life and I would not be standing at my brother's grave with Anna by my side.

"Papa and I used to fish here," she said, nodding toward the bank of the small rivulet where Jonathan and I had staked our boat.

"You shared as much, the last we were here," I said.

"I don't remember."

We stood with our heads bowed. I had nothing to say.

"Why were you here, that night, in the first place, Zebadiah?"

I did not at all expect this question from her.

"The goddamn steamboat. And those furs . . . and the American Fur Company." The struggle at Rendezvous to get what I thought was a fair price. A bastion of thieves to steal my brother's and my livelihood . . . our legacy.

"They were going to rob us of our profits." I kicked at the grave. "I would not have it!"

"Is what brought us together, Zebadiah."

Feeling comforted, I reached out my hand. She crossed her arms.

"Why have you come back here, to me . . . now?"

To protect you from being murdered, I so desperately wanted to scream. "I'm on my way to find my brother's Blackfoot wife and son," I said instead.

"You could have left from Texas."

I nodded. "Yes, I could have, but my business leaving there took me back to New Orleans and on to St. Louis. To go west brought me here . . . to you."

I could not see if she thought I was lying. Maybe it simply did not matter what excuse I gave her.

I stared at Jonathan's grave. After nine months, dirt had given way to a cover of grass. With no headstone, in ten years or so, there would be no way to tell whether he lay there at all. *Or a flood down the river could wash the grave away tomorrow.*

"Do you want a prayer given?" asked Anna.

I shook my head. Surely she remembered I did not believe in her god or her father's, the god of my white Quaker parents. The god I felt forsaken by and left for dead on the north plains at eleven years old. The god that allowed my brother to be murdered on the very ground where he now lay buried. A god who would send Willie Dan to kill someone as innocent as Anna. A god who would force me to kill him first.

"The devil is here, and he ain't no different than God," I said, and walked away from my brother's grave, toward my fate she claimed her god held in his hands.

"Bless him, oh Lord," I heard Anna say. Then, an amen whispered under her breath.

CHAPTER 36

At twilight, I stood with Anna on the rise where, all those months before, we watched the blood-red sun go down, the first time I held her and she cried, leaving tear stains on her father's shirt I wore. The Missouri looked so much closer than I ever remembered.

A lone riverboat plowed the water heading south, then east, and on to the Mississippi. One man held the rudder's handle, another leaned against the pilothouse, a trail of thin smoke drifting behind. From where I watched, in the waning light, it appeared that furs lay in packs all around them. I thought, *Hell, can't be furs, the beaver trade's played out. An' if it is furs, they ain't gettin' hardly nothin' for all their troubles.* In my mind, I spun with my fingers the silk hat given to me by Broussard . . . *poor saps!*

I turned away to the west. There was no sunset this evening for dark clouds had built up along the horizon, sweeping across the sky toward us.

Anna said over her shoulder. "Rain by midnight, I expect." She kept walking, hardly giving the river or the clouds a glance. Both dogs followed her up the trail, around the bend, and toward the cabin. Anna stopped by the door, letting them pass. As I came up behind, she stepped in front of me.

"I don't know what you expect, or who you think I am. I have changed Zebadiah; I am not the young, naïve girl you left more than nine months ago." Anna's look was as stern as any man might see in a woman, as if by losing her father, death no longer held sway. And by my leaving, I secretly hoped, gave a loneliness only she could know. At that instant, I felt her righteous sorrow, selfishly wanting to reach out my arms and hold her. Yet, I knew my feelings did not offer any shade on the present moment and stood with my hands behind my back. "With respect, my dear, I expect nothin' other than your hospitality toward someone you came to care for, savin' his life . . . an' more."

She stared at me, her eyes welling with tears and said, "Fair enough, Mr. Creed. Fair enough. Make yourself at home for the night. I'll make fresh biscuits." She nodded toward *Misun*. "You can bed your horse 'round back," and with that, she marched into her home.

Behind the cabin there lay a small stable. I entered through double doors; a tan sorrel stood in one of two stalls with a small, four-wheeled wagon stored in the back. I led my horse into the other stall. I pulled off the saddle, gave water from a bucket I found, and a bag of oats to feed him. These were left along with fresh hay for a bed, as if another horse had recently been boarded.

"Safe an' dry for now," I said and patted his rump. "Can't say for how long though." *Misun* gave a look of trust, and perhaps understanding.

I pushed open the front door. Anna looked up from the fire and smiled, as if she was truly glad to see me. I smelled biscuits and realized that I had not eaten but two, old biscuits since the morning, leaving Henry King William's inn.

"I hope you still like raccoon stew," she said. "I have half a pot left over from last night."

How could I possibly tell her about my previous evening's supper? I nodded and smiled, then sat down at the table.

She set a steaming bowl down in front of me. "I don't know who you think you're afraid of, still wearing that pistol and knife. At my table, you sit unarmed."

I tried not to appear so anxious as to lay them even on the book table, just a few feet from where I could reach if the door suddenly burst open. As much as I wanted to relax and put away my weapons forever, I could not, so I ignored her request and continued to eat.

Anna sat down across from me. "Are you expecting someone, Zebadiah?"

I took a spoonful of stew and slurped it into my mouth, burning my tongue. "Ouch! I mean, umm, this is as good as I remember!"

She blew on her spoon, then took the bite. Wiping her lips with a towel, she said, "You did not answer my question."

"Not particularly."

She stared at me. "What does that mean?"

I blew on the stew and scooped it into my mouth, then bit into a biscuit. Mixed together, it was delicious. She did not look away while I finished chewing. "Well . . ." I set my spoon down. *Tell her the truth,* I whispered to myself. ". . . there is a man, from New Orleans, who may have followed me here and . . . wants me dead."

Her chair screeched across the floor. "Wants you dead!" She rose to her feet, went to the door, and made sure the bolt was latched. Pulling back the curtain, she peered into the blackness of the night and rattled the window to ensure it was also locked. Both dogs began to whine, then Rascal started barking. Juber howled until Anna shushed them both, ordering them to sit guard at the door.

"Anna, come and sit back down, please . . ."

She turned on me, reaching for her scattergun. "You tell me everything that's going on, right now!"

I pushed my chair back but did not stand.

"What are you caught in, Zebadiah? That man you killed, his

friends or family are after you now, right?"

She spoke as if she knew my general plight, the danger I brought to her doorstep, her distrust of me now even more apparent. The rest of my story desperately needed to be told.

"Please Anna, sit back down and I will tell you everything."

She laid the scattergun on the table, eased into her chair, and again sat staring at me. This time, with a look of real fear.

"Killin' Baumgartner was not the end. But, I've come to believe, only the beginning of my troubles." I hung my head, my hands folded on the table. "The man who set up the thievery in the first place, a man name of Benjamin Brody, I found . . . and in a duel, scalped him."

Anna gave no response other than a look of disgust on her face.

I continued. "Now, I left him alive, but later, someone did kill him. While I was in Texas, I was accused of the murder. A bounty hunter came a lookin' for me. In a fight, I . . ."

I felt confused, as if I could not tell the story straight. That in my mind came a jumble of memories. Closing my eyes, I took a breath.

"A man I met in Texas, claimin' to be a friend. After the last battle against the Mexicans, he . . . he betrayed me. Took me to New Orleans in the bowels of a ship, in chains, to stand trial for a murder I didn't commit."

I felt like I could not breathe. I stood and reached for the door.

"Don't you dare pull that latch," Anna said.

I leaned back and took in another slow, deep breath. "I was in the New Orleans prison. There turned out not to be a trial for Brody's murder, and . . ."

I felt my head spinning. I did not want to continue but could not stop. "I went to prison near Baton Rouge, for scalpin' him."

I realized then how ridiculous the story began to sound. "I

ended up at a plantation, the Hydras plantation, on the Mississippi, in a gang, buildin' a road through a swamp."

"Zebadiah, what in heaven's name has any of this to do with a man out to kill you?"

"A man I knew in the New Orleans prison, a stone-cold killer, I was witness to two deaths by his hand and heard the dying screams of another, he came to the plantation and murdered someone, Margo, the wife of a close friend of mine name of Olgens Pierre. This murderer did this to show his dark ruthlessness. And that he . . . he would do it again to someone close to me, if I did not . . ."

I stopped. *You must tell her!*

Anna stared at me. "Did not do what?"

I took another quick breath. "Assassinate General Sam Houston."

"What? . . . Why?"

"A plot, the weaving of a secret conspiracy to keep slavery not just in the South, but now in the new Republic of Texas where General Houston's most likely to become president. They don't trust that he will hold to the business, that he might be swayed by the abolitionists to set all the Negroes free." I could not stop talking. "These men want Texas, Florida, and most a Mexico to join the slave states . . . to make a new country, to keep cotton and sugarcane flowin' to the north, and to England. An' whatever else needs growin' by the hands of black men and women."

I finished speaking and glanced at her to see if she followed this most preposterous tale. Her eyes closed tight, she motioned for me to continue.

"This same man that killed Margo, this devil, name of Willie Dan, he's the one who killed Benjamin Brody."

"Did you?" she asked. "Kill the general?"

"No, no, of course not! Is why I'm here tonight, before Willie

Dan finds out Houston is indeed still very much alive. To stop him from . . ." I paused, my hands visibly shaking. ". . . hurting you."

"*What?*" she shouted, her face as pale as chalk and eyes wide open. She picked up her gun again and began pacing in front of the fire. "*Me,* what have I done? I don't know these terrible people, this horrible, wicked man!"

She shooed me away from the door to again make sure it was latched.

"Why you?" she asked. "Why not this murderer just go and kill General Houston?"

I shook my head. "I don't rightly know, Anna, except maybe they thought I could get to him easier. I am his friend and confidant, you know."

"Your friend?"

"I . . . he helped me out a couple a times during the war, and I helped him escape New Orleans before gettin' killed. So yes, he's my friend."

Her cold gaze bore into my very soul. "And why me, Zebadiah Creed?"

I thought she might point her gun my way.

"Why me?" she growled.

"Because somehow, they found out that you and I . . . for even such a short time, were close."

"And you didn't kill him?"

"Who?"

"*The murderer!*" she screamed.

"No."

"Why not?" she asked, as if, in her mind, Willie Dan should have already been dead by my hand.

I could not look her in the eye. "I was beaten and tied to a chair, an' watched him kill Margo. I could do nothing for her. An' . . . then he was gone."

My face hot with shame, I did not know how to finish answering the question, except, "So no, I didn't kill him, is why I'm here now. I came as quick as possible. If I had gotten to you any later, he would find out that Houston's death was a lie, a lie I started to gain some time before the truth be told. I cried with relief when you stepped out on the porch this afternoon. I was so happy to see you safe." I wiped away growing tears. "Of all the folks in this world, I mean you no harm."

Her gaze softened. She checked the door and window locks one more time and laid her gun against the wall next to my rifle. She stood alone in the middle of the cabin, shoulders slumped, her sad eyes staring at the floor.

"Had my life not been in danger, would you've still come back to me?" she asked, looking up.

I opened my arms. "Yes, of course. I'd have been here much sooner."

"Oh, how can I trust you?" she whispered, then hesitated and slowly stepped into my embrace. Pushing away with her fists, she pummeled me hard in the chest, stopped, then pulled close to lay her head against my shoulder.

"So very long I've wished for this moment, Zebadiah."

I stroked her hair and kissed the top of her head. "As have I, my dear."

"Yet you come bringing this horror with you."

I could not say a word.

Rain pounded the roof for some time, then let up to a steady patter. By the low flickering fire, I watched soak-stained timber rafters drip water into the cabin below. Anna had placed a couple of pots and a bucket to catch the rain, but they were not enough. I stepped out of bed into a puddle, cool to my feet, the first time in a long while to feel water touching my bare soles. I moved to the fire and stood over the glowing embers, naked, with my hands clasped behind my back. Anna lay sleeping, under covers still warm by my heat. Dawn would not show itself for another hour or so. I did not want to start a new day, giving up this evening's rapture to memory. For what the future held, I could not see at all.

The dam had broken. A flood of longing desire, passion, and a desperate need for touch came pouring out of us. A first love consummated, the apple plucked from the tree and eaten bite after bite after bite, until we were covered in sweat and exhausted, leaving only the softest sound of rain and blissful sleep. Standing by the fire, I smelled her on me and began to feel again her pull.

I returned to bed, to make love with my dear Anna one more time.

CHAPTER 37

Both dogs howled.

Pistol in hand, I dashed to the window. By the morning light, I saw only the man's backside as he stood on the porch, facing away, his horse tied to the hitching post. He had yet to knock on the door.

I wore only my britches. Anna sat up in bed. The dogs settled after the man hollered, "Hey, sweetie, you up yet?"

He turned to face the door and knocked. "Anna, come to see about'cha."

I lowered the pistol. The old gentleman's gray beard nearly touched his chest. I could not see if he carried a weapon. He knocked again, harder.

The sun had just risen above the horizon, the sky a brilliant, early morning blue with the past evening's rain having washed all the dust from the air. I laid the pistol on the table and pulled on my smock. I glanced at Anna. If he's a neighbor, I thought, what a tale to tell finding a strange man sleeping alone with her.

She yawned and said, "Boonie, Boonie's here." She shimmied into her pants and shirt, brushed back her hair, and went to open the door.

I stepped in front of her. "Boonie? A friend? Neighbor? How do you know he's alone?"

"Oh, Zebadiah, don't worry. He's an old friend of Papa's, and a good friend of mine. He's just stopping in to see to my safety, my needs. Been coming 'round since Papa died. He feels better about doing it than I do."

She eased me aside and lifted the latch. My greatest urge was to hold the pistol on him until I knew for sure he was alone. Instead, I stood still with my hands down to my sides as the door swung open.

Boonie stepped across the threshold into the cabin. "Hey, sweetie!" he said and offered her a hug. His smile went to a frown when he saw me. "Well, well, I see. Here's the owner a that horse in the stable."

Anna faced the both of us. "Boonie, this here is my friend Zebadiah Creed. He's come all the way from fighting in Texas to visit, on his way to find his brother's boy somewhere up in the Rockies." She paused to gauge his reaction. His concerned look eased when she mentioned Texas. "Zeb, this here is Boonie, from Boonville, was Papa's oldest best friend."

I reached out my hand. He looked at Anna, then back to me, and gave me a strong shake.

"Well, it's certainly good to meet'cha, Zebadiah Creed. Heard all about you," he said. "Y'don't look so . . ." he glanced at Anna, pushed back his hat, and scratched his scraggly head. ". . . so hard-edged."

I felt the rough, wood floor on the bottoms of my bare feet and curled my toes. To stand there being introduced for the first time to a man so close to Anna and her father with no boots on, I certainly felt vulnerable.

"Boonie, if you'll give us a few minutes here." She nudged him toward the door. "I'll fix us a mighty fine breakfast and we can catch up on all things going on up and down the river."

Before she shut him out of the cabin, I could not tell if his slight frown suggested a little jealousy or just a natural distrust of a man standing barefoot with his dead friend's daughter.

"Finish getting dressed, Zebadiah, and then walk with him back to the stable. He'll appreciate you doing that. The second stall's where he usually ties his horse. He's funny about keeping her under a roof when he visits. He always takes the time and brushes down Ole Betty, mucking out the old hay and such. Makes him feel like he's not just visiting, but truly taking care of me."

I put on my boots and belt, eased the pistol and knife into place, and stepped into the morning sun. Boonie was about to walk his horse into the stable when I caught up with him.

"You were friends with the doctor?" I asked. "So was I."

He stopped, the horse urging him on. "He told me he saved your life, that true?"

"Sure did and I'll be forever grateful."

"Why come back? Ya left outtta here with him believin' you'd stay, take good care a her." He squinted in the sun. "You kill the men who killed yer brother?"

I slowly nodded, thinking the good doctor may have told everyone he knew what I meant to him and his daughter. So much so that strangers overheard; spies that would send word down river, knowing my history, for some goddamn reason, to hold it against me.

Billie Frieze had found out about me this way.

Boonie held the reins in one hand and shielded his eyes with the other. "Then yer back fer good, ain'tcha?"

"I have one thing left to do."

"Ah, yes, the man who told everyone that you were comin' after him, an' was gonna kill him. The man who wears the scar, same as you."

Though I should have known Willie Dan would speak so ill of me, turning the tables like that, saying *I* was out to kill *him* . . . I hid my surprise.

"Do you know where I might find him?" I asked.

Boonie shook his head and yanked on the reins. His horse followed. "Was only one night, at the tavern where the doctor an' I used to drink together, listen to his preachin'. You know the good doc was a keen preacher, if he drank enough, if ya know what I mean."

I held open the stable doors. Before slipping into the cool shade, he said, "Man's gone the next day sayin' he might be safer in Arrow Rock."

"When was this?"

"Oh, maybe two weeks ago. I'd forgotten 'til I saw you standin' in yer bare feet, Anna behind ya. Now I know yer a good man, I trust the doctor an' Anna's judgment on that. This fella, he smiled a lot, but his eyes were cold as hell. Your eyes ain't near like that." He stopped. "Why ya wanna kill him?"

"He was sent to kill Anna if I didn't kill another fella."

"Did you?"

"Nope, sure didn't."

"Hmmm," he scratched his chin. "Well, sir, good thing you're here an' I come along when I did."

I stood holding the door with one hand, vapors rising off the dew-covered grass and brush. *Gonna be hot today,* and for that instant, I felt at ease with the world. I stepped through the doorway, entered *Misun's* stall, and refilled his oats bag. He nudged me in the shoulder as if he was anxious to get a move on. "We'll be on our way soon," I whispered, stroking the horse's snout.

Boonie hollered from the back of the stable. "Meet ya up at the house. Anna sure cooks a mean breakfast. 'Sides lookin' out for her, that's why I come all this way."

I left *Misun* and walked on back to Anna. Inside, I sat at the table and watched her cook without a word shared between us. Bacon sizzled in an iron skillet with eggs ready to fry. Biscuits rose in a pan set in coals directly under the enclosed grate the skillet lay on. The sugary aroma of the bacon mingling with the delicate browning of the biscuits sent my mouth to watering.

Hearing her whistle as she cooked made me smile.

"You have not said a word about last night," she said.

Listening for Boonie's return any minute, I stood and reached for her waist. "Haven't had much privacy," I whispered, kissing her neck.

With her brilliant, blue eyes shining, she whispered, "The best night of my life, so far."

We kissed, deep. Anna dropped the fork she held in her hand. For a few long seconds, we held each other, her head laid against my shoulder.

"I think I . . ."

With footsteps on the porch, our moment gone, I let go, leaving her to stand alone at the cook fire to finish breakfast. Boonie stepped into the cabin and took a huge sniff, let out a sigh, and sat down at the table. Anna soon laid a plate piled high with bacon, eggs, and two biscuits in front of him. He went right to eating.

A grin grew slow across her face. "My two favorite men," she said.

Boonie and I glanced at one another from across the table. Anna laid a similar plate in front of me, but with three biscuits. I could not tell if he was jealous of me for receiving one more biscuit than him. I had seen men kill for less grievances.

Anna sat. "Boonie, will you be going to Arrow Rock with Zebadiah and myself later this morning? Along with holding a clinic at the Hesters' tavern, we can have an early supper before heading back."

He gave me a knowing look and said, "Of course, sweetie. Haven't been there in some time."

Anna stood and began wrapping a couple of biscuits with a towel.

"Who are the biscuits for?" I asked.

"Oh, Zebadiah, don't be jealous, they're for that patient I

told you about. His name's Andrew Butler." She paused. "He struggles to walk, though I can't seem to find anything wrong with him. The Hesters have put him up in a small room near the pantry. Claims he's on his way west with the rest of the hordes heading that a way when he came down with this mysterious affliction. I sure wish Papa was here, he would know the cause of the problem."

"When did he come to be in Arrow Rock?"

"Oh, not too long ago, maybe a week and a half is when he came to me at the tavern."

"What's he like?"

"Oh, he's sweet. Kind of a boyish face with the bluest of eyes."

"Any scars?"

Anna thought for a second, then shook her head. "No, none that I could see."

We went back to finishing our breakfast.

"What was his name again?"

"Andrew Butler."

"I'd like to meet this man," I said.

"Why, Zebadiah, I do believe you are jealous!" she said, laughing. "He's more of a boy than a man."

I shrugged and swiped up the eggs with the last of my biscuits.

Boonie cleared his throat. "Not to change the subject, but did y'all hear 'bout ole Samuel Houston, the hero general of that great war against those damn Mexicans, south a here in Texas?" He pushed himself from the table. "He ain't dead after all. It was a made-up rumor. How 'bout that," he said, winking at me. "Hell, guess I'll go an' get my horse ready. We're goin' ta Arrow Rock!"

As Boonie stepped out the door, I stood and began gathering what little things I had. Anna watched from the corner of her eye, then approached me and laid her hand on mine. "Zeb, you'll be coming back with me?"

"Of course, my dear," I said and finished packing up my possibles.

Boonie and I saddled up our horses, hitched Ole Betty to the wagon, and loaded the medical sundries. I had told Anna to bring along her scattergun, with extra shot. She stared at me, as if silently questioning a request for her to do something she had already planned on doing. The gun lay beside her on the seat of the wagon.

Boonie carried at his belt a knife and pistol along with his own scattergun held in a scabbard hung from his saddle, easy to get to.

"Ride with me, Zebadiah," Anna said, patting the seat.

Boonie nodded, and I tied *Misun* to the back of the wagon. As I climbed up to sit next to her, she handed me the gun. I laid it across my lap, and we were off.

As we came on to the main road, dust filled the air causing Anna to cough. With more wagons and riders, the dust only grew worse. Boonie rode in front of the wagon. The closer to Arrow Rock, the more crowded the road became. We entered into town, the main street running with all kinds of folks. The Hester Tavern and Hotel's two red-brick stories overshadowed the rest of the buildings. Boonie squeezed his horse into a place at the hitching post, dismounted, and stepped onto the tavern's porch.

"I'll find the owner, she's a friend a mine, an' have her clear out some a this riffraff here in front to set the wagon," he said, raising his eyebrows to me. "An' give a look around."

We sat as far to the side of the street as possible. With the scattergun still laid in my lap, I gave each man who walked or rode around us the eye, not to say a word. A sharp-dressed man stepped out the door seeming none too happy about having to move his carriage from the prominent front of the building. Anna guided the wagon to a stop. Before jumping down, she nodded to my lap and said, "Not allowed inside."

I reluctantly laid the gun in the floorboard and covered it with an old blanket. "I'm goin' in an' have a look too," I said. "I'll be back out to help with your doctor's box."

The double doors swung wide with a long squeak. Full of men sitting at six or seven tables and strewn along the front of the bar, only a few heads turned as I entered, then went back to their conversations and eating. As far as I could see, all were strangers. I stepped outside to meet Anna with her wood box of supplies. She refused my offer to take it from her hands. The room grew quiet as she entered. A large, red-faced woman came up to her, and with a smile, said, "Right this way, dearie. Let's get you set, and I'll hang yer sign out front." She shooed away a couple of customers sitting at a table by the end of the bar, wiped it off, and set down an open bottle of whiskey. Anna nodded to me and said, "Sarah, you know Boonie, an' this here is Zebadiah Creed, come to help. Zeb, Sarah Hester, owner of this fine establishment."

I bowed and said, "Certainly a pleasure."

Sarah looked me up and down with some question, acknowledged our introduction with a half curtsy, then turned to all and said, "Gents, this here is Anna Keynes, an' she'll be ministering to most a yer ails, so line up 'long the bar if you so need her services. An' don't forget to bring a few coins to drop into her glass!"

Anna sat and opened her box. A man wearing a deerskin smock and britches with blood stained across them stepped to the table and stuck his thumb out. A splinter jammed under the nail had become quite septic. With a small pair of pliers, Anna went right to work easing the bloody piece of wood from his swollen, red skin. He took a drink from the bottle of whiskey she offered him. She poured a little into a bowl and gently laid the man's thumb into the liquid to cleanse the wound. He did his best not to howl but clinched his teeth and moaned as she cleaned and wrapped his whole hand. Finished, he turned to show the crowd what she had done and, with a broad grin, said, "See there, boys! She's got the touch of an angel!" He pitched a couple of coins into the beer glass and thanked her again.

His friend stepped forward. "Now, Burt, don't go stickin' that thing up anythin' ya cain't get it out of!" he hollered, slapping him on the back. The crowd of men snickered, some shoving their way to the front. A large burly man with tattoos up his arms settled them down with the threat of a good head knocking, and they fell back into a line stretching along the bar, around the tavern's walls, and to the door, with more patients coming in.

Boonie and I stood behind Anna watching her doctor all kinds of cuts, some broken bones, fingers mostly, and a few folks with coughs they could not shake. For them, she offered a concoction from a bottle out of her box mixed with the whiskey. A couple of them thrust the glass out for more with the good doctor firmly shaking her head no. She soon needed another beer glass, for the first one overflowed with coins.

After an hour or so, she motioned the proprietor. "I've been so busy I forgot to ask about my patient, the fellow who can't walk. Is he here?"

"He's in the back an' still not walking right. Since you left two days ago, he's been asking about you constant." She scowled. "And . . . he's eating all my raspberries. Loves 'em so much I have none left for pie."

Anna glanced toward the closed curtain that surely led to the kitchen and pantry, hesitated, then picked up the wrapped biscuits out of the box, stood, and said, "I will soon return."

I started to follow. "Like to meet the fella."

"You think he's the killer, don't you?"

I shrugged. "Don't know. Might be something he'd pull, to get to you."

"Well, he's not," she said, and disappeared into the kitchen.

I stood for a second, then drew my pistol and yanked the curtain back. Through the door, and to the side of a large stove, Anna blocked the way into a small room. From behind, I peered over her shoulder to see who she talked to, holding my pistol, ready to pull her aside. She took a step backward and stumbled into me.

"Why Zeb, what in the world are you doing?"

I stared at the boy, her patient. Similar in constitution and build, and certainly crippled, he was not Willie Dan.

I placed the pistol in my belt, tipped my hat, and walked back into the tavern. Five or six new patients lined the bar, waiting for Anna to continue her doctoring. At the table sat a man slumped over with a broad-brimmed hat covering his face. A hand lay on Anna's loaded scattergun. He straightened up, raised his head, and smiled.

"Hey, Scalper, 'bout time ya got here."

CHAPTER 38

Before I could pull my pistol, Sarah stepped to the table to face Willie Dan. He shifted his gaze to her and continued to smile.

"Mister," she said. "I don't know what you think you're doing, but this here is reserved for our doctor. Now there's plenty a seats around, if you don't mind sharing. And that gun? Well, we don't allow it in here, you understand?"

"What is your name?" Willie asked, taking his hand away from the scattergun to drum his fingers on the handle of the pistol at his belt.

I slid to Willie's left, with Boonie behind him.

"Sarah, sir. My name is Sarah Hester, and if there's any trouble, ol' Jake here . . ." She hooked a thumb to the large, tattooed man who had sidled up beside her. "Well then, he will escort you out, and you can go and drink some other place besides here."

The tavern had grown quiet with most everyone now standing. Anna gripped the kitchen curtain and gasped. In her hand she held another bottle of whiskey.

Willie Dan's smile broadened. "Hey there, Anna. Ah, you're so sweet. You brought me a drink."

Boonie placed a pistol to his head. "Mister, ain't nobody drinkin' with ya. It's time to go."

Willie gritted his teeth and, over his shoulder, said to him, "You are . . . a dead man."

The front door opened. Smoke poured into the tavern.

Someone hollered, "There's a wagon on fire out here!"

In one, swift motion, Willie stood and pushed away Boonie's pistol, knocking him off balance, then turned on me with Anna's gun pointed at my belly. Staring at him, I saw only the scar on his left cheek, the skin tightening around his dead, blue eyes, and his childish, murderous grin. Just as I reached for the barrel, he allowed it to swivel downward, holding it with his finger at the trigger guard. "Yours?" he asked. I reached out and took hold of the grip. With a gentle tug, he let go.

Still staring at the scar, I aimed the gun at Willie and pulled the hammer to the second click. Boonie stood with a pistol again aimed at his head.

Willie leaned into me with the barrel of the gun I held against his gut. "I ain't gonna kill her here, too many people," he whispered, then smiled and glanced around at all the folks now staring at us. Raising his voice for all to hear, he said, "An' if ya shoot me, well, then that would be murder, now wouldn't it, Scalper."

He turned to look straight down the barrel of Boonie's pistol. "You got me," he said raising his hands and quickly ducked into the crowd, through the smoke, and out the front door.

Boonie and I followed, reaching the porch in seconds.

Willie was gone.

On Anna's wagon, the blanket and the leather and cotton stuffing of the seat lay smoldering, as if someone had started the fire, let it burn, then someone else came along and tried to snuff it out.

I tossed the blanket to the ground and stomped on the burning cloth, then used what was left to smother the seat.

"The asshole looks like he'll do anything," Boonie said, shaking his head. "Now I know why ya want to kill'm."

"Yep, he is an asshole," I stated.

A boy of maybe twelve stepped up to us. "The feller that

struck the match, well, he come back out an' went that a way,"
he said, pointing down the street. "Told me to tell the fella
chasin' him to meet at the stable." The kid squinted at me.
"That be you, mister?"

"I'll follow," said Boonie.

I grabbed hold of his sleeve. "You go on back inside an' tell
Anna I'll be only a while. Don't need you a part of this."

He tugged at his beard giving me a weary look, then slowly
turned and entered the noisy tavern.

I stepped to the street. With the scattergun in hand, I untied
Misun from the back of the wagon and walked toward the
stables.

Chapter 39

The late afternoon had slipped into early twilight. A pressing stillness filled my ears. I felt the clopping of *Misun's* hooves, stirring up the dust of the road. I asked a passerby where the stable might be. Down two blocks on the left, he said. I allowed my horse to go ahead a little, to walk on the right side of him. I did not want Willie Dan to shoot me outright, though I thought he would probably offer some loathsome words before he tried.

He indeed stood outside, leaning against one closed door, the other open just enough to slip through, his hat pulled down with a hand resting on the handle of his pistol. I stopped maybe ten or so feet in front of him, easing back the hammer of the scattergun, sure that Willie heard one, then two clicks, and laid it across *Misun's* saddle, aimed right at his chest.

He pushed up his hat and said, "You broke your promise, Scalper."

"I made no promise."

"Umm, tell me the truth, Houston's still alive and I'll be goddamn if he ain't in Texas by now."

"You're right on both accounts," I said. "And I have to tell ya." From the inside of my coat, I pulled out a scalp and held it so Willie Dan and any others watching could see. "Look at this. I cut it from your leader Broussard while Houston sat an' watched." The slightest of breezes blew the hair across my fingers. "Then we both watched him swing from a rope handled by the husband of the woman you murdered. And here I am."

He laughed hard, holding his belly. As quick as he started laughing, he stopped. "Now, Scalper . . . you must know, I was never too greatly fond a that fool. For me, he was a way in is all. I'll speak frank, I'm glad to hear of his unfortunate demise. 'Sides, it's Master John Preston who's running things, causing war against the godless abolitionists wanting to free the *Negro*. Oh, how I hate 'em. Now, how absurd is it to have them folk running all over the country like rats. You can't make money without 'em, in the fields picking cotton, cutting cane, growing rice." He paused, shaking his head, then smiled. "Course, I don't mind a few sneaking off once in a while, makes for damn, fine bounty . . . And I got to tell ya, this thing's bigger than any of those yahoos in that room watching while I sliced clean through her. And if you happen to get lucky an' kill me, well, sir, them that are the *cause* will hound you for the rest a your life."

I laid the scalp next to the gun I held on him. "Don't rightly care about any a that."

He drummed his fingers on the pistol's handle wearing a thoughtful look on his face. "What are we doin' here, *Zebadiah*? Thinkin' 'bout killing one another . . . Once, I thought we'd be friends. Still carry that hope within me. I didn't come here to kill you. I came to kill Anna." He lowered his head, narrowing his eyes into a shadow. "Because, as I started our whole talk, you broke your promise, and this needs reconciling."

I spat at the street. "Ain't no friend of yours, never will be."

"You still could if ya let go your judgment of certain things . . . 'bout life an' death, who chooses . . . an' who gets chosen."

A breath of wind eased the scalp off the saddle. With a quick glance down to see it land softly on the street, I heard the rattle of a pistol from behind. *Boom! Misun* spooked, lurching forward. I pulled the trigger, the scattergun exploding with fire out its barrel. By the clearing smoke there lay a splintered hole blown through the door where Willie stood a second before. I staggered backward into a pair of boots. Behind me sat Boonie, a pistol by his side, holding his neck. Blood poured through his hands soaking his beard and shirt. "What the hell! You were supposed to stay with Anna!" I screamed, throwing the spent gun to the ground. He looked up, as if he wondered what had just happened, shuddered, then fell backward, his eyes wide open.

Goddamn it, I whispered, then I reached for my pistol and followed Willie Dan into the stable.

The dim, blue light of dusk seeping through the doorway offered little help to see by. As I opened both doors wide, I smelled smoke, not from the shots, but from fire. Ten or so stalls lined both sides of a walking track ending with a set of closed, double doors. Smoke collected in the rafters, then drifted to the top of the stalls. I still could not see the blaze. Horses began to whinny and kick at the walls. With my pistol ready, I opened the first stall. A panicked horse streaked by and galloped out the doorway into the fresh, evening air. The smoke thickened, sinking to the ground. I opened the next stall door and let that frightened horse go free. Flames began burning down the back wall lighting up the whole stable. I coughed and tried holding my breath, then covered my face with a sleeve, my eyes in tears. The smell of burning flesh filled the stable.

From one of the rear stalls came a *yee-haw,* and out burst a black silhouette of Willie Dan on his horse. I stood before him and aimed my pistol. The horse whinnied, raising its front legs to dance toward me. I staggered backward, then fell, pulling the pistol's trigger. The horse shuddered at the shot, slamming its hooves to the ground, then stumbled forward, nearly crushing me. Willie Dan urged the animal upright, blood seeping from its neck. For an instant, he stared down at me, the fire in the rafters showering embers and ash around us. He pulled away the cloth covering his face and smiled. "Hey, Scalper, you ain't dead just yet." With another *yee-haw,* he trotted the wounded horse out the doorway.

From deeper in the stable, horses screamed. I covered my nose and mouth and released a couple more to run free. Outside, I heard folks hollering, yet no one had entered. I dropped to my knees, the building now engulfed in flames. The shape of a person loomed at the doorway. Then by the swirl of smoke, vanished.

"Zeb! Zeb!" Anna yelled out, appearing again, like a ghost.

With tears streaming, the heat blistering my face and hands, burning my hair, I crawled toward my sweet Anna. Through the crackling blaze, I heard a shot, and she was gone. *He's killed her,* I thought, and with all my strength, dragged myself a few more feet. I could go no further and laid down on the hot earth. With every breath I sucked in, smoke scorched my lungs until I could no longer breathe.

I closed my eyes and thought of the man I burned up in the beaver den years before.

So, this is how it feels . . . this is how shall I die.

Oh, Anna, I love you so.

Two hands at each arm hoisted me up and dragged me to the doorway. From behind came a crash as the fiery roof collapsed, the last of the horses screaming. Then, but for the crackle of flames, silence.

With my eyes still closed I lay on my back gulping the evening's air. I heard a voice in my ear say, "You are safe now, Zebadiah."

Anna . . . Anna, my sweet Anna is alive? I opened my eyes and reached out to feel her, to know I was not dreaming, or dead.

She gently lifted my head into her lap, brushing away singed hair from my forehead.

With all the noise of the townfolks' futile attempt to save the stable, I again closed my eyes, Anna's soothing touches the last I remembered of the evening.

Die Farbe of Heaven

Si stille! I must close my eyes, Anna soothing tenderly, the lost I read lullabied of the country.

CHAPTER 40

I shoot, and miss. From behind another tree, his face peeks out from the side, like a wily raccoon but without the mask. I reload, shoot, and miss. I glance around me. Rotting bodies lay scattered for miles and miles, over the prairie and through the trees. Turkey vultures tear flesh from bone, dogs pick through the different colored uniforms the soldiers wear. Again, I shoot, and miss. At first, I think it's him every time, the murderer, the assassin. Then, I'm not so sure for he becomes faceless with only the scar across his left cheek, and think, there are so many of us now wearing the scar.

The sky darkens with smoke. I feel the whole world burning. Dogs sit on their haunches and howl. Vultures lift up their skeleton wings and disappear into the smoke.

I shoot, and miss.

Anna whispered, "Boonie's dead."

I coughed again, my chest bruised from coughing the whole evening I lay in fitful sleep. I asked for her to repeat what she had just said.

"Boonie's dead. Shot by that monster."

I could only nod for my voice had left me.

Filtered through thin, yellow curtains, the morning sun brightened the hotel room. Anna sat in a chair next to the bed and nightstand wiping sweat from my face, cooling my forehead. She had given me medicine for my cough, though it seemed to not work that much at all. The last spoonful she offered, I refused. I did not want to become more sodden.

I turned to Anna and tried to talk, choking on my words.

"Shh," she said, placing a finger to her lips. "I know what you'll ask. Sheriff Bowen's put a posse together. He swears they're hot on his trail. And downstairs, Sarah's ordered Jake to stand at the stairs, not letting anyone up who don't belong." Anna stood, reached for the scattergun lying on the table at the window, and aimed it at the door. " 'Sides, he gets this far, well then . . ."

The look in her eyes showed a mix of fear and fierceness. I knew she would shoot to kill.

A knock came with a rattle of the doorknob. I attempted to rise up out of the bed and began coughing without mercy.

With a finger again at her lips, Anna mimicked a *shh,* and placed her ear to the door. "Who is it?" she asked, the loaded gun still cradled in her arm.

"Miss Keynes, it's me, Sarah. I'm alone."

Anna turned the key with a click and swung the door open just enough to let Mrs. Hester into the room. She held a bottle of whiskey in her hand. "Thought ya might like something for that cough," she said, offering it to me. I motioned for her to set it on the bedside table next to the medicine, stifling another coughing attack.

"Is he dead?" Anna asked.

Sarah slowly shook her head. "No word yet."

"Where's Boonie?"

"Downstairs, laid out in the room where your crippled patient was, all wrapped and ready to, well, you know." She hung her head for a second, then said, "Sometime last night, the boy up and walked away, seeming just fine to me. Said he had somebody to meet."

I lay there listening to their conversation, feeling crippled with smoke left in my lungs, helpless to do anything, to save Anna if somehow Willie Dan busted right through the door. I clinched my fists and pounded the bed. Both women turned to me.

"Ah Zeb," Anna said, reaching for the cough medicine. "Another two spoonfuls, a couple of shots of whiskey, and sleep. In no time, you'll be fit as a blue moon in September, as Papa used to say."

I took the poison and within minutes, the sun through the curtains faded to black.

I sensed the presence of someone, or something, in the room other than Anna. Once, I thought it was my brother surrounded by fireflies, a tomahawk at his belt, two fluttering scalps hung off a coup ring. I took a bite of the biscuit he offered me. Still the best biscuit I had ever tasted.

I smelled the poultice Dr. Keynes slathered onto my wounds nearly a year before in his and Anna's cabin, as I lay dying from being shot in the shoulder, cut on my face, and knocked in the head by the thieves who stole our furs.

Did I kill the bastards? I could not remember them dying. My heart still burned for vengeance, for if they were not dead, I would surely kill them, again and again and again.

Burning curtains cast dancing shadows upon the walls, shadows of war, a thousand cannons fired, a hundred thousand men in uniform carrying rifles with long bayonets attached, marching across the prairie, through towering trees. Beyond the flames, the blackest of night seeped in through the open window, the growls of dogs echoing up from the street, the room empty but for someone standing beside the bed. Willie Dan leaned into my ear and whispered, "I owed her nothing but death."

Behind him, slumped to the floor, sat Anna.

I came out of my fog, the curtains flapping in the evening's cool breeze. I breathed in fresh air and did not cough. A couple of candles burned on the table next to the scattergun. In a chair in the corner, Anna slept peacefully, a book laid upon her lap. She woke and smiled. At that very moment, I knew I wanted to spend my life with her.

"You are better?"

I nodded and said, "Seems so." My voice sounding froggy.

I pushed myself up and we sat in silence for a few long seconds, her in the chair, me on the bed, enjoying the quiet of the night.

"Have they caught him?"

She shook her head. "Jake said they thought they'd cornered him somewhere down by the river, but he slipped away."

"Hmm, I ain't surprised. He walked out of prison after killin' three men. Wouldn't be surprised if he don't have help. There seems to be all kinds of folks that would like to help him and their *cause.*"

"The *cause?*"

"To keep slavery alive an' well. Is what the fight in Texas was all about. The Mexicans damn sure didn't want it; the cotton plantation owners sure did. And so did the rest of the South's owners. Lots of dollars were sent to help fight that war, from Broussard and Preston, the two men who sent me to kill Houston and Willie Dan to kill you if I didn't. These rich men can't see any other way of livin', off the backs of the Negroes. An' they will kill anyone in their way a keepin' the money flowin'. But it ain't just the money, it's everything else that goes with bein' a white man, keepin' his power. I seen it with the Indians too and there's a war comin', for the soul of the black man, the souls of the Indians, and . . . I suppose, the soul of the nation."

I kept talking on and on, my throat still raw and damaged from the smoke. Yet, I felt compelled to ensure Anna understood completely the conspiracies unfolding around us.

She stared at me as if paying attention, yet her gaze drifted far away. She snapped back from her own thoughts to ask, "And the general's for slavery, or against?"

"Against, I suppose. I never asked him. Though if they, being the *Cause*, don't trust him enough, sending me to kill him, well, I guess that's your answer."

Anna nodded, as if she agreed. Then I remembered our conversation back at her cabin, as I had attempted to explain to her the reason why Willie was there in the first place.

We sat quiet for a while, me resting my scratchy voice and her maybe again thinking over all that I told her.

"We need to take Boonie home, so his son can bury him proper, in Boonville," she said.

With my lecturing done for a while, I asked, "Tomorrow morning we leave?"

"Yes," Anna said, then blew out the candles and lay down beside me. "But for tonight, my dear Zebadiah, let's let the big, old world spin on without us, shall we?"

CHAPTER 41

Willie Dan had shot Boonie straight through the neck, causing him to bleed to death right there on the street. The poor man never had a chance once he pulled his pistol. And now his wrapped body lay in the back of Anna's wagon, waiting to be driven home for good.

I sat holding the reins with Ole Betty waiting patiently, alert, her ears perked up like a mule's. With *Misun* again tied to the back of the wagon alongside Boonie's mare, the medicine box packed, we were ready to travel to Boonville. Jake sat on his stallion as Anna said her goodbyes to Sarah and her husband, thanking them for being such gracious hosts and allowing me to convalesce for the four days and nights it took to clear my lungs of smoke. They offered their condolences for the death of Boonie and asked us to pass their sorrow on to his son in Boonville.

"Be careful," Sarah said, handing Anna some food wrapped into a bundle. "And Jake, you keep a sharp eye for that killer. Bring her back to us safe."

Jake nodded, his horse dancing in circles, anxious to get on down the road.

Anna climbed aboard. I tipped my hat to Sarah, and we were off.

After the fire, as the townfolk cleared away the charred wood and ashes of the burned building, they had found, along with the remains of two horses, the blackened body of the stable hand. There were wounds on the back of his head that might have come from foul play. The old man was known to drink a little too much and be found in the hayloft sleeping off his stupor. The poor fellow, they said, had fallen to the ground and burned up. I suspected this not to be true at all knowing Willie Dan's history.

The sheriff raised a posse and scoured the countryside looking for the suspect, though some grumbled that since Boonie pulled his pistol first, him being shot was in pure self-defense. Still, for a day they searched, with only one possible sighting. Below the bluffs at the river's edge, a witness to the shooting swore he recognized a lone man in a small boat. Sounding the alarm, a couple of the posse hollered down for him to stop. He pushed off the shore and was carried away by the river's swift currents. Another time, Willie Dan was thought to be sighted in town near the Hester Tavern. This fellow turned out to be Anna's patient walking just fine. After Sarah Hester identified him as the healed cripple, he was released and disappeared into the night.

The morning lay before us with a full day's ride to Boonville. Though we drove against the hoards heading west, Jake rode along in silence right next to Anna, clearing the way for us to safely travel abreast. Willie Dan would not have to show his face to shoot any one of us, though I doubted his way to murder would be anonymous. Yet, desperate enough, he might be willing to kill Anna any way he could.

For a long while, she sat quiet staring out at the trees and meadows, back and forth from one side of the road to the other, passing farms, their pastures scattered with cows and fields growing patches of corn, some barley, and cotton. Occasionally, black folk, most bent over rakes and hoes, tended the crops, the same as in Mississippi, Louisiana, and Texas.

Anna seemed to pay them no mind.

"He could shoot from anywhere," she finally said, turning to me.

"Doubt he would."

"How do you know, Zeb?"

"Don't know for sure, but I think he ain't lookin' to just shoot somebody. He wants to make it a spectacle."

"For who?"

"For me," I said.

"Why?"

"Because, in some twisted way, he thinks I'm like him, a cold killer. An' somehow, he might gain my respect."

"*For killing me?* Then he is truly an evil soul," Anna said, giving me a suspicious glance. "Hard to believe there's one man in the world like him, much less two."

She turned back to the passing fields. A while later, wiping tears away, she said, "I can't believe Boonie's dead. He thought he'd gone to help you."

I nodded and with a click and a gentle slap of the reins, I urged Betty on down the road.

Near evening, we entered the outskirts of Boonville. A bit larger than Arrow Rock, with five streets crisscrossing a prime piece of land along the river, the wharf fitting up to three steamboats, plus several keelboats and a flat boat or two. By this time, the comings and goings of the day had slowed to a few folks finishing up their loads on and off the boats. The steamers would be gone by the morrow, down the river or up.

Anna guided us to a tavern near the waterfront with a sign above the door that read *Boonies*.

"This is where Papa always came. Boonie owned it but his son runs it. Boonie loved Papa coming. It's where he ministered, in medicine . . . and the holy word. After the preaching, they'd drink and sing old songs together . . . Papa spent many a night here." She hung her head, as if remembering times past with many a night spent alone in their cabin, waiting for her father to come home.

She jumped down and entered the saloon. A small crowd gathered around the wagon. A couple of folks asked who might the dead man be. I ignored them, not wanting to say before Boonie's son found out. Anna emerged through the swinging double doors with a man about my age, peeling off a smudged apron. He approached the bed of the wagon and stood staring at the wrapped body of his father.

"I knew one day he'd stick his nose into somethin' that'd get him killed," the son said with a smirk, offering no tears, no grievance, no remorse for saying such a thing about his father.

I decided I did not like this man.

"He died savin' me from gettin' killed," I said and stepped up to him with my hand out. "I'm so sorry for your loss and will be forever in gratitude."

"Hmmm . . ." he scoffed, ignoring my offer to shake, and said to Anna, "I knew somethin' like this would happen. Kept goin' up to your house." He pointed a finger at me. "Known about him for some time." He took a quick step closer. "We knew you was comin' back. He knew you was comin', Scalper."

Anna slid between us to face Boonie's son. "Now, now, Henry! Zeb didn't start the whole mess. The murderer Willie Dan did all this on his own."

Henry laid a hand on her shoulder, as if to shove her out of the way. I pulled my pistol. From the corner of my eye, I saw that Jake, still on horseback, also had his pistol aimed down at the man.

"Mister, I don't know you," I said. "But if you don't let her go, you'll be lying there with your papa, wrapped in a sheet."

Anna shook Henry off and moved to my side, both of us now facing him.

"Your Papa and mine, well they were best friends. And he

was my friend too. And I'm broke-hearted that he's lying in my wagon, with you . . . being an ass of a son right now."

Henry stared at Anna, his face showing a hurt that went beyond the killing of his father to someplace different. An instant later, his despair disappeared, replaced again by resentment. "Take him around back, maybe we'll bury him tomorrow." He spat at the ground and stalked back into his saloon. A few seconds later, he came out with a hatchet and took a swing, chopping at the *Boonies* sign, then another and another until the wood splintered into a hundred pieces. He spat again, this time at Anna's feet, and stomped back inside. The stunned crowd, but for the lanterns shining out through the doors and windows, stood in the dark. They slowly disappeared after offering their condolences to Anna.

We wheeled the wagon to the rear of the saloon. A young girl of maybe nine met us at the door. "Papa says to lay him on the table in the kitchen," she said, then untied his horse and walked off into the darkness, leaving us to stand alone next to Boonie.

We stayed the night not far from the tavern, just outside of town, with Anna sleeping in the bed of the wagon. Jake and I took turns standing watch, in case Willie Dan decided to bushwhack us then and there. If he tried anything, he would have to kill us both to get to Anna. Most of the evening we could hear whooping and hollering coming from Boonie's tavern. I hoped that it was not the celebration of his father's death, though by the way the son acted, I would not have been surprised. The morning came, we finished up the cherry cakes and jerky Sarah Hester had given to us, and headed up to Anna's cabin.

Anna drove this time while I sat with the scattergun laid across my lap. The road was not the main road and not as well traveled, though there were also fewer trees to hide behind. I remembered my dream from a couple of nights before, trying to shoot Willie Dan, or someone like him, missing every time. I hoped it not to be a premonition come true.

We rode in silence for a long while. I would glance at her as she looked straight ahead. Then from the corner of my eye, I would catch her quick glimpses toward me.

"I have to tell you, Zebadiah Creed," she said, finally breaking the silence. "After you left, then Papa died . . . leaving me all alone in that cabin day after day, night after night, with only the dogs for company, I welcomed Boonie's friendship. Mostly his talk and also his help around the place. But then . . ." She paused as if to collect her thoughts exactly. "Sometimes, when he didn't visit, Henry would . . . come calling."

I knew. I felt it between them as they stood facing each other outside the tavern, next to Boonie's body, the hurtful look in his eyes. I said nothing to allow her to continue.

"It was just a few times, but enough where he got the idea," she stopped, "about us." Then, "Oh no, not you and me, Zeb! About Henry and me."

At that moment, my heart broke for her. Not for her wanting or needing companionship, but for the times she was so lonely that she would consider a man like Henry, and that I left her to this.

I did not know what to say except, "I understand."

She smiled and gave the reins a good snap. "On there, Betty . . . *home we go!*"

Late afternoon, we drove past the privy and the corral toward the cabin. Anna yanked hard on the reins saying, "Whoa, Betty!" Jake pulled his pistol. I raised the scattergun and stood on the buckboard to get a better view of who sat on the porch in front of us with both dogs by his side.

"My horse run off an' I cain't walk no more," hollered the boy.

Anna leaped to the ground and asked, "Andrew, is that you?"

Then I recognized him. Anna's crippled patient from Arrow Rock.

What the hell is he doin' way out here? I thought and held the gun pointed straight at him. For some damn reason, at that moment, I felt as if I knew him from sometime long before. A fearful feeling ran cold through my very bones.

The kid looked right at me and smiled, his perfect teeth flashing white in the sun.

CHAPTER 42

Jake lowered his pistol and got down off his horse. I kept my gun pointed at the kid.

Anna reached him, asking, "Are your legs not working again, Andrew?"

He nodded and tried to stand, grimaced, and fell back to the porch. "They worked for a while, long enough to get on down the road. But then I couldn't feel 'em when I rode my horse and was afraid to dismount. So I asked around where you lived an' came to find you. Then, like I said, my horse run off, and here I am."

"You was headin' west?" I asked, now standing in front of him with the gun lowered but ready.

He looked up at me, his eyes squinting in the sun, and slowly nodded. "Yes, sir, headed to Oregon, I expect."

"But ya came back east."

"Yes, sir, where her cabin is." He raised his hands as if it were obvious. "Dr. Anna is the only one who'd help me with my ailment."

Anna turned to me. "Now, Zeb, you leave Andrew alone; he is not a threat to me or you, you hear me?"

I stared at her, then at Andrew. Sitting in the noonday sun without a hat, I gave him a real hard look. Tall and lanky, his hair swept to the side, thin for his age. The kid smiled, as if he could not help himself. I could not get past his perfect teeth.

"Do I know you?" I asked.

He shook his head. "No, sir, I swear to you we never met. That is 'til you saw me that other day in Arrow Rock."

"Yes, when you barged in on us, suspecting him of being somebody he isn't," Anna said. She sat down next to Andrew. "Now, tell me, you can't walk at all, just like before?"

He shook his head again and said, "Just like before. The feelin' in my legs just gave out."

Rascal sauntered over to me and sat by my side. Juber stayed on the porch with Anna and Andrew.

"Well, let's get you inside and out of the hot sun," she said.

"If ya can't walk, how'd ya get to be sittin' comfortable here on the porch?" I took a step forward. "An' how come you ain't hurt from falling off your horse? I don't see no scraped skin, no broken bones, is what usually happens when somebody . . . falls off his horse."

Anna quickly rose to face me. "Zeb, you leave him alone. Now I know he's got an ailment . . . I just don't know yet what it is."

I held my ground, with her gun still ready in my hand. "There's something about him. I'll know soon enough, and when I do . . ."

"You'll do what, Zeb, kill him, then scalp him? Or is it scalping first to let 'em know what it feels like to have the top of your head cut off? Just like you showed me once."

Anna had turned on me, trying to protect her young patient, mentioning an instance between us I was not particularly proud of, me showing her one late afternoon, the day before I left to go after Baumgartner and Rudy all those months ago, how I would take a knife and scalp someone. I knew down deep she might still be frightened that she would see me do it.

She opened the door, let the dogs in, and then with help from Jake, dragged Andrew into the cabin and placed him on one of the beds next to the curtained partition. I stayed on the porch for a while, watching the elm trees, keeping an eye out for anything out of sorts. Jake lifted the box of medical supplies and laid it on the porch, then grabbed the reins of both our horses, climbed into the wagon, and with a nod, drove off toward the stable.

If the kid's horse threw him, it would surely return, I thought.

I did not believe him. There would be no horse coming back, if he rode in on one at all.

Behind a post on the porch lay a traveler's bundle. I picked it up, sat in one of the rocking chairs, and untied the string holding it together. A small pistol and a shooting bag lay wrapped in two sets of clothes. I un-cinched the bag. Beneath a small powder horn and a handful of shot balls, wrapped in another piece of cloth, sat a pocket watch and chain. I raised them up in front of me. The gold chain untwisted, spinning the watch until it slowed to a stop. I held the timepiece in my hand noticing a small dent on the back with what appeared to be a streak of dried, black blood staining the silver. Inscribed on the front cover were two letters, AB. I opened it with a click. Loud ticking broke the hot, afternoon silence. A picture of an older woman fit perfect inside the cover. The time, 4:03.

Hmm, AB . . . I thought.

I closed up the watch, wrapped it in the cloth, and buried it in the bag, then added the pistol and clothes, tying the contents together again into a ragged bundle. From inside the cabin, I heard talk, then Anna laughing, sounding like she was having a rare, old time. I smelled biscuits.

I sat for a while longer, alone on the porch with the kid's bundle beside the rocking chair, the scattergun across my lap. *Gonna be a hot night with all of us stuffed in that cabin.* I muttered, *might have to sleep out here.* I stood and stretched, then leaned the gun against the wall and stepped to the door.

Anna had the kid in bed, propped up against the inside wall

of the cabin, the same as where I rested when she and the doctor tendered me back to life nearly a year before. Juber sat at the bedside, the kid rubbing the dog's head. Rascal lay by the cook fire near Anna, her back turned and bent over the grate stirring something steaming in a pot. I stood just out the door swinging the bundle in my hand, staring at the kid, him doing his best to ignore me. I swung up and let go. The bundle flew across the cabin, hit him in the chest, and landed square in his lap.

"Yours?" I asked.

Knocked out of breath, he leaned over clutching his personals.

Anna rushed to his side and brushed back his hair. Glaring at me, she said, "Zebadiah Creed, why in the world did you do that!"

I strode on into the cabin. "Ask him how he was going to make it to Oregon with just two pairs of shirts an' britches, a pistol, and a pocket watch. Go ahead, ask him."

"I would imagine his horse carried the rest he needed," she said. "Right, Andrew?"

The kid, gaining some of his breathing back, nodded and whispered yes.

"But he was able to grab this just as he was bein' thrown . . . right Andrew? Or did ya climb down off your horse, shoo it away, an' walk over to the porch carryin' your pistol?"

Andrew's face turned a bright red. Still holding tight to the bundle, he looked away from the both of us.

"Not a very good damn liar, are ya, Andrew?"

Anna stood upright.

"It ain't like that," he said.

"Well, tell us what it's like, kid."

"Andrew, can you walk?" Anna asked. "Now, tell me the truth."

"Stand up," I said, thumping two fingers on the handle of my knife.

I heard boots on the porch steps.

Anna looked past me and asked, "Who are you?" Then she sucked in a shallow breath.

With the click of a hammer pulled and the barrel of a pistol placed square to the back of my head, I knew.

"Willie Dan, ma'am, come to rescue you from this murderin' scalper."

CHAPTER 43

"Call the dogs off else I kill him right now," Willie Dan said, still holding the pistol to my head. Rascal and Juber had yet to attack, snarling at him from a few feet away. All they needed was a prompt from Anna.

He grabbed my shoulder and pushed me farther into the cabin. "Put 'em outside."

"Where's Jake?" Anna asked, her voice shaking.

"Well, ol' Jake was layin' up the horses, and now he's lying next to one all peaceful. And he won't be in for supper, so I reckon I'll be takin' his place." He pulled another pistol from his belt and leveled it at Anna, then Rascal. "Now I hate to kill a dog; it's like killin' a child. Done it before, but don't like to. Now get the goddamn dogs out the door."

No one moved. The dogs continued their barking.

Willie Dan dropped the pistol a little. "Andrew, I saw you from afar pettin' these mangy yappers. They seem to like you. How 'bout you take 'em out and while you're there, pick up that ol' gut buster Zeb left by the chair an' bring it on in."

Andrew swung his legs to the floor and stood right up. Anna uttered a deep growl as he strolled to the open door. He leaned down, patted his leg, and whistled. The dogs quit their barking and sat staring at him, then turned to watch for a signal from Anna.

"The dogs, outside," said Willie, still holding the pistol to the back of my head.

With a finger, Anna motioned them to follow. Rascal and Juber did as they were told and out they went. Andrew walked back into the cabin with the scattergun cradled in his arms, as if he had carried one forever, closed the door, and stood by the bed to my left.

"Something sure smells good, but . . ." Willie Dan sniffed. "Seems like the bottom of the pot might be burnin'."

Anna did not move.

"Time for supper," he said, again pointing the pistol at her.

I glanced at the kid, with him holding the scattergun, staring at Willie Dan.

"You're goin' to kill her, ain'tcha?" asked Andrew.

"What?"

"We come here to kill 'em both. Not just him but her too," said the kid.

"Well, yes, it's why you're here." Willie paused, his hot breath on my neck. "Her for sure, that was the deal."

Andrew lowered the gun from a cradle to hold it with both hands, his left at the fore-end and his right one at the grip, finger on the trigger, pointed to the floor.

I felt the barrel of the pistol ease slightly from the back of my head. Willie still pointed his other pistol at Anna.

"I would like some supper, though, I'm starving," he said.

Anna had not moved a muscle, her stone face pale as a ghost.

"I don't want you to hurt her," said the kid.

"Well, sir, again I say, that was the deal. I come up here to kill her, an' I got your skinny ass up here so you can kill him an' make your papa proud. But ya only get him after he watches her die. Other than that, you ain't got no say in the matter."

"I do," he said pulling the hammer back with two clicks and raising the gun.

The same time Willie Dan shot at Andrew, I pulled my knife, swiveled, and gutted him twice in his belly, swift and deep, to the hilt, like he did to Margo. Anna took hold of an iron skillet and swung it at his head. He tried to duck but could not. The force of the blow knocked him sideways to the floor toward the closed door. He still held a pistol in his right hand and raised it to shoot her. She jumped at him, slamming the skillet down, his fingers crackling as they fractured. She stood over him, his right ear smashed and bleeding. He reached for his belly with his left hand, poked two fingers through his shirt into the wide gashes, and looked up at me. "Didn't even feel that," he said, then touched the side of his swelling face. Wincing, he turned to Anna with a crooked smile. "Now that was a whopping." He leaned his head back against the door, both dogs now howling and scratching to get into the cabin. "Will you shut those mutts up?"

Anna's arms began to shake as she stood over him holding the heavy skillet. She sucked in a short breath, then another, and another. She said, "I let those dogs in, they'll fight over which one will eat you when you're dead." The skillet slipped through her fingers to the floor.

Willie took a deep, gurgling breath, then said, "Ya got me, Zeb. I suppose we ain't ever gonna be friends. Damn, was lookin' forward to . . ." He coughed up blood into his hand. *"Damn."*

I heard footsteps near the cook fire and swung around to see Andrew, unharmed, still holding the loaded scattergun. He bent over, picked up the pistol Willie Dan dropped, and pointed it at him. Anna moved back toward the bed. I wiped the blade of the bloody knife and slid it into my belt, then pulled my pistol and stood next to her. The dogs had quieted down some with only whimpers heard from the porch.

"Cousin . . ." Willie said to Andrew.

Andrew answered with, "You killed my godfather."

"Ya bring that up again, now?" Willie shook his head, grimacing in pain. He shrugged and said, "He needed killin'.'"

It began to dawn on me who this kid might truly be. "Benjamin Brody?" I asked.

"Nah . . . Billy Frieze," Willie said, smiling up at me.

I gulped at the two words, a name from my past I least expected to hear from this bastard who lay dying in Anna's cabin.

Willie continued, "Ended up killin' both brothers. Shot Billy in that field as you and him . . . stole those slaves from Broussard." He coughed, spewing blood into his sleeve, then groaned, grabbing at the cuts in his gut, trying to close them back up. Blood flowed into a pool on the floor. "*Shit . . .*"

I pulled my knife and leaned over Willie, the blade at his forehead, and grabbed a fistful of hair. Without a flinch, he took another gurgling breath, sighed, and said, "*Hey, Scalper,* your friend Grainger shot Billy first . . .*"

My belly turned inside out, and I felt for an instant Billy's murdered, dead body pressing me into the black mud of the Louisiana bayou, him being shot twice after helping me to safety from Broussard's plantation. The memory of Margo played in my head, her lying on the floor dying, run through with a knife.

Willie Dan stared up at me and said, "Go ahead . . . *Scalper.*"

I glanced back at Anna. She had turned to face the wall.

"*Scalp me, you goddamn savage!*" screamed Willie Dan.

I shook my head and whispered to him in his ear, "*I ain't you.*"

Andrew took a step and placed Willie's pistol to the back of my head and said, "You can kill him, but you ain't gonna do him like you did my daddy."

I let go of Willie's hair and stood holding the knife. "You're right, I'm not. He don't deserve to be scalped."

The kid and I stared down at the dying man on the floor.

"Your, your daddy . . ." Willie stuttered, then coughed, with blood flowing from his mouth, down his chin, and onto his shirt. "Your daddy shoulda killed him when he could, the chickenshit."

The kid turned the shaking barrel to Willie's head, and cried, "Cousin . . . no!"

"Yes, sir, a coward he was, an' you're just like him. You ain't gonna kill my friend Zeb here, he'll kill you first." Willie took the barest of rattling breaths. "Yes, sir, a couple a real pieces of chickenshit you are!"

Boom!

The shot blew a hole through Willie Dan's cheek and on through the door. Andrew dropped the pistol to the floor, the scattergun now aimed at me.

On the porch, one dog howled, another yelped in pain. Anna reached for the door and tried jerking it open but could not for Willie Dan's head still blocked the way. She took hold of his legs and dragged him across the floor, now slick with blood. Rascal pushed himself into the cabin barking, scurried back out to the porch, then in again, wanting someone to follow him.

Anna opened the door wide, Juber lay just past the foot jam, on his side, whimpering. She lifted the dog into her arms, carried him inside, and laid him on the table. "Bring me my box," she said. Neither Andrew nor I moved. With a look of disgust, she stepped onto the porch, lifted the box of supplies, and carted it in. Opening the lid, she pulled out white pieces of cloth and applied them to the hole shot through the dog's side. No matter how much she tried, the bleeding would not stop. Within a minute, Juber relaxed, exhaled, and lay still. Rascal began to moan, then to howl.

Anna pressed her fingers against the edge of the table, knuckles nearly busting through the skin, her eyes filled with tears. "You killed my dog," she said, now staring at Andrew.

With his face crimson, he let the gun drop slightly. I moved toward him, my knife still in hand. He turned to me and ordered, "Put all your weapons down, right now, else you're as dead as him."

I knew that he could kill me. Hell, he just shot his own cousin. If I went along, there might be a chance for me to live through the rest of the day.

I laid my knife and pistol on the table. "What do you want?" I asked.

"We're taking a walk," he said, and motioned us both toward the door.

"Who are you, really?" asked Anna.

Andrew stared at me. "The man you killed and scalped that night in Sophie's parlor near a year ago, way back in New Orleans? Well, sir, he was my daddy, Amos Baumgartner. And I aim to kill you where he killed your brother . . . right here in Missouri, down by the river. Where you shoulda died that night too."

CHAPTER 44

When we reached the rise overlooking the Missouri, Andrew started talking.

"My daddy told the story many times, at the fire, after supper, mostly drunk. Mama got tired a hearin' of it, tellin' him to stop in front a the children. Turn us all into thieves like him she'd say. Hell, he was proud a what he done, proud a makin' a livin' thievin'. It's all he done his whole life. Put a good roof overhead, kept us fed an' in clothes. You know, bein' a good father."

Anna and I walked before him with a scattergun aimed at our backs, not able to do anything but let him talk.

"He never did mention killin' nobody, to us children anyway. But then, one night, his friend Mr. Jacks come 'round. They start swappin' tales an' soon Daddy's drunk enough he don't care who's listenin'. 'Sides, I'm now old enough to hear daddy talk real talk, ya know. Man's talk. Anyhow, 'long with takin' the furs, which by the by, brought a pretty penny for my family, he tells of these two brothers. Stupid men he's claimin', gettin' caught on a sandbar in the middle of the river and how him an' his partners ole Jeffery an' Rudy pull 'em off . . . only to catch 'em sleepin', right down below here, where we're headin' now."

We reached the island, jumped the narrow stream, and on through the trees. I smelled mint. The scent from the night Andrew insisted on telling us about. The story of the evening when this poor kid's father murdered Jonathan.

"He said your brother threw a hatchet ten foot an' split Jeffery's head near in two. Is that true?"

From over my shoulder, I answered, "Was a tomahawk."

"Ooh wee, like to have seen that. Never cared for him anyhow . . . when he used to come 'round the house and . . . around my sister." He trailed off the last words, as if suddenly struck by a foul memory. Then, "Yep, liked to have seen him dead."

With dusk coming on, the katydids came alive. We entered the clearing. The sun hung low through the trees. Shadows crossed my brother's and Jeffery's graves. The dogwood tree drooped in a sad way, losing its shape. Though it grew on an island surrounded by water, there might not have been enough to keep it flourishing. Or perhaps, the evil deeds done there cast a curse upon this land and blood-soaked tree.

I turned to Andrew. "So, look upon Jeffery's grave. Hell, he's lucky to be buried at all, thanks to this woman and her father. And my brother's, who your daddy killed. Shot him in the head as we were tied to that tree over yonder. Our blood still stains the bark."

Anna also faced him. "Why have you brought us back here?"

He raised the gun and aimed it at my chest. "I'm to kill him, like he killed my daddy."

I took a step toward the kid and spat at the ground. "Your daddy came at me with a knife, my brother's knife he stole, an' me fightin' . . ." I raised my fists clenched so hard my fingers felt like they would break. "With only my bare hands."

I dropped my arms and stood straight. "Have to say, I don't feel bad about your daddy dyin'. He was a thief and a killer, an' I'm sure Jonathan wasn't the first man to die by his pistol."

Three more steps and I was nearly on him. I sucked in a breath and hissed, "Yes, sir, I don't feel bad at all! What I feel awful about is that it had to be me doin' the deed, 'cause now you're standin' here and . . ."

I stopped and touched the scar burning on my cheek, then stared past him to Jonathan's grave. Visions of the last year of my life rushed through my mind, like a whirling thunderstorm, with me standing square in the middle. I caused it all. No blame could be laid upon anyone else. I chose to sell our furs down-river rather than to the fur company up at Rendezvous. I chose to seek bloody revenge against the man who killed my brother. I traveled to Texas to appease my guilt for the death of my friend Billy Frieze. And I alone placed my dear Anna in the gravest of danger. Yet . . .

I glanced over to her as she waited for what came next in her life, to grieve the death of the man she had come to love, or to bear the senseless killing of a son come to seek vengeance for his father's death.

I took a couple of deep breaths and slowly unclenched my fists.

The kid slid both his boots back a step, his eyes welling with tears, and raised the scattergun to his shoulder. "It's my right."

I shook my head and spoke. "All killin' does is get more men killed. I can own up to that and will carry the burden of the men I killed 'til I die, includin' your father. But you . . . you don't have to. Revenge ain't so sweet. It's a cold-blooded way of livin'. Always lookin' over your shoulder 'til somebody like you, the son of a dead man . . ."

Words caught in my throat. I looked down for a second, then stared right at him.

"It never stops, never, 'til you gain the courage to put the gun down."

The katydids paused their singing, filling the forest with silence.

Anna moved between us. "Lower the gun, Andrew."

"Get outta the way, Anna," he pleaded, his face glowing red by the last rays of the sun. "You're the only one who seemed to care 'bout me."

"It's because you've got something special shining through your eyes, and I'd like to get to know it better." She paused for a second and nodded to me. "But I won't have you hurting my friend here."

"I shot your dog," Andrew said, wiping away his tears.

She looked at him and sighed, "You sure did, but you didn't mean to."

There blew the faintest of breezes, rustling the leaves of the dogwood. The last breath of the day. The katydids started back their singing. Beyond the kid, near the two graves, a firefly lit up for an instant, offering a tiny light to the looming darkness.

"No harm will come to you, I promise," said Anna.

She gently lifted the gun from Andrew's hands, offered it to me with a tender touch of my sleeve, and gathered him into her arms.

CHAPTER 45

Arrow Rock, late October 1836
There comes a time of morning when, if one listens close, the river sounds like conversation. Between two folks or a thousand depends on the water's calling, and who shows up to do the deeds necessary to tell the tales. Through our adventures come meaningful lessons for us all to heed, to live another day or die by our thoughtless, selfish acts, only to find that it may be a simple conversation that saves us from ourselves.

Thus, up and down the river we shall go until we find a landing suitable, though brief, for one to call home, to share a joyous word or two each morning and evening with those we have come to love . . . and to listen closely to the tales of all rivers, blue rivers of heaven.

Anna glanced across the table. "What are you writing?"

Embarrassed to show her, I placed the quill pen into the inkwell, leaned over, and laid my arm in front of the paper, shielding my words. "Nothin', just some things I've been thinkin' about."

"You writing a book?" she asked, with a questioning smile upon her face.

I looked up and smiled back. "Maybe . . ."

"Well, Mr. Creed, I would not be at all surprised if you were," she said, and went back to mending my smock.

The smell of raccoon stew cooking on the fire filled the cabin. Biscuits rose to brown in a pan on the coals. With supper nearly ready, I heard boots tromp up the steps and onto the porch.

Andrew poked his head through the open door. From under the table came a low growl from Rascal.

I do believe he's grown taller since the summer, just like his papa.

He smiled, showing his perfect teeth, and said, "With all those thorn bushes gone outta the corral, I expect to be buyin' a horse soon."

Andrew walked on into the cabin and dipped himself up a cool drink of water. "Are we goin' to Arrow Rock again tomorrow?" he asked. "With winter comin' on, I hear there's less and less travelers who might need doctorin'. Wanna earn just a little more coin for my pockets." He sat down with us at the table. "Lookin' forward to the cold though . . . an' ain't never seen snow before."

"Long about late February, early March, you'll be done enough with winter and be expecting spring any time," Anna said, laying my smock in her lap to rub her swollen belly.

I nodded in agreement, folded the piece of paper in two, and sat with both hands crossed on the table.

The raccoon stew sure smelled good, and with a bite from one of Anna's fine biscuits, what more would a man ask for.

ABOUT THE AUTHOR

Originally from Oklahoma, **Mark C. Jackson** is an award-winning author and songwriter, as well as the writer of the series *Butch Cassidy and the Sundance Kid* for the podcast *Legends of the Old West*. He is a standing member of the prestigious Western Writers of America and the San Diego Professional Writers Group. Mark resides in Chula Vista, California, with his lovely wife, Judy; their cat, Mr. Kitty; and their dog, Hazel Nut. This is his third novel of the series *The Tales of Zebadiah Creed*.

www.markcjacksonwriter.com

The employees of Five Star Publishing hope you have enjoyed this book.

Our Five Star novels explore little-known chapters from America's history, stories told from unique perspectives that will entertain a broad range of readers.

Other Five Star books are available at your local library, bookstore, all major book distributors, and directly from Five Star/Gale.

Connect with Five Star Publishing

Website:
  gale.com/five-star

Facebook:
  facebook.com/FiveStarCengage

Twitter:
  twitter.com/FiveStarCengage

Email:
  FiveStar@cengage.com

For information about titles and placing orders:
  (800) 223-1244
  gale.orders@cengage.com

To share your comments, write to us:
  Five Star Publishing
  Attn: Publisher
  10 Water St., Suite 310
  Waterville, ME 04901